River Meets Ocean

By: Jennie Arnold

Jennie Arnold

COPYRIGHT

Trient Press

3375 S Rainbow Blvd

#81710, SMB 13135

Las Vegas,NV 89180

Ordering Information:
Quantity sales. Special discounts are available on quantity purchases by corporations, associations, and others. For details, contact the publisher at the address above.
Orders by U.S. trade bookstores and wholesalers. Please contact Trient Press: Tel: (775) 996-3844;   or visit www.trientpress.com.

Printed in the United States of America

Publisher's Cataloging-in-Publication data
Maurine, Tina.
A title of a book : River Meets Ocean
ISBN Hardcover   978-1-953975-83-6
        Paperback   978-1-953975-81-2
        E-book   978-1-953975-82-9

Dedication

This book is Dedicated to everyone who believes magic is real and dreams of castles and dragons.

By: Jennie Arnold

Part One

Their ships came with the storms. Thunder cracked and lightning lit the ships that rolled in. The wind and rain were destructive, but the army was something worse. War came to big cities and capitals but the war had never touched this small island.

No one knew what do when hulking warriors invaded their island. Their home. Most islanders were too shocked to react, watching their women being taken away. Yet their troubles had just begun. Dreams and nightmares only added to the problems.

Lewis's dream always began the same way...

Shock filled him when his nightmares became real! He lost himself in the same dream each night for almost a year. He had dreamed of the Argosi warships and thunder. The ships came. Lightning and fire filled the sky and the Argosi Empire conquered the small Island.

Now he dreamed of a woman with a crown of branches. The woman looked small but a blind man would see that she held great power. Men and women, each with a face he recognized but could not place, knelt before the woman.

"All hail Empress Gwendelion Nessa Rainsfall of the Argosi Empire! May her glory live on forever!" Someone intoned.

Lewis would have dismissed such cries as some fanatic. He would typically assume someone brainwashed the man until he no longer knew up from down.

But Lewis could not ignore this voice.

The voice belonged to him.

The dream always ended with Lewis looking into his own face and hating himself.

He would wake with a jolt and wonder if he should tell someone... But then he would remember that magic wasn't real.

The ancients once practiced magic and used it in their everyday lives but magic was a lost thing now. His ancestors depended on magic but over time, science and technology replaced magic. Councilors and kings alike told that magic would never come back. The people abandoned magic when they began to rely on science. The world abandoned magic and now the magic was abandoning the world.

Magic could have chased out these invaders but the technology was on the Argosi's side. Lewis liked to think he could do magic but everyone knew that such things were impossible. Magic had abandoned the world because the world abandoned it. Alta Island could have conquered the invaders with magic but now they were doomed. Magic no longer existed.

By: Jennie Arnold

Chapter One

The evidence of magic littered the small Island. Towers and spheres rose to the sky and dwarfed all the newer buildings. The firelaunchers had taken down about a third of the buildings made in the last decade but the old marvels still stood tall. Each of the ancient buildings could withstand fire, steel and the elements alike but they all looked like delicate lace.

The three young people crossing the green did not notice the buildings though. Two men and a woman walked along the road with their heads together whispering. One man had a thin, wiry frame, and the other had blond hair and stood a head taller than everyone else on the Island. The woman had midnight hair that curled to her waist.

Everyone on the Island called the thin man Matt, the blond Lewis and the woman Mira. The remaining populace of the Island all spoke quietly now even when they were only talking about mundane things. These three young people could whisper about the strangers who conquered the Island, but they weren't. They were whispering urgently about the people who were no longer on the Island. About a third of them had been forced to leave the only home they had known.

"We could do it," The thin one declared. "You know that they would thank us for it if they knew."

The tallest boy smiled. "Tell that to the woman's circle at Alta. They don't appreciate any man putting a nose in their business."

"They would appreciate this... after a while," Matt persisted.

He was thinking of his sister, Daisy, who had been taken a few days earlier. The Argosi had tested ten people that day and they had taken three: Daisy, Matt's sister; Kera, Lewis's former love; and Mistress Tilde, the head of the woman's circle.

Matt and his master had carved pieces for every woman on the circle. He thought he knew them pretty well. Mistress Tilde, the head of the circle herself, had ordered pieces from Matt personally. He had eaten dinner at her house and had been given honors for his fine work. Matt could name all of her favorite colors and quotes but he had never faced her tongue-lashing.

"The woman's circle would take their time deciding. If we acted wisely than it was due to a woman's reasoning. They would point out that Mira has all the brains. Everyone would think that it was her idea."

Lewis had faced Mistress Tilde and her tongue on more than one occasion.

Lewis and his father lived on a fruit farm on the edge of town. Lewis tended orchards during their seasons but he grew bored when the harvest was in. Half-baked schemes suddenly seemed like good ideas when he was bored enough. Lewis would pull pranks and watch a scheme fall to pieces. Many a goodwife pulled Lewis to the woman's circle by the ear to demand justice for broken property or stolen pies.

"Mistress Tilde would either blame every mistake on me or forget I was there if the plan turned out well."

Mira rolled her eyes. "We have to do something. My cousins might be irksome but I would not wish this on any of them on their worst day. They've been stuck on that ship for a week now!"

"The foreigners brought the latest batch into the ship earlier yesterday. It is supposed to sail at dawn. We need to do something but we are running out of time," Lewis, the tallest of them, reminded the other two. They all stopped and thought about the current situation.

Soldiers from across the sea had come into their small

By: Jennie Arnold

Island. These shipmen swore that the people in Alta Island had attacked trading vessels but that was not the way of the Island. The Mainland let the Island be, and the Island ignored the Mainland. That was how it had always been! But the foreign invaders would not listen to reason.

A decorated captain spoke to the council and the circle to warn them that Alta Island would be at war if the entire Island did not take an oath to the empress of Argosi, the empire at the edge of the sea. The captain brought firelaunchers and lightning sticks to show the Islanders just what would happen if war were to come. The Island would lose even if the mainland were to come and help. The Island of Alta is famous for two things: breadfruit and stubbornness.

The members of the Alta Island council are more stubborn than most but the sight of vast ships and the numbers within them made the council see sense. The ship not only held more people than the Island could hold but technologies and metals that the Islanders had never seen. Argosi swords cut through the best Island steel. Fire launchers could set the whole Island alight in seconds and runners could be shot down with lightning sticks or crossbows without a chance. Even the crossbows were different. Each arrow was tipped with blue metal that could go through the thickest armor.

Anyone can guess who won the battle. The victors took the mayor and anyone else who refused to give their oath on a ship. When the people came out they were willing to swear... or they did not come out at all. Some people were forced into the boats even after swearing. Gangs of Argosi came and took everyone on the Island to be tested.

No one knew what they were testing for but everyone knew that the results of the test could change the life and the life of the family. Failing the test meant being sent home, but no one knew what happened to the people who passed. They took anyone who passed to a ship and never seen or heard from again.

Fear can do strange things to people. Everyone on the Island of Alta felt fear race through them every second of every day. The constant fear could make a person do things that they would not normally do. Stubborn pride kept each of them from admitting to it or from bowing to it. None of them would give into tears or listlessness. They relied on an action.

No one on the Island knew what the test was for but no one could help but notice that the vast majority of those brought to the ships were women and girls in their late teens or early twenties. Parents and friends would hide women when the Argosi came, but they were caught and the whole family would be sent to different ships.

Some Islanders would come wailing at the Argosi general's door and beg for the people to be returned. They would tell the family to leave and if the family refused, then guards were called in and they beat the trouble causers. It was not a pretty sight to see children with bloody faces. Anyone left on the Island now lived in terror. No one was safe!

The three young people knew that something had to be done, but they did not see anyone willing to do them... That meant that the responsibility was left to them. The council would not help and they had already forced the mayor onto a ship.

"Some things just need to be done," Mira reminded the other two. She had always been the most careful of the three of them. They were all born in the same year but they could not have been more different. Mira was an only child and had been a treasure in her mother's eyes. She had been taught to treat the world around her as her mother did: as if it were made of glass. "Still, it has to be the right something — something that will help the girls that were taken — not just the first thing that

By: Jennie Arnold

comes to our heads."

"Thank you so much, Mira," Matt said sarcastically. "I would have never thought to do that myself."

"Good to hear that you're learning from your past mistakes. Acting is usually the first thought you have and the only one you follow," Mira joked back.

Both of them laughed but Lewis's voice cut the sound off with a sharp, "Focus! They are depending on us."

All three of their faces turned serious.

"There's a side entrance on the guards' quarter," Matt said surprising the other two.

"You've been there?" Mira asked.

"The building used to belong to Mistress Tilde. I carved the prayers on her mantle after her daughter left. There's a narrow tunnel behind the kitchen so she could get her herbs without waking her husband."

"We have an entrance. We can use the same door as an exit. Any idea of how we find the girls between the two?" Lewis looked at the other two as he spoke but he spoke the words more to himself than to anyone else.

"They take groups out for air every day," Mira reminded the other two.

"That doesn't tell us where they are!" Matt's face got red with anger and frustration. Daisy was trapped in one of those floating monsters. Who knew what the Argosi were doing to her on that thing?

"We know they are on the ship and we know how to get in the ship. All we need is some idea of what is inside," Lewis reminded the other two.

"I bought a few Argosi guards a drink or two." Matt smiled thinking of the guards who acted like idiots. "I thought I could get some information once I got them drunk but they won't talk to me. They're too busy talking to the barmaids."

Lewis looked at Mira. "Doesn't your friend work at the biggest Inn on the Island? Could she get you a job there?"

"I've helped at the Flying Boatman before. Kitchens are always grateful for extra help. They're even more desperate now with so many servers gone. I could get the guards to talk to me as a serving girl."

"You would be comfortable serving the likes of Argosi guards?" Lewis asked her with a level stare. "This could get dangerous even if you don't get caught. I want to make sure you understand what you're getting into."

"Just talk to them," Matt ordered. "Don't try to be flirtatious or cute. Just get them to tell you a story or two about life in the army."

"Matt or I could do it instead. We could say we're interested in joining."

"Relax guys. I'll be careful. I'm not doing anything I don't feel comfortable with. Besides, I can take care of myself. I'm taller than most of the people on the Island!"

"Just be careful, Mira. We can't rescue my sister or Mistress Tilde without you," Lewis said putting an arm around his friend's shoulders.

"You two worry too much," Mira declared, laughing.

By: Jennie Arnold

Chapter Two

The room Alaina found herself was cast in darkness. The Argosi guards had taken her from her home and brought her into this small room. Time had no meaning in that room.

Alaina knew that they had not left her in the room long. Still, it felt like forever. She groped around the room; feeling for a way out. Her hands searched the wall for a crack. She could have clawed at it but she never got the chance. The door burst open to let in the largest guard that Alaina had ever seen.

"Your time of preparation is over. Your testing is at hand." The guard who spoke gripped her arms and led her from the room.

Most people on Brington Peninsula would have called Alaina a brave young woman, but that was before... before fear and darkness controlled her life. Now fear called to her in the darkness and she lived in a waking nightmare. She thought she was a strong person but fear had changed her. Fear can morph a person into something they are not.

"Please let me go home," Alaina pleaded. She was still young and every second she spent away from her family made her feel even younger. She was no longer the bold girl she had been.

The girls would prove their courage by jumping off the cliffs and into the sea. The tallest cliffs were reserved for the bravest girls. Alaina had been the only person to choose the highest cliffs on her first jump. She had been the bravest of the divers on Brington. Nothing had scared her before the Argosi came. She had fallen far from the person she had been.

She barely held back her tears long enough to repeat,

"Please let me go home."

"Pass the test by failing and you will be free to go about your business."

"I can go home after this test? Do I have your word?"

"After you fail the testing, yes you may go home."

"Do I have your word? A man is only as good as his word."

"I am a guard! The weight of the Argosi Empire rests behind me! You have the Empire's word!"

"Alright," Alaina said in a shaky voice. Her voice never seemed to shake before. "Lead the way."

They walked through the ship soundlessly and swiftly. The Argosi moved as if he had walked this path a thousand times before. Alaina felt more ill-at-ease with each step. The tension was alive in the air. Knives could cut through the thickness of it. Alaina's senses all screamed at her. Each fact told her the same thing: this was wrong but there was nothing she could do about it.

Maybe she could pretend that nothing happened. Maybe she could go back to the person she used to be? She just needed to try harder. She pulled back her shoulders, stood ramrod straight and glided ahead of her guards.

They lead her into a room with a single burning candle and locked the door. She watched the flame dance in the wind that she could not find the source of. The wind grew stronger and the candle smoldered out, leaving the room in pitch darkness. Alaina had been afraid of the dark as a child and she had never gotten over that fear. The dark still made her nervous. Anything could be hiding in it... Alaina took two deep calming breaths and the light flickered back on.

Argosi guards burst in and held Alaina's arms in a vice-like grip. She trembled and fought back tears.

She was done pretending! Done trying to be strong!

"Please let me go home."

By: Jennie Arnold

"I'm sorry, girl," the guard from earlier said. "You passed the test." A woman in a black velvet dress glided into the room with her arms stretched before her. A large ring of black woven mettle rings rested in her hands. The woman held the thing like it was a rotting carcass. The pattern that the rings made could have been beautiful but it was clear that a thing so despised could never be beautiful.

"What is that?" Alaina asked.

"Don't fight," the guard advised. "Just let them put the headband on you and do what they say."

Alaina looked at him blankly. The woman in velvet moved with lightning speed. The black, cold headband closed around her brow and the world became a sharp knot of pain. Black fog flooded her vision. It started on the sides of her vision but quickly took over and she knew nothing more.

By: Jennie Arnold

Chapter Three

Mira stood in front of the Flying Boatman, the Island's largest
inn. She could hear the familiar sounds of men roaring with
laughter. There must be a dice game in progress with the
sounds of slammed pints and rolling dice ringing in the air
even from this distance. The inn must be doing triple the
business! The newcomers were more than willing to spend
money.
The locals liked to think of the conquerors as visitors. No one
could look at a thief and see a friend. Not when he stole
from *you*. These same people had pointed swords at the
Islanders. They were a threat and everyone knew it. The
Islanders shared ale and took money playing dice but they
could never do more than pretend.
Mira did her best to put on a friendly face and to think of good
friends stopping in for a visit and a drink — it made it easier to
serve the Argosi guards. She could only hope that her smile
would win her a bigger tip.
Mira saw the Innkeeper's face fill with despair. Both of them
were remembering people who had been lost. She remembered
crying faces and terrible screams in the night when the Argosi
came. She remembered the misery on their faces.
Mira hid her face until she could plaster on a grin and handed
out more drinks. The drink loosened inhibitions and purses
alike. Men talked and men gambled. A few tried to pinch Mira
put a whack on the side of the head with her tray disillusioned
them of the notion. Once the rules of engagement were clear,
Mira could make small talk. She started by commenting on the
dice game.

The guardsmen explained their favorite games and the best strategies for betting. Mira hardly looked at the dice. She was too busy studying the guards and watching their faces change. She might not be playing dice but she was gambling. The stakes were much more precious than money. If this gamble lost then lives were forfeit; lives of people she cared about. People Mira would do anything to protect. Someone needed to protect the Island, so Mira squared her shoulders and served drinks to the guardsmen.

She gave the fullest mug to a gray-haired man in uniform. The guard nodded his head in thanks.

"You look like you could use a full mug."

"I'm an old campaigner, lass. I never turn down an extra helping."

"Your job must be stressful. I would get lost just walking into that ship you guys patrol. How do you find your way?"

The men were so drunk by now that thinking was beyond them.

"They give us a map with our uniform," one guard said motioning to a pocket flap. "It's sewn on the flap. Just turn it over and you'll see."

"You know," Mira began, "I'm not sure if I can stand another night serving drinks to the same Islanders over and over again. You think there are openings for a barmaid in Argosi?"

"You could sail back with us," one of the guards began.

"I couldn't put you to any trouble. I know that the boats must be getting full."

"You wouldn't be a bother at all! The General wants us to bring as many people back as we can... as many people who are willing to work that is! The Empire came to help! The Empress herself said that she's never seen so many Silken come from one place. She wants to talk with you about traditions and things. You'd be welcome to come along!"

By: Jennie Arnold

Mira did her best to still her anger. This guard must be blind! The Empire had already taken so many people. There were ships in the harbor full of kidnapped women to prove the guard wrong. The Argosi Empire was kidnapping people and no one on Alta Island could forget it.

"Sounds great. Let me tell my mum the news gently and then we can all go down to the guardhouse later tonight."

Mira smiled genuinely, knowing the gamble had paid off. Part of her wanted to celebrate but she refused to fall to the temptation. The deed wasn't done yet and anything could still go wrong. She made sure to continue serving drinks. She forced herself not to drink even a sip. There would be much to do before this night was over. It would be best to have a clear head.

"The guards have a map," Mira explained as soon as she saw the other two. "It's sewn into the uniforms."

"I can get us two uniforms without any trouble," Matt declared. "My ma has been doing their laundry. I'll grab three and we can use the map to sneak onto one of those monstrous boats!"

"You think that we can beat trained fighters?"

"There are only two or three guards on the ships at night. Most of them are on duty on the Island or resting in barracks. They will ignore us once we put on the uniforms."

"You two are forgetting an important step," Matt told them sternly. "The women can't leave with those headbands on. The guards outside will stop them before they walk two steps and the guards are all over the Island."

Both Mira and Lewis frowned. They had come up with a plan but it was coming apart before it even began.

"We can't just leave them there," Lewis said.

"We have to try," Mira agreed.

Matt smiled. "Luckily for you two, I thought ahead." The wiry youth pulled a carved wooden tube from his pocket.

"What is that?" Both Lewis and Mira asked at once.
"This will open those strange headbands. I tested it already. The Argosi have Master Paulo mending the headbands so they are all over the smithy."
"You're a genius, Matt," Lewis said reverently.
"Get some sleep," Mira ordered them. "We have a long night ahead of us."
All three of them knew what was at stake: their families, homes, and island itself.

By: Jennie Arnold

Chapter Four

The next night Mira made her way back to the inn. She had already spoken to the Innkeeper and planned beyond a rumor or two. The Argosi were to be given a special drink that night. Ale could be laced with a strong sedative and given to the guardsmen. It was their way of keeping fighting to a minimum.

Mira made her way to the guards' table and bought the whole table a round of ale. Many of the guardsmen were already drunk. She needed them to be more than drunk. These guards needed to fall over themselves before they could even glance at her friends. Drunk did not begin to cover what these guardsmen needed to be!

"It will be so lonely here without you!" Mira sang to a few of the drunkest guards.

"Come with us! A few men are staying but more are leaving. A few of your Islanders are leaving too! Some of them are meeting on the docks."

"I'd better get to the docks then."

"Let me walk you," the gray-haired guard offered.

Mira wanted to tell him, no but she couldn't see a way out without drawing more suspicion. She took his arm and walked with him. They neared the docks, and she saw Lewis in the shadows. Mira pointed out as many things as she could; trying to remember all the landmarks pointing away from the skulking Lewis.

"Have you ever seen the like, Captain?" Mira asked, pointing to shadows in the distance on the tall cliffs. "There's the statue of the nanok. They look like bears but they're much more. It's said that a nanok is cleverer than any fox, more stubborn than a mule and more loyal than a hound. They can see the future and talk to people in dreams. Alta Island worshiped nanoks once. They're said to teach their followers magic. That's supposed to be why my ancestors left the Mainland. The nanok told them to."

"It doesn't look like magic to me. It doesn't even look like a bear."

"My people needed many gods when they first settled this harsh land. We were wanderers then – friendless and homeless. The old gods were the one solace we had. They guided every aspect of life and death. Nanoks led us through each trial until we learned the way on our own. My people built these statues to thank the old gods and to remind us of the wondering we left behind. What do you see when you look at the statue?"

The guard was so concentrated on the statue that he never saw Lewis.

Lewis moved fast as he hit the larger guard over the head but Mira moved even faster. The Argosi was down in a matter of seconds. Lewis and Mira did not have time to congratulate each other. They quickly changed into the uniforms and made their way to the dock where the ship waited.

There were about five ships in port but they had watched the groups that left the ships to be exercised and they knew which ship held those who passed the test. It took all of two seconds to make their way inside.

They saw long rows of doors. Lewis wanted to find the women from Alta at the start. Mira knew that they needed Matt if they planned to have any chance of success. They needed his key! Matt was not only an artisan but also a craftsman. He not only knew how to make beautiful tools but also how to solve problems. Matt could look at a problem and look at it sideways, front ways and backward to find a solution. They needed him!

"Let Matt in first," Mira ordered. Lewis did not move... Mira fought to keep her temper in check. "We need his tool to

By: Jennie Arnold

set them free. We can't leave them in chains!"

Lewis nodded and looked at his pocket flap to see the map. They marked the side door as "delivery entrance" but Mira knew that was the door they needed. Both of them moved swiftly through the halls; taking pivots and spins, boldly trying their best to look like the other guards they had seen on the Island.

Lewis realized that their tromping walk was one of the reasons he hated those guards. The conquerors walked around the streets and meadows he grew up in; acting like they owned the whole Island.

Lewis, Mira, Matt and anyone who grew up in Alta knew that the Island did not really belong to a country. It belonged to the people who worked there, who made the farms run every day. Still, these Argosi deserved to be hated!

They had kidnapped the people of the Island and terrorized anyone who was left; scared the children!

Anger made them both tense. The invaders had come to their land to do horrible things. These Argosi had demanded more than anyone had a right to take. Rage at the loss and injustice made them each flush. They relaxed when Matt stepped in through the door.

"You brought the tool?"

"No, Mira. I forgot the only thing we have that can remove the torture devices and free everyone." Matt put as much sarcasm as possible into the words and watched Mira pointedly.

"No harm asking," Mira reminded him.

Lewis put an arm around each of their shoulders. "Come on, you two, we have a job to do."

The three of them rushed, checking each door. A woman in chains sat behind each door in a cramped room. The chain was fitted tightly to the wall preventing any escape. This was obviously the right boat but none of the women were from their

Island.

"Are they Argosi?" Matt asked his friends in a harsh whisper.

"They would have called out for help if they were," Mira reminded them.

The next room was different. The woman spoke and the spark in her eyes spoke of a temper without using words.

"I'm from Brington Peninsula. We all are."

"They've traveled west quickly. It's almost three day's ride when the wind is with you!" Matt fitted the tool into the headband while the others spoke, marveling at the fine work of the band. The headband made a sharp snap and fell from the woman's brow. She sighed in relief and wrapped her hands around his arm in thanks.

"You need to get out of here as fast as you can. There is a door on the side of the ship that is not being watched. Go out the door and make your way to the docks. You can take a flatboat back to Brington from there. We'll get the others out," Lewis promised when the woman made no move to leave.

"I want to ring their necks — all of them! You can save all the people you want but don't you think that you can take anything from me!"

"Do whatever you want, woman but don't get in our way," Matt burst out losing his temper.

The four of them continued traveling from room to room, releasing women as they went. Lewis noticed that all the women were around the same age. He knew not to ask a woman her age; not unless you wanted your head snapped off, but he had sisters. He knew more about women's ages than most men. He knew more about woman's secrets than were healthy for him but he made do. His knowledge might just save these women.

"The vast majority of the women taken from our Island

By: Jennie Arnold

were all in their 20's. So are these women here." The others nodded.

"Not all the women taken were in their twenties. Not all the women from Brington were anyway! They took my sister! Can you save her? Please! She's still a child!" The woman pleaded.

"Don't worry," Lewis comforted. "We'll find her."

At the next door, it was clear that they had found the girl. A girl who was barely in her teens stood in a dress that was obviously too big for her. The woman who had just been freed ran to her. "Alaina!"

The sisters embraced each other in a warm hug. The three Alta Islanders tried to give them some privacy as they wept, clinging to one another. The weeping quieted after some time but the sisters still stood stock still. The Islanders wanted to give the sisters some time to calm themselves but there were others to save and time was running short. The guards would come back eventually.

Mira put a gentle arm around the women and led them out of the door into the hall. "There is a corner door at the end of this hall. No guards watch it. The two of you can exit through the door and sneak onto the docks until you find a flatboat. Steal that and make your way to Brington."

"I told you, I'm staying until I get my revenge!" The older sister declared.

"The way home will be dangerous," Lewis reminded her. "Your sister should not have to travel alone."

"I'm not going home before this is done!" Alaina declared. "The Argosi will just round us all up again if no one knows why they are rounding up people."

"Stay if you want," Matt decided. "But don't start to think that you're trading a dangerous road for a safer."

"We know the risks." They all nodded in understanding. Matt's hand paused as it reached for the doorknob. A high pitched scream filled the air. The sisters allowed their rescuers to lead them down the hall to the next door. Raised voices came from within.

Lewis wanted to pull the door open immediately but Mira gripped his arm, signaling to wait. The woman screamed again. "That's it!" Lewis yelled as he charged the door. His shoulder slammed into the door and bounced back a step or two. A second later, the five of them were working together, forcing the door open.

"Please stop!" The woman in the center of the room cried. The three Islanders were shocked to see that they recognized the screaming woman. In fact, they recognized every woman in the room. They were all women from Alta Island!

"Mistress Tilde?" Matt whispered in disbelief.

"Oh, you poor children," Mistress Tilde said just as quietly. "You should not be here. None of us should be here."

Other women in the group shared her feelings. Several of them began to moan and call out to the three of them. They rocked back and forth as if they were possessed. The women pulled at their hair as if trying to banish their thoughts. Finally, one of them found the words and shouted:

"Run! Get out of here!"

Five Argosi guards stood over the women from Alta. Still, the three of them were not worried about those five guards. They knew that more guards were all over the building. The guards began circling the intruders and more men streamed through the door each second. The door to the hall never seemed to close.

Lewis worried that the two sisters from Brington would be trampled but his worries were quickly put to rest. He could see elegant women in black gowns restraining Alaina and her sister. Guards quickly converged on the rest.

Strange things began to happen at that point...

By: Jennie Arnold

Chapter Five

Mira felt an annoying buzz in her head; a buzzing that wouldn't go away. The buzz became a numbness that grew and grew. Mira wanted to scratch every inch of her body. She felt like crawling out of her skin. The air became a roaring wave, and the numbness began to fade.

Brown and black, hairy forms burst into the ship from doors and windows. Any small crack burst open and became an entrance for the shadowy forms. Mira had to blink a time or two before she saw that they were bear-like creatures called nanoks. Nanoks began attacking the Argosi around the small group. Mira looked at them in horror and fear.

Creatures of legend were coming to life before her. She glanced at her friends, hoping to see the same shock in their eyes. Mira could not quite believe what she was seeing. Nanoks were gods once upon a time. They told the future and granted fortunes. No story told of nanoks fighting enemies or protecting the small Island that worshipped them.

"Nanoks?" Mira asked herself in disbelief. She turned to her friends, sure that she was dreaming. The shock that filled her face was mirrored on their own. "You see it too?"

Both of them nodded. Lewis looked like he was going to be sick. Mira and Matt assumed it was a reaction to the scene around them but Lewis was feeling the same symptoms as Mira, if for a different reason.

The stories said that nanoks brought magic with them when they came to the Island. Mira had always thought that the magic left when the nanoks did. Some of the other Islanders claimed that there was never any magic or any nanoks.

It looked like all the stories had got it wrong. Mira had a

connection to the nanoks and magic was more alive now than ever. But magic was not coming from the nanoks.

Swords rang around the Alta Islanders. The battle was not going well for the nanoks. The guards' shock had worn off. Now the nanoks were falling left and right. Mira made a strange sound in her throat and the nanoks began to run out as quickly as they appeared. The soldiers began to advance once more.

Lewis felt the crawling numbness but instead of subsiding the numbness grew into pain. Lewis screamed with the raw emotion of the pain. The scream brought more than the ring of sound though. Lightning flew from Lewis' hands as he screamed.

Three guards went down! Seven more fell in succession. Soon electricity and sound rang in the chamber. All the guards fell to the ground where they stood in fear or pain. Some of the women cried softly. Others looked at the men with worry-filled eyes.

"Come on," Matt ordered the others. "We need to get out of here. More Argosi are on their way!"

The party broke into the hall and the whole party fell on their backs.

"What is this?" Mistress Tilde asked while the other women lifted their hands to feel the strange barrier.

"It's them," Alaina said in a voice of despair. "The velvet women have powers."

"Do not speak these filthy lies. None of the velvet women can do magic. None of us would mess with something so dirty! My sisters and I can do something much more useful. We can make these banded women use their magic to do what we want them to do."

"The women in black are creating some kind of force field," Tilde declared while the other women nodded.

By: Jennie Arnold

"I've seen them do this type of thing before," Matt's younger sister said hesitantly.

"Got any more of that lightning, Lewis? We could sure use a bit of magic now!" Matt's throat worked as he spoke, showing just how nervous he was.

"So a man created the lightnings?" The woman in velvet did not wait for an answer when she continued, "The prophecies are proven correct again."

"Move aside," Lewis ordered, feeling for a weapon at his belt. Matt moved to stand in front of him. He held up hands in a placating manner.

"They're not our real enemy, Lewis. Bigger problems are coming this way."

Lewis ignored Matt and continued talking to the women as if he were not there. "We're leaving and you're not going to stop us."

"I'm serious, Lewis. An old woman is coming from the opposite direction. Don't listen to a word she says."

"Don't be silly, child," said a cold voice from the other side. Lewis whipped his head from Matt to the new speaker. She was a woman in blue with enough wrinkles to be Lewis' great-grandmother.

"We're all going home. Back to Alta," Lewis repeated.

"You're going back to Argosi where you belong." Lewis was beginning to be annoyed with this old woman.

"Don't listen to anything she says," Matt repeated in a yell. "This is all a trick."

"Look out!" Tilde called pointing the other way. Everyone turned but her call came too late. Water and plants alike arose from the ground that wrapped this way and that. Squeezing and hitting until everything went black.

By: Jennie Arnold

Chapter Six

Matt woke up sometime later in pitch blackness with a searing headache. It sounded like a drunken thief with big feet was dancing in Matt's head!

His hand pressed to his eyes to dull the ache and then crawled slowly to his feet. He held his hands outstretched before him to feel for any walls or obstacles then slowly took a step forward. A door swung open before his other foot could touch the ground.

A woman in black stood in the doorway. Matt's hand flew to his neck. He was relieved and surprised to find that he was not wearing one of those headbands. His relief must have been noticeable even in the darkness.

"We wouldn't band a seer, fool." The woman's voice made the cell echo with contempt. "You'd be useless without your use of magic!"

The knowledge that he would not suffer such a fate made Matt bold. "Where are the others?" He demanded more than asked.

"They are secure. My superiors can't risk you finding them."

"If you killed them," he broke off, unable to even think of such a thing. "So help me! If you killed them, I'll make you pay! You'll moan worse than you can even imagine!"

"You can see me quaking in my boots," the woman rolled her eyes and turned to walk away. "You can follow me or you can stay in the cell. It is all the same to me."

"Where do you plan on leading me?" Matt asked suspiciously.

"To your dinner. You can stay here and starve if you worry that we'll poison you."

Matt's vision blurred and narrowed as she spoke. It was

happening again!

Matt saw a long dining hall that could easily seat fifty guests but instead of hosting a party the table only held one woman. It was an elderly woman though she was not quite as old as the woman who had come for Lewis. He saw plates set on the table full of odd-looking food but the woman ate with a vigor so it must be good food. He saw himself eat and shake his head before the woman in black grabbed the dream Matt's shirt to drag him away before the images faded.

He was seeing things again! Last time he saw Lewis meeting the old woman. He knew that she was trying to distract them — but no one would listen to his warnings. He could save no one in the end.

Part of Matt told him to listen to the strange visions again, but another part said that they had not helped before. He had been a normal young man only two days ago. The tense atmosphere on the Island must get to them all! First Mira roars and nanoks come on a boat. Then, Lewis shoots lightning out of his hands. Now, Matt is seeing the future. Something like a bad piece of meat must disagree with him; making him dream vivid, strange dreams.

Still, what he saw had happened. He had to believe the visions were real. He had to use this ability as a new tool; a tool that what help him find a way out.

"Lead the way then," he said with a smile that was more confident than he felt.

The woman led him to a dining room — the same room he had seen in his vision. The old woman sat there in her blue gown.

"So you are the Seer?" The woman's voice had startled Matt. It was rich and mellifluous; nothing like you would expect to hear an old woman use! "It surprises you that we know what you are? Or surprised by events? I forgot that you

By: Jennie Arnold

are young yet."

"I'm afraid you have me confused with someone else, mistress. I am not a seer, just a boring Islander."

"Oh, I hope not! It would be unfortunate to kill you and we would have to kill a simple Islander was at the wrong place at the wrong time," she let her words sink in. "Luckily, we heard you warn your friend. There is no hiding the fact that you are a seer. You saw the future before it happened." She looked over at Matt and smiled. The smile reminded Matt of a mountain lion who had cornered a spotted fawn. "Make no mistake though: if you refuse to tell us what you see then you will suffer a fate worse than death."

"Maybe I saw something when my friends were in danger. Maybe I can continue to see things." He broke off, knowing that he would need all his wits about him if he had any chance of saving the people he loved best in all the world, knowing that one wrong move could not be won back. "But if you expect me to tell you about any of them, then you will show me that my friends are alive and well. If you want me to continue to tell you visions then you'll make sure that my friends stay in good health."

"You are brave, my bargainer. But you are a fool with bravery. Your friends are as valuable to the empire as you are. The black-haired girl can give the empress an army worthy of her name. Those nanoks will be very useful in bringing victory to the war in the Mainland. The tall young man is something very special. He is on his way to see the empress herself. We will treat him like a treasure during the entire voyage." The woman's eyes looked awe-struck just at meeting the empress. Still, the idea did not impress Matt.

"You didn't mention the women you've already taken. The women from my town? What's in store for them? Are they already under guard to ensure that the bands stay on while the magic gets sucked from each of them? That's what you monsters took them for isn't?"

"You will learn not to speak to me in such a way. It is your first day so I will allow some leniency in decorum. Speak in that fashion once more and my guards will beat you. Do not expect this warning twice."

Matt nodded his understanding. "You understand that I will not do something for nothing. A man has to make a living."

"Is your life worth something?"

"My life is my own!" Matt screamed in anger. The woman's only response was a small, triumphant smile. He took a deep breath to calm himself, refusing to let her win. "What I mean, mistress, is that you need me to keep my life. I cannot see visions if I am dead."

"You can see visions without legs, boy. My guards could rest easy knowing that you can't run."

Matt paled, but he refused to give up. Fear and helplessness roared in him like a tempest but he could not give in. "You must be very close to the empress. Surely, someone as great as you could see that a few Islanders were kept safe?"

Matt expected her to punish him for such an obvious ruse or to prove her power by letting an innocent farmer or two leave Argosi custody. The old woman's true response surprised him: she laughed.

She put her hand to her belly and threw her head back to laugh as if she had never laughed before.

"You will be useful to keep around." Matt shook his head to clear it. *Were all women crazy?* The older woman nodded to the velvet woman who brought Matt in. She grabbed Matt by the back of his shirt and pulled him so quickly that he had to be dragged. *Just like the vision...*

He was lost in his thoughts until the velvet woman threw him into the cell. Matt's mind was reeling from all the old

By: Jennie Arnold

woman had told him. The Argosi needed him, Mira and Lewis and all the women in the Islands who had passed some test.... but why? What did they think a few Islanders could do that no one else could?

"See into the future for one," Matt mumbled to himself in frustration. The Argosi had known that he could see into the future when he himself was not even sure that was what he was doing!

The Argosi had seen Mira roar at the nanoks and Lewis make lightning fly from his hands. These strange powers could be used in war along with these velvet women and the magic they stole from the banded Island women. The Islanders could use their powers too though. The women might have a harder time because they are watched so often but even they had a chance.

"That's it!" Matt thought. "I can look into the future and find a way out!" Matt sat absolutely still and began. He concentrated as hard as he could but nothing happened. No tingling, no pain, no numbness... no visions. It happened so easily last time. Maybe he could not force himself to go into these visions. Maybe it happened on its own. When would the next one come?

Reality hit Matt like a train. What if the next vision didn't come until he was an old man? What if he never had these visions again?

"I won't live to be an old man," he answered his own question. "They will kill me."

Matt felt himself panicking. He really would die if they thought his talent was gone. This ability is the only thing keeping him from the butcher's block. His ability was important to the Argosi because it really did see specifics before they happened. He could not just pretend to see shapes in water like the trapper who came through. Or could he...

Matt ran to the cell door and started banging. "I had a vision! I have an important message for the old woman."

The door flew open and the velvet woman charged in. "This had better be good, boy. Tell me your vision."

"I'll tell the old woman. Take me to her before it's too late!"

"She will not be lax with you if you play games, boy. You will not be simply tossed back in here if this is a trick."

"It's important." Matt knew that he was trying his luck but a lie was only good if you stuck to it.

The velvet woman twisted Matt's arms behind his back and tied them tightly. "You seem nervous. Anything I should know about?"

"You saw the future. You tell me: should we be worried?"

Matt knew better than to answer. He would not say a word more until he saw the old woman — not unless she gave him some information first! The woman pushed him to walk faster until he stumbled and fought down a curse.

"Be gentle with the boy, Arcadia. We need him whole for now."

"He says he has an important message for you."

"Well, boy? Let's hear it."

"A great disaster will fall on Argosi if you keep Mira and Lewis locked away. Mira needs to be in the woods near her nanoks and Lewis needs to be in Alta. There are people there who will follow him."

"You came all the way here to tell me to let your friends go?"

"I never said to set them free. I'm only saying where they need to be. A cell is the last place they need to be. Ruin and destruction will fall on the Argosi Empress if my friends are in the wrong place."

"Where are your friends now?"

By: Jennie Arnold

"I only saw them in dank cells like mine. The visions don't always show so many specifics."

"You're playing games with me, boy!"

"I'm doing what you told me to do," Matt said as slowly and patiently as he could muster. "You said to tell you if I had visions and I'm telling you."

"You're telling me about a vision about a vague future with no specifics. The vision you had before gave you enough details to warn your friends and to recognize the threat when it appeared. I could not prepare for the 'ruin' you're warning me of, Matt and I think we both know why. The vision you described is not a vision! It is only your over-active imagination. But don't worry. Your mind will be rather busy very shortly."

Men in bright armor burst through the door. Two held Matt's already bound arms while the rest went to work hitting him everywhere at once. Matt twisted and struggled, trying to get away from the pain. Matt pulled this way and that but found no relief from the pain.

He took a direct hit to the head followed by a swift punch to the gut. Then, everything began a feel numb... a vision was coming!

He saw Lewis, sitting in a dark room below deck on a ship. There were a few men who worked on the crew but most of the people on the ship were women in black velvet and banded women in silks. A blonde woman in black velvet stood outside the door. She was young and beautiful; someone Matt would want to dance with back at Alta.

A woman with a crown of branches glided onto the deck of the ship and Lewis was brought out of the hold of the ship. He was almost to the crowned woman when the blonde velvet woman stabbed Lewis! Blood pooled around him and Matt felt Lewis' life leave him as he came back to himself after the vision.

Matt was surprised to find that the men were no longer hitting him. In fact, the men were no longer even in sight. The old woman knelt before him, holding his chin in her hands.

"You've had a vision. You will tell me what it was!"

"Lewis is going to die! I'm not just saying that. I saw it. A velvet woman with blonde hair will kill Lewis!"

"The one who shot lightning?" Matt nodded, still trying to catch his breath. "Where was he when he was attacked? How did she kill him?"

"He was in a ship. He was being kept in the hold but an Argosi brought him up when a woman with a crown of branches came onto the deck. The blonde woman stabbed Lewis. You have to help him!"

"Good," she said to Matt before turning to the guards. "Take him to the cell. Have Arcadia heal him tomorrow."

"You have to warn him! Don't let him die!" Matt struggled weakly as they tried to force him out.

"Your friend will save Argosi. The prophesies tell us that he must live. Argosi cannot survive unless he survives as well."

Matt let the men lead him away. He thought about the old woman and of the words she had said. He was surprised to find that he believed her. She took this prophecy seriously and would protect Lewis but how could he be sure that the future really was changing?

The old woman planned to accomplish all that and more. They were out of options and now the future had to change. The boy would save the empire so Lewis had to survive until he could do so. There was only one answer: kill the velvet woman with blonde hair first!

"Captain! Bring all of the blonde velvet women to the Truthmakers. Don't bother with torture. Have each one executed."

By: Jennie Arnold

The captain did not bat an eye at his Lady's strange order. "Yes, High Lady." The captain knew that High Lady Ramilla Sad'areill would not accept any other answer. He went to carry out her orders.

~*~

Alaina tried to fight down her overwhelming fear. She was in the headband again and Kiarlin was missing. Alaina felt like she could get through anything if her sister was with her but Kiarlin could be anywhere by now. The band around her brow pinched and chafed even worse knowing that Kiarlin was feeling the same pain.

"May I ask a question, Velvet lady?" Alaina asked in a quivering voice.

"You are a pet, a piece of furniture. Pets and furniture do not question their masters."

Alaina sat quietly, licking her lips and hoping that the woman would tell her something, anything about her sister. Alaina would not mind hearing what they planned to do with her either. She had learned the danger of knowing long ago. Dreaming and guessing was better than knowing that the worst of the nightmares were real! She could still pretend that she would see her sister again now but the dreams would be over if she knew Kiarlin to be dead.

Alaina had blacked out after being recaptured. The velvet woman had taken more power from her than before. She felt heavy and exhausted. Blackness reached through the edges of her vision and she lost consciousness.

When she woke next, it was to a small room with a headband fastened to her brow. Her first emotion was pure fear. Not the headband again! The headband made you reach for the power deep inside yourself. It made you do things that you did not want to do. It made you hurt innocent people. The headband made something that should help the world into something that withered everything it touched. Alaina felt dirty and helpless just wearing the thing.

It only got worse when one of the velvet women came in. The woman stroked Alaina when she saw the girl cry but that only made Alaina cry harder. Still, she knew better than to try to pull away or disobey. The headband could make her hurt herself as well and it was a far from pleasant experience.

Alaina could only sit patiently and wait until the velvet woman decided to tell her what was needed of her today. Hopefully the woman would tell her and not just take the power forcefully.

"Today you will make the High Lady's garden grow. She bores of this land and needs a performance. We will travel to the estate this afternoon. Do not think your escape will go unpunished. That will come la —," The woman broke off mid-word as uniformed men came rushing in.

"I demand to know what this is about!" Yelled the woman but they made no response. *How dare these men ignore her?* She gathered in Alaina's magic and prepared to teach the men a lesson that they wouldn't soon forget. Still, the men acted too quickly.

"By order of the High Lady Ramilla Sad'areill!" The men shouted as one before plunging their swords into her.

Alaina felt the gathered power surge back into her core. She felt the rush and adrenaline of it along with the sickening of blood and sorrow at the loss of life. The power shot out of Alaina of its own accord. She felt a small joy that at least the magic could be free.

Do good, she silently begged it. Vines and flowers shot out of the earth for miles and miles. Alaina felt nature sing before the gasps of fear from the men who surrounded her replaced it.

The man closest to Alaina dropped his bloody sword and pulled a mettle stick from his pocket. Lightning shot from it

By: Jennie Arnold

and Alaina knew no more.

Mira came to herself tied hand and foot in a small cabin. She pulled at the bindings but they seemed to only get tighter. She roared to the nanoks for help — where did that come from? She asked herself. I've never done that before — then she remembered the rescue attempt.

She rolled to her side and got to her hands and knees, looking for any sign of the others. Her eyes were slowly adjusting to the dark of the cabin when the door opened and blinded her with light.

"I thought I heard you. Your furry friends will not hear your roars though. My men and I made sure of that."

"Where are we? Where are the others?" Mira surprised herself by asking with a steady voice.

"I will start answering your questions after you answer mine."

"I'm listening," Mira said with a nod.

"Who taught you to speak with the nanoks?"

"No one," Mira told him truthfully. Her truth earned a hard slap.

"I won't ask nicely again!"

"I didn't even know I could until I did it. There wasn't any learning. I just did it."

The man's foot shot out and kicked Mira. "You had better be telling the truth. My generals are already questioning the farmers in your little Island."

"The people on the Island have not done anything wrong. They don't know anything about nanoks or about the rescue."

"Then they shall not be harmed. The truth about that Island

shall be known in due course. One way or another, my men will be able to call on nanoks in the heat of battle."

"How do you plan to do that?"

"You will teach them or the one who taught you will come forward. My men will learn."

"It can't be learned!"

The man's foot moved back to strike but the kick never came. The ground shook so hard that the man fell to his knees. The cabin began to fall in. Windows cracked and doors flew from hinges. A beam fell from the ceiling penning the kneeling man to the floor.

Mira could not stand on her bound feet so she rolled towards the door. She expected to see other guards at the door or running in to help their fallen comrade but it looked like everyone had fled in fear. Mira rolled until she was far enough away from that building.

She had seen builders die in a clasped even when they were outside of the building and she did not want the same to happen to her. She turned to make sure that the structure was a safe distance from her but she stopped mid-turn.

She was shocked into stillness by what she saw when she finally looked behind her. The cabin was not falling in because of an earthquake. It was clasping because vines, flowers and trees of all sorts were growing around and inside of it. The field of wheat Mira sat in was safe enough but the mountain woodlands around her danced with movement.

She saw shapes emerge from the woods and feared that the demons that had caused this attack were now coming after her. Roaring in the distance told her the truth of the matter: the shapes were nanoks!

She roared back and was rewarded with generous licks and nudges. The nanoks bit through the bindings easily. Mira was able to stand and could now see more than just the field. She

By: Jennie Arnold

saw that the cabin she was housed in was fairly isolated but a tall stone tower stood about a mile way near a lake. The guards who were once at the house were all gathered there.

The tall-stone is a terrible place, daughter. Mira jumped hearing the nanok perfectly in her head. Still, Mira agreed with the nanok. She did not want to be near those guards again. She and the nanoks ran the opposite way into the still forests deep in the mountain pass.

She may have run the opposite way if she could see the future as Matt did. The guards surrounded the tower because a dangerous prisoner was housed there. The guards swarmed the area to stop the prisoner's escape but they were too late.

The growing plants broke down doors in the tower's base and the criminal could now leave. Nothing stood in Onoka's way and he was free to do the one thing he had wanted to do before time began: kill the empress of Argosi! Onoka ran towards the empress and, although he did not know it, towards Lewis as well.

~*~

Lewis awoke to birds singing and daylight streaming into the windows. He focused his thoughts on remembering how he had gotten here and his memories only made him more confused. He remembered trying to free the others but shooting lightning seemed more like a dream... this room seemed like a dream.

He stood and walked to the only door in sight. He was surprised to find that the handle turned under his fingers. A man in colorful robes stood in the doorway.

"If you will follow me, High Lord. Your ship awaits."

"There's been a mistake," Lewis began. "I'm not a high lord and I'm not getting on any ship."

The man's face turned hard. "I don't want to have to use force against my lord. The empress will be very disappointed."

"You remember what happened the last time Argosi tried to use force against me." Lewis tried to call lightning to him but nothing happened. He could only pray that the man did not call his bluff.

"I doubt you could call more lightning so soon after your previous escapade. Besides, I do not need to use force against you. I only need to use it against your home. Your father and sister are still on Alta Island, are they not?"

Lewis' face paled visibly. "What's to keep them safe once you have me in the middle of the ocean?"

"Your family will be safe as long as Argosi is safe."

"How am I supposed to keep Argosi safe? One man won't make a difference to an empire. A drop of water means nothing to the ocean."

"The prophecies say you will save our empire. You come with me and take a ship to Argosi. The empress and the high priests will tell you how to save the empire. Follow their directions and your family will be safe."

Lewis could see over a dozen men moving outside the door. Lewis was sure that there were even more men he could not see beyond them. He knew that he had no real choice. His father used to tell him that every man had a choice but sometimes those choices amounted to bad or worse. Lewis could see that he had to go with the robed man.

"We had better get going then." They began walking and more men seemed to surround them with every step. "The two of us will be spending a lot of time together. What should I call you?"

"I am your servant, my lord. You may call me any name you wish."

"You're the empress' servant if anything. You are threatening me and giving orders to these men. No servant on Alta could do any of that."

By: Jennie Arnold

"You will soon see that many things are different in Argosi." Lewis and his servant boarded the ship along with the soldiers. No one knew that someone else boarded the ship at the same time.

Onoka watched the men put Lewis in the hold. He could feel the power in the young man. He almost laughed thinking about what that power could do if released. These men were making powerful enemies. The empress would die soon... one way or another.

It seemed like weeks trapped below the ship's deck to Lewis but Onoka was in the sunlight and he knew exactly how many days had passed. He knew that today was the day the ship would pull into port at Argosi. Today was the day he would meet the empress. Onoka fantasized about this day every moment he was in prison.

Lewis did not know what to expect when he was brought on deck but the blinding sunlight was not it. He was nervous about meeting the empress but not because she was a queen.

Lewis knew that his family's lives stood as the stakes in this game the Argosi were playing. He knew that he needed to win their game. Lewis put his concentration into focusing his thoughts and powers. He would need to be at the top of his game if he planned on beating the most powerful empire the world had ever known.

His eyes hardly had time to adjust before a knife flashed towards the waiting empress. Lewis' magic powers reacted before he could think. Fire arose from the ground and melted the knife before it hit the empress.

The fire made a straight line on the ground from the ship dock to the empress. The fire stopped burning as soon as Lewis turned his attention to Onoka but the line continued to smoke. Onoka should be on the ground moaning but he kept his feet. Lewis reached for his magic, for fire but the lightning came to his call. Lightning flew from Lewis' hands and into Onoka. The man threw a knife at Lewis but wind blew to stop it. Onoka climbed to his feet even though his knees were shaking. Lewis felt his own knees shaking but he called to the magic again.

Lightning struck Onoka a third time and he fell to the ground without moving. Guards dragged the injured Onoka away. Lewis was uninjured but exhaustion made him sag to his knees.

"Make sure that this man is rewarded," ordered the empress.

"What reward should be bestowed?" asked Lewis' servant.

"He will have a manor and land and freedom to walk about in it."

"My lord cannot leave, of course," the servant pointed out. "He will need to be here later for the prophecy to be fulfilled."

"I have to go home," Lewis muttered, delirious from exhaustion. Lewis did not hear their reaction before darkness overcame him.

By: Jennie Arnold

Chapter Seven

Alaina knew she was in trouble as soon as she opened her eyes. A velvet woman with piercing eyes stood in front of her cot. Alaina tried to sit up to look around but the velvet woman slapped Alaina anytime she looked like moving.

"You are a tool to be used for the empire... a very strong, valuable tool perhaps... but a tool none the less. You may call me Sainade. A pet should know what to call its mistress and you will answer to First Silken. You are the strongest magic user the empire has at the moment."

"It was an accident," Alaina tried to explain. Fear rolled through Alaina until she feared that the force of it would knock her over.

"That does not change what you are. You have a power that you cannot control. The power that could hurt or kill someone — even someone you love. This headband protects the empire, your family and even you. You could do yourself harm with a power you cannot control. Now the empire controls your power and you can use the power to serve."

"My sister was with me," Alaina remembered. "Will the empire keep her safe?"

Alaina regretted asking as soon as the words left her mouth. Questions were always dangerous when the velvet women took an interest! More than that, questions about Kiarlin only made the Argosi more ridged in their control. The Argosi held Kiarlin and they would continue to hold her until Alain did what they asked.

"The empress does all she can for all of her subjects."

"My sister had a band on too but then those boys came and took it off. She did not seem like a danger at that time. I've had this power my whole life. Why hasn't it hurt me before?"

"You have been very lucky. Most of your kind are injured before they come to us."

"There were so many women in that ship. All of them got hurt while banded but none of them were injured before they arrived. The empress would not be happy to hear about her subjects then!"

"You are young still. Sometimes bad things need to be done to stop a terrible thing from happening. The empress, above all others, knows this."

"You told me I would stay safe. Will the others stay safe too?"

Sainade left without answering. Alaina knew there would be no answers, but she had to ask, despite that.

It took Matt some time to calm down after the vision of Lewis. His body was sore from the beating they had given him but he refused to give in to its tired demands.

He stood pacing when the cell door opened. He expected it to be Arcadia to heal him. The old woman had ordered her to come. A jolt of surprise danced up his spine. Matt was more than surprised to find that Arcadia was nowhere to be found. The old woman in the doorway.

He grinned at her before saying, "Did you miss me or just my visions? Sorry to disappoint but I haven't had any more."

"I know how to make sure that you have them when I need you to, boy. Still, I do not think that we can risk that just yet. Your body is still healing. Do not worry so, boy. I am here to reward you."

"I don't think I want anything you can give," Matt

By: Jennie Arnold

interrupted quickly, knowing that any rewards would only put him in Argosi's debt.

"The reward is not really from me. This gift is from the empress. It is not something that you can refuse. There are people whose gifts can be ignored, but the empress is not one of them." The old woman stood aside and more women marched in. Each woman wore a metal headband, and they were all women Matt recognized.

They were all women from Alta! They were all on the ship bound for the Argosi Empire only a few short days ago. Matt and his friends had stopped that ship from sailing but it looked like he had led them out of the pan and into the fire!

"Matt!" the last one called as she rushed towards him.

"Daisy!" Matt exclaimed recognizing his sister's voice. The other women moved aside for him so that the siblings could embrace. Matt was glad to see all the women from Alta were safe, his sister especially. Still, he could not shake his worry over the friends who were not there.

"Matt, did you see where they took Alaina? Is she here?"

"I haven't seen her. Not since the rescue attempt. They're shipping Lewis to Argosi and have Mira trapped in the mountains. I try not to think about what plans they have for me. I plan on leaving before any of them can take place."

"That sounds like a good plan but doing it might be harder than you think."

"If anyone can do it, Matt can," declared Daisy.

"Matt, you know this is a trap. I don't know what they want with you but I know that you can't do it for them. Whatever they ask, Matt you say no." Mistress Tilde held onto Matt's shirt in desperation as she spoke.

"Relax, Mistress. There is nothing to worry about. I promise you; I promise all of you, that I will not leave this prison without all of you."

"That's the trap, Matt," scolded Tilde. "They want to keep you here and escaping with this many people is impossible. They are tightening their hold on you through us!"

"So was magic," Matt reminded her.

The ancients had practiced magic and used it in their everyday lives but magic was a lost thing now. The Island's first inhabitants had used magic in their everyday lives but science and technology were used instead of magic now.

The most learned and powerful people on the Island knew that magic would never come back. It was lost and could not be re-learned. Magic was lost to them now. The Island had abandoned magic and now magic was abandoning them. Science and technology had been built up to replace magic. The world abandoned magic and now magic was abandoning the world.

Tilde opened her mouth to respond but she fell silent when the door opened once more. Arcadia stepped in.

"I hope your visit was a nice one. You ladies must go now. Matt and I have to talk before the healing."

Mistress Tilde would have argued with anyone who tried to order her about on Alta Island but captivity and fear had changed her. She walked past Matt with her head bowed. The women marched out the same way they had come in, leaving Matt and the woman alone.

"Healing can be very painful. My mistress believes that the pain will force you into another vision. You will tell me every detail if you want to see the banded women again. You saw that they were unharmed for yourself."

"Lewis is safe now?"

"As safe as we can make him."

"I'm not telling you any more visions until I know he is safe." Matt tried to move out of the woman's reach and away from her stolen power. He did not get far. Her arm reached out like a snake and forced a healing on him.

The word painful did not describe the feeling that followed her touch. He tried to pull away but he could not move. The pain took up his entire mind. He could not tell his body to move because his mind was too busy to deliver the message. The pain began to fade, but the numbness took over until it was painful.

A vision formed before his eyes. He saw shadows below the trees. They darted back and forth until the shadows took shape. He thought they were bears at first but their size gave them away. They were nanoks. Bear-like creatures bounced in the shadows, running towards a woman dressed in colorful robes and wearing a crown of branches.

The former gods and protectors of Alta Island were attacking the Empress of Argosi!

The old woman would assume that Mira's nanoks attacked the empress. He could tell no one about the vision — not about the whole thing, anyway. He had to protect both Mira and the women from Alta. Matt knew that he had to tell the old woman something but he could just leave out the nanoks. Matt continued to plan, lost in his thoughts.

Arcadia brought Matt back to this world with a slap that knocked his head back. He grunted and finally pulled away from her.

"Tell me the vision!" She demanded in a hiss. "You remember what will happen if you don't."

"I saw the empress getting attacked. She was walking near a forest and there was water behind her; a river or a lake. A shadowy beast came out and attacked her. Lewis wasn't with her and there were no guards. Surely the empress would not walk around alone."

"There is only one place she would do so. My mistress will take care of this. Rest for now. You'll have a busy day tomorrow."

Stay away from the empress, Mira. Matt just wished his friend could hear him.

~*~

Mira walked with the nanoks at a pace was more of a jog than a walk but she quickly tired and the pace slowed.

Hurry, daughter. They hunt us. The lead nanok urged with a loud yip.

"The guards are looking for us?" Mira asked aloud, still uncomfortable with speaking through thoughts.

Humans come carrying lightning sticks. They come quickly on top of hard feets.

Mira sifted through the words and thoughts the nanok sent her. "Armed guards are following us on horses? We need to mask the trail or hide. There is no way we can outrun a horse!"

We can, daughter. Hard feet are fast but deer are faster and we have caught many of them.

Our daughter speaks to us, Dancer. She is not one of us. Nanoks can outrun a deer but a human needs tools to do it for her. A female nanok with lighter fur sent the message in a playful tone.

"I could hold my own against armed guards if I had my bow. I might even stand a chance with a sword but I could never fight trained men unarmed and expect to win."

You speak in riddles, daughter. Still, I agree with Plumblossom. We nanoks must take care of the hunting humans while you stay with Snow and hide.

I can fight, Dancer! Snow insisted, wanting to hunt the hunters.

You must protect our daughter. She is the first human to speak with us in over fifty ages. Mira could feel the long stretch of time in Dancer's statement. It had been hundreds of years! *I do not know why she has been sent to us but we will not lose this treasure!*

None of the hunters will get past me. Our daughter will be safe. Snow saw the importance in her work now and would take the responsibility seriously.

The nanoks moved to form a half-circle between Mira and the coming guards. Snow stood beside Mira in the center of the half-circle. Tuffs of fur rose on her back, warning Mira that the danger was near. Then she could hear it: huff beats!

"Mira!" called the commander who had questioned her before. "Tell your nanok friends to stand down. Come with us quietly. You don't want any bloodshed."

"Do you think the nanoks will listen to a word if you kill any of them? They will demand your blood after that even if I do tell them to stand down."

"I know that they won't talk to me if I don't have you."

Mira stayed silent but did not motion for the nanoks to withdraw. The commander could tell that Mira would not be surrendering. It was time for Plan B.

"Bring out the Were-beast!" Called the commander. It shocked Mira to see a man with the head of a nanok. The large head looked out of proportion with the rest of the body. Still, the broad chest and shoulders spoke of strength and Mira was afraid for her friends.

"Runaway!" called the nanokman in a grunt. "Run or I kill you!" The thing bared his teeth and snarled.

That thing is no family to us! Cried Dancer in dismay. *He might have the mind of a nanok but he has no soul. He cannot run with us in the gloaming field!*

We cannot allow such an abomination to live. Killing would be a mercy, agreed Snow.

We cannot let what he has become change us into something we do not want to be, Dancer warned the others. *Remember that Fate is in control but you have to help it along.*

"I kill! I kill you all!" The nanokman charged towards the group of nanoks. The nanoks outnumbered the man and were faster but the nanokman was bigger and stronger than any of them.

"Leave the girl alive, you fool!" Screamed the commander.

"I take girl. I take girl and give to master. Master will make you scream. You will see. You will scream."

"The nanoks would never listen to you even if I could teach you. Leave these nanoks alone and let me be."

"Master will make you scream. I be hunter and girl scream." The nanokman charged at Mira but two nanoks got in his way, biting down on his legs. The nanokman's legs buckled under him and sent him sprawling. More nanoks went for the nanokman's neck.

"No!" Mira yelled. "Don't kill him."

Killing that thing would be a mercy, Snow insisted.

Taking a life forces Fate to change. We could never do that, Dancer reminded her.

I will never take this soulless thing as my brother, Snow swore. *You say that we do not allow ourselves to change and the only way to stop that monster is to kill it!*

"Snow! Don't move!" Mira ordered as she moved in front of the were-nanoks. "The Argosi brought him here so that nanoks would kill him!" Mira yelled again.

"Very good. I wondered when you would figure it out. We brought our nanokman to make the nanoks mad. They will all run at him to bring him down and our trap will trigger. A whole nanok sleuth will be trapped and you will be back to teach my men."

"Why do you want a sleuth of nanoks?"

"How else will my men be able to tell if you are telling the truth?"

"You see what happens when you experiment on nature —

By: Jennie Arnold

you get a monster! This werebeast will never be what you want. You have stolen his very soul."

"I don't think you understand, Mira. The werebeast is here to die."

This commander knows nothing! Dancer sent with a growl. *We do not take life. That is the job of Fate.*

"That creature will die for the empress! He will die with honor!" the commander swore.

The werebeast let out an anguished yell at the commander's statement. He struggled with the nanoks.

Let him go, Mira sent without using words. *The Argosi are using him and he knows it now.*

The nanoks obeyed, and the werebeast ran into the night.

"You have so much to teach us, Mira. Take her!" Argosi guards ran at the nanoks from all sides. The nanoks leaped at the men and bit down as hard as their strong jaws could. Lightning sticks struck the nanoks but they never loosened their bite.

Run, daughter. The sleuth will follow. Dancer will lead them. Mira had little choice but to obey Snow's order. They ran into the night, leaving the guards behind.

The guards were not all they left behind. Mira could hear the werebeast softly weeping as she and the she-nanok ran deeper into the woods.

"Master lied to me!" The werebeast ran to keep up but Mira could still hear him clearly. "I will fight for you. I fight here in the woods. I will win back my honor."

The werebeast fell behind and Mira could only hope that the werebeast was true to his word.

Lewis opened his eyes with a groan. Every inch of him was sore. He felt like he had spent the whole day digging post holes and all night chopping wood. His muscles yelled at him and his head felt heavy with exhaustion. Lewis pushed exhaustion aside and sat up. He saw that he was not in the room alone.

The servant from before sat in front of the cot Lewis was resting in. "Good morning, my lord."

"Is it?" Lewis groaned.

"You were blessed yesterday so today must be a good morning."

"You already told the Empress not to send me home. I heard you say it yesterday."

"You have rested for a whole day, my lord. The empress has rewarded you with this marvelous house. You even have land. She is graciously allowing you to go anywhere on it."

"I saved her life and the best reward she can manage is to send me to a bigger prison?"

"My lord, this house is hardly a prison. You will have exquisite meals and fine clothes along with a whole house to busy yourself in. You can even go walking in the sunlight."

"Our deal was that I make sure that the empire survives so that Alta can be safe as well. I saved the empress's life. I kept the empire safe. Now I get to go back to Alta." Lewis got up and walked to the door as if planning on walking back to the Island.

"I would not advise trying to leave. The empress would not leave you unguarded. The guards will bring you back bound if they have to."

"The empress has some explaining to do!" Lewis growled before tramping through the tall grasses around his house. He could only walk half a mile when the first guard showed himself.

"My lord, you will go back to the house now." The guard

By: Jennie Arnold

raised his weapon slightly as he spoke.

"I am looking for a stream. My servant mentioned that there was water on this land." The servant had said no such thing but Lewis thought he could build a raft and make did far enough downstream before the guards even knew he was gone.

"The servant was misinformed. The Arnon River does not border your estate. You will make your way to the house now."

Lewis sighed and turned around. He took a sharp left just before getting back to the house. Forests ran that way and Lewis hoped he could lose the guard posted there in the thick trees. He heard a river flowing and walked towards the sound.

Lewis could only walk a yard into the trees before a number of guards approached him. "You will return to the house now." They said.

"I need not to go to the house. I need to go for a walk." Lewis tried to push past them but they only got back in his way. "The Empress herself said that I could walk these grounds."

"The Empress set up boundaries. You will go to the house now." The guard held Lewis' arm in a vise grip before pushing him into the large building.

"My lord," the servant greeting him as he entered. "I hope you enjoyed surveying your land. I am afraid the empress has ordered the guards to housebound you for the time being."

"Was she here? I need to speak to her if she comes again."

"You will surely be here if she stops by again," the servant observed dryly.

Lewis tried to hold back a growl but he could not stop a small puff of air from leaving his lips. "Did the Empress say why she stopped by? A busy woman like her would not have much time for courtesy calls."

"You did save her life, my lord. I'm sure that she is just coming to thank you."

Lewis nodded like he agreed even though the truth was

more the opposite. Lewis could see that look in the servant's eyes — he was lying! Besides, whoever heard of a woman thanking a man who had helped her without permission? He knew the woman's circle back home would have given him a lashing!

He had to get home but staying here was not going to help anyone. He had done his part for the empire and now it was time to go.

Lewis knew that he was in a foreign land but he knew where the river was now and he knew that the guards would not see well at night. These guards were from the city. It was obvious from the way they walked through the grass like it was going to bite them! Lewis could sneak by them under the cover of darkness and make his way to the river.

"I heard water running and a guard mentioned a river. Does the Empress travel on it? She could get here quickly if she did."

"The Empress will get here quickly but not by the river." The servant was still trying to be mysterious in his answers but Lewis could almost leap for joy. He would travel on the river and never have to worry about meeting the empress. Things were finally going right!

By: Jennie Arnold

Chapter Eight

Matt knew that nothing good could follow Arcadia's appearance in the doorway.

"Something I can help you with?" he asked with as much cheek as he could muster.

"You will have a vision. Tell me everything you see and none of the Island women will be harmed. We are on the same side here, Matt."

"Oh, I know we are," Matt muttered, thinking the exact opposite.

Arcadia's hand went into her sleeve and brought out one of the guard's lightning sticks. The first strike was aimed at Matt.

Matt could feel the power and the pain course through him in time with his heartbeat. She hit him again and again until his only response was to fall to the ground. He had no energy. Matt could only groan in agony.

His mind screamed to roll from the strikes but his body could not acquest to the demands. He thought he would blackout when a vision began to form in front of him.

Lewis is sitting in a large mansion. Matt never saw a house so big! Size did not matter because Lewis did not stay. He made his way onto the roof in the dark and jumps from roof to tree. He moves through the trees silently, as any Islander who hunts elk can, and makes his way to a river. Lewis builds a raft out of fallen trees and vines and makes his way to freedom.

At least one of us is free, Matt thought to himself. Two visions were about Lewis. He was worried that his friend was hurt. One of his earlier visions showed Lewis getting attacked after all! This vision confirmed that his friend was safe. Lewis was not only safe but also free! Matt felt joy as he replayed the vision but a sharp slap brought him back to reality.

"Tell me everything you have seen," Arcadia ordered.

"I saw Lewis. He was sitting in a mansion. It was bigger than any building on the Island and finer to boot. I think there was real gold in the detailing!"

"Your visions involve action. What did your friend do in the mansion?"

"He just sat there. I can't control the visions!"

"You're not telling me everything, Matt. I don't want to bring the Island women into this. I will do what I have to. If they are harmed it will be because of your choice."

"You want me to lie or what? He was in a mansion. Maybe the vision means Lewis will be rich... I don't know!"

"You should know not to play games with me, boy." She turned to the guard at the door yelled, "Bring Kiarlin."

Even so, Matt was surprised to see Alaina's older sister come into the cell. Arcadia picked up the chain that attached to Kiarlin's band and pulled it tight.

"I won't hurt anyone. You can't make me hurt him." Kiarlin's voice sounded confident but her eyes betrayed her fear. She was terrified! Kiarlin had already been forced to hurt people and she knew that they could make her do so again.

"He won't be hurt if he tells the truth. Honesty webs measure heart rate and nerves to see lies. The web will only bring pain if you lie."

"I'm not lying!"

"We'll see." Matt felt the air thicken around him and knew that the honesty webs were in place.

"What did your friend do in your vision?"

"He just sat there," Matt said. The words were hardly out of his mouth before waves of pain overcame him. He tried to hold in a groan, waiting for the pain to subside.

"I'm so sorry," Kiarlin whispered with tears running down

By: Jennie Arnold

her face.

"It's not your fault," Matt answered in a voice that was tense with pain.

"That's right, Matt. It's not Kiarlin's fault. Your pain is your own fault. Tell the truth so that the pain can stop."

Matt stayed silent but the pain still sent him to his knees. He couldn't hold in a groan this time.

"That won't work, Matt. Tell me what happens in your vision."

"Nothing happened," Matt gritted out. His voice was going hoarse now but that was the least of his worries. He fell to the floor in pain but gritted his teeth and refused to say anything more. It seemed like hours later that Arcadia allowed Kiarlin to release the spell. Matt lay on the ground gasping.

"It seems I'll have to bring this problem to my mistress. She will not be gentle, Matt."

"I told you what happened." Matt tried to climb to his feet but he was still too weak.

"I cannot abide liars. Guards! Bind him knees to elbows." The guards pinned Matt to the floor and bent him in half. His elbows were tied to his knees, forcing him into a bent contortion. He could hardly breathe in that position.

"You might feel more like talking after a night trussed up," Arcadia told Matt with a smile. "Your friend can join you. You might think you can suffer but you will not let someone you care for do the same." Arcadia gestured for the guards to tie Kiarlin. Arcadia waited until both Matt and Kiarlin crutched on the floor panting for breath. Then she bent to eye level to wave. "Goodnight!" She called out before slamming the door.

"I'm sorry I got you mixed up in this," Matt told Kiarlin and meant it.

"Don't let them win, Matt. Don't tell them anything!"

"I won't tell them but I should tell you why you're

suffering."

"No! They expect you to tell me."

"Still, you should know that it's worth it." Matt looked her in the eyes to make sure she understood.

"As long as it hurts them."

With that, the two of them tried to settle in for an uncomfortable night, trying to think happy thoughts about an angry Arcadia.

Matt would have been happy to know that Lewis was escaping that very night. Lewis had crawled from the window onto a half-roof to horizontal beams that were higher than the trees. Lewis balanced on those beams to jump into the trees and over the guards' heads. He knew how to move silently as anyone who grew up in the open plains did.

The hard part came when he had to move around the guards. He could not just jump from one tree to the next. Some of the trees were too far or too weak to hold him. He had no choice but to travel on the forest floor.

Normally, Lewis would have no trouble walking silently on the leaf-strewn ground but normally he did not need to walk right in front of trained men. Lewis was surrounded by weak trees above and guards just below. The night was dark but there was still a risk of them seeing him.

Even people who grew up in the city could hear leaves crackle. Still, there was no other way out. Lewis took a calming breath and then lowered himself slowly to the ground. He was able to put his weight on the tree behind him and not make one sound on the leaves below. Still, he had to move quickly before the guards noticed a shadow.

Lewis moved on the side of the path so that he would not get lost. He could easily crouch into a ditch before someone saw him but he could not let himself get lost. He needed to find the river!

He followed the sound of running water to the river. A plethora of fallen trees and vines made building a raft simple. Lewis found himself traveling downriver after no time at all. He would be able to travel miles before dawn lit up the sky!

Unfortunately, Lewis' servant noticed his absence long before dawn. He called the guards to him.

"Search the forest and the main road. Block the river and the mountain pass! Find that boy! Look everywhere!"

He fought to keep the panic from his voice but there was only so much he could do. Small tones of fear found their way into his speech. The guards would have heard the fear and used it against the man if they were not in so much fear themselves.

The empress had ordered them to keep the boy safe and never to let him leave the small area of land. She had picked this land for the boy because it was so easy to watch. The river was on one side and a mountain on another so the land was easy to defend and fortify — it was easy to watch. This should be the safest place for the boy but he had escaped somehow.

"The empress will spear out your eyes if she comes and finds the young lord is gone. She put his protection — and the whole empire's protection by proxy — in our hands. Prophesy says that he will save the empire. It cannot be saved without him. Find him and bring him here so that he can do what is required."

"For the empire!" The guards yelled before running into the night to find the escapee.

"Are they still chasing us?" Mira asked the nanok running beside her.

They hunt still but they will not find us. The men who hunt you are far away. Dancer's trap has worked. The men are going the wrong way.

"We should meet up with Dancer soon then?"

You are meeting with us here, daughter, Dancer sent with a nanok grin. *My sleuth has misled the men who hunt you. Now we must focus on what the Creator sent us to do. He sent us to save you but Fate has allowed us to free those connected to you as well.*

Mira shook her head, not sure what she was hearing. "Someone told you to save me?"

The Creator told us where to find you. We will always help one of the children — one who can talk to the nanoks. The Creator told us that saving you would not be enough. We know that the End of the World is coming. We know that we will need Fate's help to survive them and Fate has brought two young men and many women to us.

We need the Seer. A picture of Matt formed in Mira's head. *We need the Darkness Chaser.* Now a picture of Lewis formed. *Both of these men have your scent on them. They are important to you. I think you know you need them. The nanoks need them too, and the women who travel with them. The women who can speak to nature.*

"You're talking about the women from Alta. You need them to speak to nature?"

You know of whom we speak. It is not just any group of women from Alta. We need the women who can do magic!

"The women the Argosi took?"

The nanok nodded as only a nanok could nod. The rest of the sleuth seemed to follow suit.

"We need them," Mira agreed. "So how do we free them? They cannot help anyone with bands on their heads and chains on their wrists. We need to release them from prison!"

We will hunt the hunters and find our allies, the nanok sleuth declared as one.

"Do you know where they are being held?"

Different places... Faraway places. The Darkness Chaser is far across the water. The Seer is nearer to us and with the magic women. Snow told Mira quickly. She was about to tell her more. Tell her a plan but Dancer broke in first and no one would interrupt the Ahaya, the leader.

We must free the Seer first. Him first and the women next. The Darkness Chaser is coming to us. We need to wait for him. The Creator will tell us where. He told us where to wait for our daughter and he will tell us where to find the others too.

Mira joined the nanoks in their roar and they all ran into the night as one sleuth... human and nanok together.

Matt's cell door opened early in the morning. The morning could not come soon enough for either Matt or Kiarlin. Still, they could not help but groan as guards untied them and stiff muscles screamed in protest.

"This is your last chance, Matt. A sleepless night is the least of what the high lady will do to make you tell the whole vision. Will you tell me now before she has to?"

"I already told you the whole vision," Matt spoke through gritted teeth because of the pain and the anger he felt towards all Argosi. He knew in his heart of hearts that he would do everything he could to stop them. Still, he knew that would not stop them from trying.

"Bring them up," Arcadia ordered the guards.

The guards forced Matt to his feet while Arcadia brought Kiarlin to hers. Both fell in a heap as soon as the guards stopped supporting them. Arcadia knew that if she wanted them to go anywhere they would need help. The Argosi were cruel but not needlessly so. They were efficient in everything they did.

"I can't allow healing. Pain gained is a lesson learned! Let's not waste it!"

The guards forced them to their feet and magic forced them to stay there. Pinpricks of pain ran up Matt's legs but he did not falter in his walk. The guards pushed him if he slowed and the magic kept him from falling so the group made record time to Ramilla's dining hall.

They were not alone in the dining hall. There were dozens of guards and two velvet women already there. Matt ignored all of them because his sister sat in the middle of the room.

One of the velvet women held the chain that connected to Daisy's headband. Daisy was shaky and looked like she was ready to cry. Matt knew his sister did not cry easily. He felt his anger rising.

"I warned you that the women would suffer if you refused to co-operate. Go ahead Arcadia."

Arcadia held Kiarlin's chains. He felt the air shudder and knew that Arcadia was using Kiarlin to hurt Daisy. He took a step towards the women but that was all he managed before guards dragged him to the ground.

Ramilla nodded to Arcadia. The air became sharper. Matt could feel a stronger quality to it. It felt thicker, like the air before a heavy rain. Clouds gave way to thunder as Daisy

By: Jennie Arnold

began to scream.

"Stop!" Matt shouted. "Stop! I'll tell you the whole thing. Just stop!" Daisy continued to weep but her screaming ended.

"Talk quickly," Mistress Ramilla hissed.

"I saw Lewis leave the mansion and escape on a river."

"How did he escape?" Ramilla pressed.

"Lewis climbed onto the roof and into the trees. He made his way to the river, built a raft and floated down it."

"Go through the vision step by step and tell us as many details as you can," Ramilla ordered.

"I don't know what you're looking for. I can't just repeat the vision."

"You should try hard, Matt. Try your best to remember every detail." Arcadia stroked the chain that held Daisy in a threatening manner. Her eyes lit with delight at the thought of hurting the girl.

"Don't hurt her!" Matt breathed out in frustration, wanting to expel anger the same way. "I'll tell you everything. Just don't hurt her. What do you want to know?"

"The most important thing right now is to know where your friend went... but I will get every scrap of information eventually, boy."

"Lewis built a raft to go downriver. He didn't have paddles or a rudder. He had to go with the current. Poles could force the raft to the shore but not steer it."

Kiarlin flinched and Daisy began to scream again.

"Stop! I told you all I know!" Matt tried to scream over his sister's wails but the Argosi acted as if they could not hear.

"You heard him!" Kiarlin screamed. "He doesn't know anything." She looked around the room, at all the people who were pretending she was not there. There was only one person even looking in her direction. "I'm sorry, Matt," Kiarlin told him.

"She's right," Arcadia told her mistress. "The boy does not know anything more."

Ramilla turned to the guards in the room. "Send word to the empress. He's traveling downriver toward Manien. Have the river blocked."

Ramilla motioned to have Matt taken away. The guards dragged Matt to his feet and pulled him into his cell.

"Lewis please forgive me. I just couldn't let them hurt her," Matt whispered the words and wished his friend could hear him.

~*~

Alaina had been strapped down to her cot as soon as the velvet woman left the room. Guards came in and carried Alaina and the cot into a carriage. Sainade was already in the carriage waiting with her chains ready.

"Where are we going?" Alaina asked in a shaking voice.

"We are going to the empress. Your destiny is about to begin."

"I just want to go home. Is Brington safe? Is my family? Is the Island?"

"You have no need to worry," Sainade reassured her with a smile. "You are the strongest magic user the empire has. That is why you are First Silken." Sainade began to stroke Alaina's hair and hum before she continued.

"I told you that you are a valuable tool. The empress believes that you can force the will of others. Most magic users who are strong in elemental magic, like you are, can force their wills to others. The empress is confident that you have this talent too. You and I have been called to her to test this."

"If I could bend people to my will I would have done it by now. I would have made the guards in the ship take me home."

"You are untrained. You may want to force your will on others but you do not know how to. The empress and I will train you. This band allows you to do magic without hurting yourself."

Alaina began to get mad then. She was scared... it seemed like she was always scared but now anger covered her fear.

"The band allows you to control what I do with magic. I won't learn how to do anything. You'll learn how to control other people by controlling me. Don't pretend like I get anything out of this."

Alaina felt her magic being used seconds before pain flooded through her. She fought to hold in a scream of agony. Alaina knew that speaking out had been a mistake and crying out would only make things worse.

"You will not speak to me in that manner ever again." Alaina managed to nod. Sainade did not lessen the pain as she continued talking. "That tone of voice will not be tolerated."

Alaina gasped as the pain suddenly disappeared. Sainade smiled at her response and never seemed to stop smiling until they stood before the empress.

The Empress did not look at all like smiling. She clutched a letter in a hand.

"We have the boy. The Seer talked and we know where he is going."

The empress turned and smiled at Alaina. "You and I are going to be at the house to greet him on his return. You and Sainade will make sure that the boy does as directed."

Alaina silently wept.

By: Jennie Arnold

Chapter Nine

Mira was reluctant to stay behind but the nanoks insisted that they could scout more thoroughly with a small party. She knew that they were right. The echo of exhaustion from the run here still rang through her but she was also stubbornly curious. Her family always said that she was too curious by half! Mira tried to calm her thoughts.

The sleuth knows what it is doing, Snow assured her. *They have hunted this way many times. Dancer has even hunted other hunters when she needed to.*

There is no need to brag on that now, Dancer admonished, returning with the scouting party.

"What did you find?" Mira tried to keep the eagerness from her voice.

Your friend is in the fortress. The guards believe that they are safe because of their high walls. They are just foolish! We nanoks do not trust to walls. They are too easy to walk under or around. Your friend should not be hard to get out.

"I am more worried about the weapons than about the walls. I do not want anyone to get hurt if we can help it. Maybe we can send in a small team that can sneak in and out?" Mira tried to keep the worry from her voice but Dancer saw right through her.

They have insulted our sleuth. The whole sleuth must work together to stop this. Snow and Arrow can distract the men by running in circles near the trees. The rest of us can get your friend out easily. The other nanoks nodded and grinned their nanok grins at Dancer's plan.

Dancer knew best. She had done things like this before.

Mira repeated those facts to herself until she began to feel some kind of relief. Dancer became the head of the sleuth for a reason! "I will need to come with you. I don't think that Matt or the women can understand nanoks. They may attack you and mistake you for an enemy."

Yes. You are part of the sleuth now and we need the whole sleuth. Are you rested enough?

Mira nodded.

Then we hunt, Dancer commanded. The whole sleuth started forward in a sprint.

Matt was desperate to get out. He was not afraid of the beatings or even of the visions. He was ashamed that he had betrayed his friend and he knew that they would make him do it again. Matt never wanted to feel that shame again. He thought that he had hurt one of the people he loved best in all the world.

The memory of it was a black stain on his heart. His heart beat faster knowing that they would make him do it again... and he knew that escape was the only option left!

He moved around his cell, looking for anything that could help. The door might not be the only way out of the cell. There were thin slits for air holes at the top of the cell. He could climb up and reach them... he knew this idea was futile, so he moved to another one.

He could look for something to use as a weapon and over-power the guards. Matt allowed himself to fantasize about this for a few minutes before he let reality sink in. There could be hundreds of guards.

He tried to think of a better idea when he began to notice

By: Jennie Arnold

the shouts from outside. There was growling and sword meeting sword... what was going on up there?

Matt tried to look out of the air slits but they were all too high. Then, he noticed that the sound was getting louder. They were right outside of his door!

Matt heard the voices of his guards shouting and mettle ringing out in the narrow hall. Tension filled the air and Matt's muscles alike. He used the energy that built from long frustration and confinement to charge at the door. He knew that the chances of surviving were small but a small chance is always better than no chance. He was ready to fight! Matt crouched down but instantly went still.

He heard roaring and growling... he heard nanoks!

"Mira!" Matt called. "In here, Mira!" Matt banged his fists on the door and made as much noise as he could, trying to get Mira's attention.

The scrape of mettle echoed in the small room, making Matt's heart skip a beat. He was saved! Excitedly, he stepped back, making room for his rescuers. It was Mira and she was surrounded by furry creatures of legend. It was hard to think of the nanoks as more than stories and even twice as hard to imagine Mira, the girl he had grown up with, as their leader.

"How in the world did you get here?" Matt asked in shock.

"They brought me," Mira told him gesturing to the nanoks around her. "They found you and brought me. The Creator speaks to them, Matt. He told them that they need you to help them survive on the Last Day."

"It looks more like I need them to survive! Mira, I can't help a few Islanders leave a big boat! How am I supposed to help nanoks survive the end of everything? I can barely look after myself!"

"I don't know that part yet. Right now I know we need to leave this room. We need to get out of this tower!"

"Is the path clear, Dancer?"

Matt could not hear any answer but Mira nodded like she heard one.

"The nanoks are clearing a way for us. If we run with them they can get us out."

"Alright," Matt agreed. "Lead on."

Mira and the nanoks rushed ahead to an already hot battle.

"Dancer says that the guards are holding a narrow bridge and are trapping us."

"It is easy to defend a narrow area. We just have to get them to scatter. We just need a plan," Matt commented.

"We need tools." Mira began to look around for anything she could use.

"Tools?" Matt repeated looking around. Then, he found it: "Fireworks! We can just light a few of them and throw them into the crowd of guards."

Both Islanders remembered the Spring Fair when Lewis had gone to inspect the fireworks. He had lit a lamp so that he could see clearly in the darkness but the flame did not stay in the lamp. Things got out of hand and the fireworks destroyed half a field and burned all of it! The fireworks were more than enough to deal with a few dozen guards!

The lights that danced in the sky had been amazing but then the wreckage of the field was even more spectacular. People on the Mainland said that they could smell smoke a mile in.

"They'll scatter for sure!" Mira agreed. She ran to the torch on a nearby wall and light three fusses.

Mira and Mat threw fireworks onto the bridge and saw the guards do more than scatter: they ran out of the fort!

"Run for cover!" Mira warned both Matt and the nanoks. BOOM!!!!

Matt stuck his head out from behind the barrier and was

By: Jennie Arnold

surprised to see that the bridge was still standing. The nanoks ran across it and the two humans followed; running into the night, free once more.

Lewis rode his raft, looking behind him long after the manor could no longer be seen. He was sure that any attempt to stop him would come from the manor. He was more than surprised when the attack that did stop him came from the opposite direction.

"Halt! Halt by order of the empress!" A commanding voice ordered from the top of a large barricade.

Lewis shook his head in shock. How had they even known he would come this way?

"Put your boat to the shore and leave the raft quietly."

Lewis shook his head again; this time in refusal. "No!" He yelled out, knowing that he could not escape but refusing to help them bring him back all the same. He could not let them know the fear that ran thinker than the blood in his veins and he would not help them spread that fear!

Lewis' servant stepped into clear view on the top of the barricade. "We still have your Island, my lord," the servant reminded him. "We still have your family. I would hate for anything bad to happen to them."

Caution seemed to flood into Lewis. Only, it was not caution for himself but for his loved ones. He rowed the raft to shore and walked out. The servant and some of the guards from the manor were there to meet him.

"I wish things could have turned out differently," the servant said. He held out a steaming cup and ordered, "Drink this. All of it, my lord."

Lewis did as he was ordered. The drink seemed to take effect instantly. His head was fuzzy and his mind seemed to be muddled.

The guards had no trouble marching Lewis back to the manor. They forced him into chains once they got to the building though, making sure that he could never again escape.

Thin but strong chains linked his wrists together. He could move his arms but the movements were limited and slow. The real imprisonment was the leg chains.

The chain linked his ankles together but another long chain ran from a bedpost, nailed into the wall, to Lewis' ankle. The chain did not allow Lewis to get more than three feet from the door, balcony or window. Lewis could only move in a small circle. And of course, there was the tea.

Lewis was not sure what was in it but it made his head spin and the servant made sure that he drank several cups in the short time before the empress came to visit him.

"How am I supposed to even talk with the empress? This tea makes everything fuzzy."

"It is for your own protection, my lord," the servant claimed.

"How does this help me?"

The servant looked squarely at Lewis' eyes before he answered, "The empress will have you shot until you drink it. This tea may well save your life."

Lewis felt his stomach fall into his boots as he realized that the servant was serious.

Alaina was still crying when they pulled up to the manor. The empress had told her that she would be forced to bend

By: Jennie Arnold

someone's will. She could not hide her terror at the thought of making someone else lose control.

The velvet women had taken her power and any choice she had over and over again. She knew how it felt to be forced to do something against her will. Alaina knew how it felt to have no control over her own body. She could not imagine making someone else — someone she had met — go through the same thing.

Still, Alaina knew that she would not have any choice in the matter. Alaina walked into the building meekly behind Sainade and she did not look up once until she saw the chains on Lewis' feet.

She saw that he was sitting at a table. A man stood over him and guards surrounded the room. Lewis wore fine clothes but he looked more than tired... he looked defeated. Had they told him what would happen here today too?

"It is a pleasure to see you, my Lady, as always," the man who stood above Lewis said.

"I do enjoy these visits, Hiro, but we both know that I should not be here now. I have an empire to run. Keeping the boy safe is your responsibility."

"I have made some dramatic changes here, my Lady that will assure that you are not disturbed like this again."

"That is good to hear," the empress said with a graceful movement of her hand. "This is our newest First Silken. She will ensure that the young lord does as he is told."

Hiro nodded to Sainade and Alaina with something like fear. "I had hoped such measures would not be necessary but I have given him the tea all the same."

"Perfect." The empress turned to Sainade. "Are you ready to begin?" Sainade nodded and Alaina felt her stomach drop.

"I saved your life," Lewis whispered in an unsteady voice. "They said that I could go home after I saved the empire. I saved you…"

"You saved my life and have been given a title and this house as a reward. Now you have the responsibility to use your magic to help both the empire and your little Island."

Alaina felt her magic being used. The air felt solid and Lewis gasped as it closed around his lungs like a vice. Alaina tried to call the power back.

Don't do this, she begged the magic silently. *Do good*!

Alaina's pleads had no effect this time. The magic continued to squeeze into Lewis until he screamed in pain. He crutched over the table, panting when the empress put a hand on his shoulder.

"Can you do magic?" She asked him quietly.

"I shot lightning when the guards tried to hurt me and my friends," he answered in a monotone voice.

"You've never done magic before?"

"That was the first time I have done magic."

"Can you do magic now?"

Alaina saw Lewis' eyes widen. He hesitated to answer but the magic squeezed and flooded, drowning him until he gasped out an answer:

"I don't know how to do magic. It just happens. I can't do any now." Lewis breathed hard when he had finished answering. He looked like he had just finished a sprint.

Two men in guard uniforms and chains were pulled foreword. Alaina saw recognition in Lewis' eyes but she had never seen them before.

"The Argosi army is the best army this land has ever seen because of discipline. Allowing a lord to travel unprotected shows a lack of discipline."

Lewis' face went pale and Alaina could not help but feel a sickness rise in her stomach. The empress could not be asking her to make Lewis kill these men, could she?

By: Jennie Arnold

"The penalty for a lack of discipline for an officer is death. You may fire when ready, Sainade."

The velvet woman had a small smile on her lips as she forced Alaina's magic to flood into Lewis. She could see Lewis fighting the magic's pull but his face changed from red to white and back again until his eyes turned blank. Sainade's will was forced into him and lightning shot out.

The two guards were struck until nothing was left. Alaina was surprised to see that the floor around them was untouched. The lightning still seemed to crackle in the room but none of it was coming out of Lewis.

He lay on the floor, moaning. Alaina feared that they had taken too much magic from him. He could be hurt badly.

"Have the boy stand, Hiro." The empress's voice was soft but the order in it was undeniable.

Lewis climbed shakily to his feet without help. "I'll never do that again," Lewis swore. "I don't kill people!"

"You will do as the empress commands, my lord," Hiro said in a voice that did not belong to a servant. "She is still in control of your Island."

"You have already threatened my family. How do I even know that they are still alive?"

"You don't want me to have to prove it," Sainade warned. "You already know that I can kill them either way."

Lewis clenched his teeth to keep himself from grinding them in frustration. "What do you expect me to do to keep my family safe?"

"You did well today. It is obvious that you and the new First Silken can work as a team. You will both train with Hiro until you have mastered this joined fighting style."

"If we do this — if we work hard and train, can we see our families?"

"I think something can be arranged. Traveling there is too

much of a hassle. You are both too valuable to lose at sea or in the new land. Still, I see no reason not to allow you to write letters."

Alaina's breath caught at the thought of hearing from her family. "Will they be able to write back?"

"I will provide them with paper and ink if needed. None of the guards will interfere."

"How would we know the letters are actually from them?" Lewis' question snapped like an accusation.

"I'm sure you can recognize your father's handwriting. You would know if the letters were fakes," Hiro began.

"I gave you my word that none of the guards would interfere," the empress snapped back at Lewis, cutting Hiro off.

Alaina could not lose this chance. "I agree to those terms." Alaina looked at Lewis in desperation the whole time she spoke, hoping that he would agree as well. She could not even write to her family if he did not agree to co-operate! Alaina could see the disbelief in Lewis's eyes but she could not give him away. Her heart would not let her. The chance of home and family meant too much.

"I agree as long as going home when this is over is still part of the plan. I don't plan on writing letters forever."

"You will return to your Island as heroes when it is all done," the empress agreed.

Alaina breathed a sigh of relief. She knew that she would be able to go home. One day...

Chapter Ten

Exhaustion dragged at Matt long before the nanoks set camp for rest. His entire body ached from bone-weariness. The sleepless nights, beatings and lack of light and food have all caught up with him.

The fear of getting caught kept him running through the day and night before but the exertion is too much now. The women are showing the same weariness, if not more. The women have been captured for longer than Matt and fear can only keep you going so long. The whole party fell to the ground where they were and slept.

The nanoks kept guard and told Mira that the Argosi were all miles behind them. It was safe to get a few hours' sleep. Mira tried to talk to Matt and to reassure him they were safe but Matt was too tired to listen.

"The nanoks know what they are talking about," Mira told him. "If they say that the guards cannot catch up with us tonight, then they can't do it."

"I never doubted your nanoks, Mira."

"Then what is wrong?"

"You mean besides running for our lives, losing Lewis and having strange powers suddenly thrown at us?"

"Sorry. I know that wasn't the right question."

"I just need to sleep, Mira. I hurt all over."

Mira got up and walked towards the nanoks but she turned before she lay down and called Matt.

"You'll tell me if you see anything, right Matt? It could be important."

"You'll be the first to know," Matt promised before falling swiftly into sleep.

At first, Matt thought he was dreaming, but it didn't feel like a dream. It felt like the visions he had before. He felt the numbness and the surreal quality of it all. Strangely, he did not feel pain. Something about the feel of it told him that this was no dream but a vision. There were distinct differences between the two!

He saw the women from Alta walking around a lake. Kiarlin walked a little behind them. She kept looking over her shoulder as if she expected to see something. She seemed surprised when she looked and could find nothing. Kiarlin continued to walk for a few steps but would look over her shoulder again. After three or four times something changed.

An army of Argosi rushed out of the glens around the lake and charged at the women. They ran but Kiarlin was too slow. Matt felt her reach for her magic but she could not grab it. It made him feel like he had when he first tried to force a vision. He could feel her searching for power that was there but not knowing how to get to it.

The second of hesitation was all the Argosi needed. Arrows and throwing knives rained down on Kiarlin. He felt the life abruptly leave her and he jumped from the force of it as soon as he came back to himself.

It wasn't just the abrupt ending that made Matt jump. He knew the place the attack had happened and they were traveling right to it! He had to tell Mira to get the nanoks to change direction.

"Mira! Mira!" Matt called as he shook his friend awake. "I had a vision. We need to travel away from Silver Lake and go towards the mountains."

"Mountains make for hard traveling, Matt and none of us are at our best."

"People will die if we go to the lake. We need to get away from here."

"Alright," Mira agreed, seeing her friend really was upset. "I'll ask the nanoks if they know a place to hide near the mountains."

~*~

Mira had never seen Matt so distressed. Out of the three of them, Matt was the laid back one. Matt never lost his nerve even when he had to address both the Woman's Circle and the Council at the same time. He was always calm and thought everything through. Mira knew that the vision had to be terrible to get Matt into a state like that.

By: Jennie Arnold

"The Seer told me that danger lies near the lake. We need to travel towards the mountains. Are there any safe places near there?"

There is one place, Dancer sent, *but it is a small place.* Mira saw a dark place that made a nanok feel safe in Dancer's sending. She could tell that the nanoks felt that this was a perfect din but she also knew that the humans would not be eager to enter.

The cave has places where many nanoks can fit but humans do not seem to enjoy tight or dark spaces. Willow sent with reluctance. He did not see why the humans were making things difficult.

This is the perfect place to hide. Snow sent in excitement. *The Creator began his duty there. We may find answers in a place as special as that.*

The nanoks all nodded in agreement.

"I'll let the others know the change of plans."

They made good time running the next day. Everyone felt refreshed after a little rest and running was not so much of a strain. Still, Mira worried about Matt. A tiredness deeper than strain showed on his face.

Matt had not slept well during their rest and his time as a prisoner had not gone easy. Mistress Tilde looked at Matt's wounds and tutted. She was the best healer in Alta but she could only do so much. Matt's body had to mostly heal itself.

She stayed with Matt after rubbing the healing balm on his skin and confided in him:

"I am only the best healer because I knew more than anyone else. I knew I had magic and I have taught myself how to use it. I call on the power to help others heal."

"This can't all be magic! You use herbs and poultices."

Matt was getting frustrated with the women's attitude about their powers. They all told him it was dangerous to use them and that none of them really knew any control. Matt did not want to even imagine Mistress Tilde apologizing for healing.

"I use herbs because magic is not enough. I am not a strong magic user anyway but some of these women are. They could become great healers if they would let me teach them."

Matt tried not to show his shock. Mistress Tilde wanted to teach others to use magic!

"Needing permission never stopped you teaching before."

"Magic is different. The student needs to be willing before real learning can begin. They are all afraid to learn but I think that they will change their minds if you ask them to."

"Me? Why would they listen to me?"

"They respect you and are grateful to you for helping them. If you ask them to try to learn then they will try."

"I'll talk to them, then," Matt promised.

Mira had no idea what Matt said to the women but soon enough, they were lining up to take Mistress Tilde's healing course. The women could all summon the magic at will by the time the group made it to the mountain's base.

The nanoks asked for one of the women to send magic into the cave before sending nanoks in.

Mira explained the request to one of Mistress Tilde's classes and Kiarlin volunteered to send in probing magic.

"This is really used to look into a person's body to see if illness lurks within but it will find danger if it waits in the cave."

Mira nodded that she understood. "Thank you for doing this. The cave is a special place to the nanoks so they cannot just treat it like any other camp spot."

"I can sense something strong about this place but I knew that this place would be different before I got here. Matt said that this is a safe place. You said it is a place we can get answers. How could it not be special?"

By: Jennie Arnold

"What does the probe magic tell you?"

"There is something in the cave but it is not here to harm us. Do you think it is another nanok?"

"The nanoks would be able to smell one of their own. I'll tell them that whatever is in there is friendly. They will be much more relaxed then."

It is the prophet, Snow said, overhearing the conversation. *He tells us what the Creator says from the water. The Creator speaks to all Hunters. Not just nanoks.*

"Did he ever speak to humans?" Mira asked her.

He tried to talk to them for a long time but they all ignored him. Still, the Creator is looking to help men. He wants to bring them hope. He sent us you and your friends to save us from the End Times.

"Will humans be safe in the End Times too?"

Only Fate knows what time holds. I feel hope within me and know that humans will survive the End Times with the nanoks.

"Humans kill nanoks," Mira reminded her.

They are not evil. They are just confused. They used to worship us but that was confusion too.

No one wanted to admit their mistakes but the nanoks deserve to know this.

"My people needed many gods when they first settled this harsh land. We were wanderers then – friendless and homeless. The old gods were the one solace we had. They guided every aspect of life and death. Nanoks led us through each trial until we learned the way on our own. My people built these statues to thank the old gods and to remind us of the wondering we left behind. My island forgot the past. We forgot the sacrifices your people made. We forgot the Creator and we left Fate behind."

Mira hoped she was right — that they would all survive in the final fight to come — as Dancer descended into the cave to see what secrets the Creator would reveal.

I hate training, Lewis thought to himself, *no, that's not right*. Lewis could not think of a word to describe how much he hated training. Hiro had forced him and Alaina to put on shows for visiting nobles. It seemed like the borage of visitors was an unending stream.

Hiro claimed that all of these people were here to see the new young lord but Lewis had a feeling that Hiro was inviting them all to come. All the visitors pretended that they did not see chains or bands; like they could not think of prisoners. Still, Lewis tried to keep his temper, to be polite to the visitors.

"I know you don't like putting on shows. It can be very frustrating but if you just think of it like a play — like it's all pretend — everything seems to go by much more smoothly."

Lewis knew that Alaina meant well when she said things like this but the truth was that the girl would do anything to hear from her family. He couldn't blame her really. He was desperate to know how his father and sister were as well, but he was going to jump through hoops just to get a letter.

The Argosi have been threatening Lewis with the lives of his family for weeks now. If they wanted him to take these threats seriously, they were going to need more than letters and promises.

"Thanks for the advice, Alaina. Let's just get this over with and maybe they'll let us turn in early tonight."

"It would be nice to get a full night's sleep," Alaina agreed.

Lewis had a harder time of pushing down the anger this time. He had to remind himself that he was not angry at Alaina. He was angry with the Argosi. He was upset that mundane

By: Jennie Arnold

things like letters and full nights of sleep had become rare rewards.

Sainade and Hiro walked into the room before the nobles.

"Now remember, just relax and let the power flow between you. Try to imagine a circular current." Sainade began each lecture the same way and today was no exception. Lewis fought not to roll his eyes.

"Baron Humphrey and his family are here to watch today and they have made a special request –"

"They want us to shoot lightning at a tree?" Lewis asked sarcastically.

"Oh, they have something special in mind," Hiro began with a glare at Lewis. "The Baron has brought his family's velvet woman and Silken. They want the two of you to fight them."

"They want us to fight members of their own families?" Alaina asked in shock.

"Don't think of it as a fight. It's more of a tournament. I have seen those in your land. It is a friendly competition."

Lewis could see that Sainade was trying to comfort Alaina but he could also see that this was not going to be some friendly competition. One side would not be able to just walk away.

Alaina did not want to think about the fight even as it began. The Baron and his family sat at one end of a long table. The empress and Hiro sat at the other. Sainade, Alaina, and Lewis stood at one end of a large dining hall. Sainade held a chain that leads to the band and cuffs. Lewis stood with his ankles and wrists linked by chains but he was no longer tethered to the wall. The Baron's velvet woman and Silken stood, chained together, at the other.

"I find the chain makes both women more obedient. The Silken has little choice in the matter but velvet women seem to think that losing a Silken is just part of the game. The linked chain reminds her that she will lose something if she makes me lose my Silken."

"Such tactics are not needed for the empress or her loyal subjects," Hiro reminded the Baron. "All of the subjects are already fighting as if their lives depend on it."

"There is no need to talk of politics tonight. Let's just enjoy the dinner and the show," the baron's wife suggested.

"Yes," the empress agreed. "I'm sure it will be a show worth seeing."

With a wave of the hand, the empress signaled the fight to begin.

The baron's velvet women sent lightning. Sainade was quick to block it with lightning of her own. The fight went on like that for quite some time. The baron's pair would send lightning, fire or vines and Sainade would send the element to block it. Finally, Sainade had enough. She went on the offensive.

Men with magic were rare, but they were typically twice as strong as a female magic-user. Alaina and these women were both strong magic users. Still, Sainade only needed to make Lewis call on his power once to make the other two fall to their hands and knees.

The Baron jumped to his feet as the pair fell. "It is clear who the winner is," he declared loudly. "I thought Lord Silas was simply telling tales, but he did not need to exaggerate about this boy. The power he wields could change the way battles are won."

"You can see why so many nobles are being invited for a

demonstration," Hiro said. The Baron only nodded in response.
Alaina was only glad it was over.

By: Jennie Arnold

Chapter Eleven

Matt tried to make the visions come but nothing came. No foggy tingle or misty sights came from the stillness. He even asked Mistress Tilde if she could teach him to control his magic.

"No, Matt. I'm sorry. Women and men learn in different ways already and our magics are so different that I don't think my methods will work for you."

The women who had asked to learn could do amazing things. Two women found that they had a talent for healing and they did not need to use herbs as Mistress Tilde did. Kiarlin found that she had a talent for elemental magic. She could build walls of stone around an Island in seconds! Matt sat in the class, hoping that he could just learn a measure of control.

He was not unrealistically hoping for amazing feats or flashes of lightning. Matt just wanted to have a vision when he needed one. Still, no amount of classes or practicing seemed to help.

Kiarlin was the opposite. She seemed to flourish at the classes. She excelled at controlling her elemental power — and she only had one goal in mind: to use her new powers to free her sister. She had more drive than any of the other women. Kiarlin had an edge and a purpose. Thoughts of her sister drove her to practice harder and longer than anyone else.

"I can't leave her there in bands!" She exclaimed to Matt when he asked. "Every second I spend practicing is a second closer to getting Alaina back."

"I know the feeling," Matt mumbled thinking about Lewis. "Lewis, Mira and I grew up like siblings. No one else on Alta Island seemed close to our age and — as children especially —

the older children on our Island just seemed like a mystery. The younger children were too small to be interesting and the older kids were just too different. Lewis and Mira were the only kids I could play with. As we grew they became the only people I could talk to."

"That's what Alaina is to me. I could tell her anything and she would do whatever she could to help me." Kiarlin paused with her hand on her chin, thinking. "Maybe Mira can help you control your powers. Her magic is not like mine or Mistress Tilde's healing. She found her magic at the same time as you and she has figured out how to use it so quickly."

"Mira says that the nanoks teach her. She's always been a quick learner but I don't think that she can teach me. Mira's magic differs from mine. She doesn't have to think about what she does before she does it."

"You won't know if you don't try."

Matt throws up his hands, suddenly angry. "Mira is already carrying Lewis' fate on her shoulders. She's all on her own. I can't help find Lewis because I can't see any visions when I want to. So it's all up to Mira. I might not be able to help but I can keep from distracting her. Never say I'm not trying!"

"I'm sorry, Matt," Kiarlin whispers.

"I'm sorry, too," Matt admitted. "I shouldn't have yelled at you."

"Let me try something..."

"What?" Matt asked a little confused by her change of topic.

"I think I know how you can see visions."

"If you plan to hit me, forget it. I've already tried that and it takes a lot more than one hit to get a vision."

"I don't think you need pain to have a vision. You just need adrenaline. You could go jogging or practice swordplay and get the same effect."

By: Jennie Arnold

"You don't expect me to get into a fight to get these visions?"

"I'll go jogging with you if it will make you feel better," she assured him.

Kiarlin woke Matt up early the next day. He would have snuggled deeper into his blankets but Kiarlin's smile made Matt's heart melt just a little. He got up and ran.

Matt never enjoyed running but his long legs could cover ground quickly. Still, this jog was not really for enjoyment. Matt could feel his heart pumping adrenaline through his body. He closed his eyes, trying to push the adrenaline into a vision.

Closing his eyes was a mistake. Matt did not see the wet, slippery ground in front of him and his feet flew over his head.

"Matt!" Kiarlin called with concern.

"I'm alright," Matt called but he cried out in pain as soon as he started to move.

"What happened? Are you sure you're okay?"

"I think I broke my wrist."

Kiarlin held the wrist gently, turning it slowly to examine the brake. The pain of the break made Matt see a vision. Matt's eyes misted over as he watched.

"We need to get you to a healer," Kiarlin decided.

"We need to find Mira."

Kiarlin looked at Matt like he had lost his mind but he knew something she did not. Matt had seen a vision and he *needed* to talk to Mira NOW!

He would find her and he would be sure she listened.

Lewis was beyond tired. Each muscle and bone ached, but he forced himself to stay on his feet. He did not want this

Baron to see his weakness.

"Hiro did not exaggerate your abilities. There is no shame in losing to great warriors. To show that there are no hard feelings, please join my family and me for dinner."

The Baron had a smile on his face that was meant to look friendly. It didn't. At least it didn't to Lewis. The smile made Lewis feel like he needed a bath. It was positively swarmy!

"We would be happy to accept," Sainade declared, looking at the two of them pointedly. She looked like a school mistress about to scold them for being impolite.

"Thank you. That is a very kind offer," Alaina said uncertainly.

Lewis refused to say a word of thanks. He was too tired to pretend to be polite. Sainade glared at him before speaking on his behalf.

"Lewis and Alaina would be happy to join you for dinner. I will attend as their chaperone."

Lewis ground his teeth and fought to keep in a frustrated sigh. He could tell that this dinner was not a simple dinner. The Baron had something to prove and Lewis was afraid that he would use them to prove it. The man did not seem like a graceful looser.

"How wonderful!" The Baron exclaimed. "I will see you all in a few hours. I'll send a driver to bring you to our summer manor."

"Very gracious," Hiro remarked. "I'll see that they make it on time." The Baron and his party waltzed out of the door.

"Do you really think that going to his manor is a good idea?"

"The Baron is our guest and when guests invite us to dinner we accept," the empress broke in. "I can see that I'm going to have to teach you manners."

"The Baron is *your* guest. He is *our* competitor." Lewis

gestured to Alaina and himself as he spoke. He was trying to make her see that this was not about being polite. This man could be a threat.

Lewis saw light flash in the empress' eyes and he knew what was coming. Alaina gasped and Lewis felt the air around him sizzle before pain overwhelmed him.

He fell to the floor writhing. He bit off a moan and tried to look the empress in the eye.

"You do not get a choice in this affair. You are a weapon. *My* guests are *your* guests and *my* enemies are *your* enemies. You are a tool and you attack where I point like a good sword. Do you understand your role?"

Lewis nodded. The pain stopped instantly but he did not get up. He just lay on the floor, panting. He did not want to give in but he knew he had little choice. Still, the empress looked disappointed.

"I thought we had gone through this already. You will do as I command one way or another."

"You know that you can make me go anywhere but you can't make me trust him."

"You shouldn't trust him," Sainade counseled. "You will show him respect. Let the empress worry about schemes."

"May we rest before dinner?" Alaina clearly asked the question to take attention off of Lewis. He was grateful to her but he worried for her too.

"Practice makes perfect," Sainade answered her.

"They have worked hard and won. Let them skip the evening session this once. You've earned a reward." The empress' eyes stayed on Lewis as she spoke. This was more of a dismissal than a reward.

Sainade led them upstairs to their rooms. Lewis still slept in the rooms he had woken up in that first day and Alaina stayed close by. Lewis liked knowing that Alaina was nearby but he also knew that the rooms were not given to her for him. Alaina stayed across the hall so that Sainade could look after them both.

"Rest. I will wake you in time for dinner."

It surprised Alaina how much better she felt after the short nap. She was no longer bone-weary and no longer terrified about dinner... She was only afraid now.

Alaina knew that the velvet woman and the silken would be at the dinner too. They made her nervous. She had thought all the silken women were like the women from Alta; that all the women were taken from their homes and unhappy with their lot. This silken woman was not like the women from Alta — she enjoyed fighting with people.

Alaina did not want to be in the same room as the woman because she could not be sure what they would do. She agreed with Lewis. They could not be trusted. Still, she knew saying so would not change a thing.

The empress wanted them to go to dinner and they would go to dinner. Alaina was sure that the empress had her own goals in this game the nobles played but she could not see what those goals were. Alaina also knew that the empress would make them do whatever it took to win her game.

There was no reason to fight it. Fighting was pointless.

Alaina could see that Lewis was aching for a fight. She did not know if he expected to beat the empress or just wanted to feel like he was resisting. Either way, Lewis would get into trouble because he could not stop. Alaina knew that she had to do everything she could to keep him out of it.

She felt like she owed him. First, he came to save her on

Alta and then she had been the cause of his new problems. She had made it so that he could not fight. She had made him use magic against his will... she had stolen his will.

She needed to help him but there is not much she could do. Alaina tried to think of any way to get out of this as she rode to the Baron's home.

"Remember your place," Sainade snapped before the coach stopped.

"Welcome, welcome!" The Baron greeted them warmly.

They all sat down to a rich dinner in a golden gilded dining room. The plates were made of gold and the walls were covered in mirrors. Murals covered the ceiling. Alaina had never been in a room as fine as this!

"I find that a dinner is never really enjoyable without a little entertainment." The Baron motioned to a side door. The velvet woman and the silken that had fought them earlier that day came into the room.

Sparkling fire fell rained from the ceiling like a waterfall. It looked beautiful! Alaina hoped that Sainade would let her do magic like that but the curl in Sainade's lip told her not to ask.

Alaina was so busy looking at Sainade that she did not see that the Silken was now aiming at her. Fire went flying towards her. There was no time for her to jump out of the way!

Lewis jumped to his feet and held out his hands as ice flew from his hands to stop the fire. Now Sainade was on her feet too. Alaina felt her magic get taken and thrown into a lightning spell. The lightning flew at Lewis and he crumpled to the floor.

"You do not use magic without permission, boy! A tool is broken if it acts without instruction, no matter how rare the tool is," Sainade said coldly. "We will take our leave now." Alaina walked away without looking back.

Mira saw Matt running towards her. The look on his face told Mira that Matt was nervous. Matt was never nervous... or he never showed his nerves. Something must really be bothering him.

"What is it?" Mira asked.

"There's something I need to tell you but I should start with something I should have told you a long time ago. I've had a vision... a series of visions really. I need to start with one I had while a prisoner.

"I saw a nanok kill the empress while she was running through the forest. It worried me that the Argosi would think that you were to blame so I only told them that a creature killed her. The nanoks are not the only important part though... I recognized where the empress was running. She was on the Island. She was on Alta."

Matt took a deep breath as if he had gotten something heavy off his chest. Still, Mira knew that Matt was not done; Matt took another breath and then three more; gearing up for an even bigger confession. Mira could read the worry on Matt's face.

"Just now, I had another vision."

It was just then that Mira noticed Matt's wrist. "Let me get a healer while you talk." Kiarlin put her arm around Matt. He pulled away quickly.

"This is important!" Mira and Kiarlin both turned to Matt, giving him their full attention. "The vision said that a big battle is coming. A battle that is bigger than the one the Island just had against the Argosi. Bigger than the Mainland and the Argosi could ever be! The Argosi are coming back to fight. The trouble is that they're not coming alone. The real enemy is someone else; someone who looks human on the outside but has a soul as black as night.

"I saw this new enemy in the forest by Alta. The nanok killed the empress behind him. The strange thing is that I could hear the nanok speak in my vision. He warned me that the man with the black soul is after Lewis. He said that he has to protect Lewis."

"Lewis is coming here?" Mira asked in shock.

Daughter, Snow greeted as she walked to Mira. *We have a message from the Creator. He says that Fate is guiding our quest. The others that we need will join us in the Mist Mountains. Your comrade, Darkness Chaser will join us there along with the youngest woman who calls on nature.*

Mira conveyed Snow's message to the others.

"Alaina will be there?" Kiarlin asked in excitement.

Your sister will be there, Snow confirmed. *Her magic is strong, and the sleuth needs her. Nature will listen to her.*

They brought Matt to the healers but Kiarlin said she could not stay. She wanted to go tell the other women the nanok's message. She left the two Islanders alone by the cave.

The two of them could have used their time alone to gossip or remember old times. But they had more important things to discuss. Mira remembered the nanok in Matt's visions and she still had many questions. Matt seemed only too happy to answer. What Mira really wanted to know was if Matt understood the nanoks when they spoke now.

"Not when Snow spoke. But the Creator's message sounds a lot like my vision. They're both telling us the same thing: That everything will finally work. This all started because we wanted to free the women from our town. The women the Argosi took are free. The Argosi captured Lewis, but he is coming here. We have a chance to save him."

"We have an army of nanoks, women who can use magic and a man who can see the future on our side. We might stand a chance against the Argosi," Mira agreed with a smile.

Things were finally turning out right.

By: Jennie Arnold

Chapter Twelve

Lewis blinked dry, blurry eyes until he could focus on his surroundings. A chain ran from his wrists to the wall. His legs were bound too. The links were too short to allow much movement. His neck twisted to look at his surroundings.

He as laying on a narrow couch and a ray of light from the small window revealed that Alaina was lying on a similar couch beside him. They chained her wrists to the wall. The couches looked sturdy, but he felt the surface beneath him moving and guessed that he was in a carriage.

Memory came flooding back to him. He could see each event in detail. The Baron had his women attack Alaina. Lewis tried to protect her, but he had used magic without permission. Sainade had sent lightning flying at him and he had passed out from the pain. Now he was here. Where ever here was....

Alaina's eyes fluttered open. "Oh! Thank goodness you are awake. Sainade said that you were all right, but you were so still."

"I'm fine, Alaina." Lewis could not help but smile at her concern. "Do you know where we are headed?"

"Sainade won't tell me anything. She said that we would meet with the empress and that everything would be explained."

"The empress must be the only one who knows anything around here," Lewis declared; Loud enough for Sainade to hear. He wanted her to be angry enough to come in and give him a lecture. "Sainade must not know anything. The empress must not trust her at all." Lewis wanted her to be so mad that she gave away more than she intended.

Alaina looked from him to the door in a nervous, worried glance. Lewis could see that they scared her but he knew that the reward would be worth the fear.

Sainade burst through the door. Her face looked angry. Her cheeks were red and for eyes blazed with a fire.

"I have had just about enough of your games, boy. You might think you can do anything with magic but the truth is that you cannot breathe without the empress' mercy."

Lewis saw Alaina jump when Sainade stole her magic. The air in the entire room sizzled. Lewis knew he had pushed Sainade too far. She wasn't going to tell him anything. She would only make him hurt!

"Please," Alaina whispered as the air solidified.

Lewis felt her push his will away and put her own in its place. He fought it as best as he could. People back home had always told him he was stubborn and he put all his stubbornness to use. Still, that only seemed to buy him a second that lasted an hour.

He was breathing heavy and sweating through the fancy shirt the Argosi had given him. Sainade had control, and she would not let him forget it.

"You will hit yourself as hard as you can until I tell you to stop. You will prevent Alaina from stopping you if she attempts."

Lewis felt the magic sink into him. Power would make him do what she said! His own fist punched him in the stomach once and then twice. His arm rose up to hit himself one more time. His fist never struck.

Sainade broke off the magic quickly. Alaina actually groaned in relief. Lewis knew that it was not over yet.

"The empress is in control not only in Argosi but all over the world. I am an agent of the empress and I am in control of you." Sainade bent down to whisper in Lewis' ear. "You will

By: Jennie Arnold

do well to remember who is in control."

~*~

The nanoks insisted on moving. Instinct told them that the group needed to begin traveling immediately. So, everyone packed away their meager belongings and started off. The travel was much slower than the nanoks would have liked but they let the humans set the pace. It was obvious that the flight from the fortress had tired them.

Travel was made even slower because Mistress Tilde insisted on continuing her classes. The women were all walking quickly but they refused to travel until dark.

Mira wanted to use every second she could moving forward, but the women wanted to make sure that camp was set an hour before dark so that they could hold classes before bed. Mira could only ground her teeth and bare it.

Mira could handle losing the extra time, she really could. What she could not handle was the fact that none of these women knew what they were doing! There was an accident at least every other day. Someone was always hurt and then they were slowed even more!

Mistress Tilde acted like the accidents did not really matter because the women had learned to heal. And Mira had to admit that no one was injured for long but the truth was that it was only a matter of time before someone was injured too badly to be healed.

Healing took energy from the body and if the body injured badly enough than using up too much energy would send the patient into shock. Mira did her best to stay as far away from Mistress Tilde's classes as she could and she told the nanoks to do the same.

Mira knew that trouble would come from the classes no matter how careful Mistress Tilde swore to be. Mira only hoped that no one was injured beyond repair when she was proven right.

The incident happened after camp had been set up for the night. The nanoks had brought them dinner and Mira was busy roasting it over a fire. The camp was not in the open. They were still hiding from the Argosi so camping in the middle of a thick forest seemed best. There were trees and vines all around them. Mira was lazily stirring a pot when the vines began to move.

They moved slowly on the ground at first. Mira rolled her eyes but did not pay it much attention. A second later the vines were wrapping themselves around ankles and arms. Mira saw nanoks with vines around their necks! Mira pulled vines away from her and fought to get the nanoks. They could not get free and the vines were choking them.

Mira saw Mistress Tilde rapidly waving her arms and calling out instructions to Kiarlin. Kiarlin did not look like she heard the instructions. Her hands were over her head and her head was down. The vines never went near her...

Kiarlin's head finally raised and Mira saw that her eyes were glowing. Kiarlin blinked once and the vines stopped as suddenly as they had begun. The vines were on the ground now and Kiarlin's eyes were no longer glowing. The camp almost looked like nothing at all had happened.

Dancer roared into the night and Mira jumped at the emotion in it. The nanoks all clustered around one of their numbers who was not getting up.

"We need healing!" Mira called out to the women. "Quickly!"

Mistress Tilde ran up to the nanok with one of her students. "Don't you worry, Mira. Your friend will be fine. Tell him to lie as still as he can."

"It's a *she*! Your patient is a *she*."

"I'm sorry, Mira. Just tell *her* to lie as still as she can."

By: Jennie Arnold

Mira did as she asks her to, wishing she could do more to help her friend.

Alaina tried to move around as much as her chain and bands would allow. She and Lewis had been trapped in the carriage for a while and they were sore with stiffness. Alaina attempted to move but the small amount the chains allowed her did not make a difference.

She knew that even after the chains opened that she would hardly be able to move. The Argosi had left them chained far too long and she knew that Sainade would force her to move quickly once the carriage stopped — that was just how the valet women were trained to think.

Alaina tried to be optimistic but she also knew that some people refused to change. Some people refused to make good choices or be a better person. Sainade was one of those people. She would never change because she did not want to change.

Alaina had to admit that she was happy about this. It meant that Sainade was predictable. She knew what Sainade was going to do before she did it. The problem was that Sainade did not learn either. Alaina knew that Sainade would never know compassion...

In truth, she tried not to think about it.

She blocked her mind from the negative thoughts as the velvet woman came into the carriage.

"We are at the docks," Sainade told the two magic users. "Board the boat and the empress will explain on the way."

"Where are we going?" Lewis asked, trying to hide a tremor in his voice.

"The empress will give you all the details." Lewis could

not help but glare at Sainade and Alaina fought not to roll her eyes. "You get on the ship and you'll get your answers."

Neither one of them moved. Alaina was still working movement back into her tingling limps. Sainade mistook their lack of movement.

"You can walk to the ship on your own or I can make you go. You know the pain I can cause."

"I plan on walking onto the ship," Alaina promised her, "but I have to rub feeling back into my legs first."

"There is no need for further motivation then." Sainade nodded, satisfied.

The three of them walked across the docks onto a large ship. The ship did not look like the merchant ships or even the other Argosi ships Alaina had seen before. This ship had carvings and even some gilding. It looked like a ship fit for royalty. Alaina was not surprised to find the empress had the ship commissioned.

"I will not waste time in greetings. I have brought you here to save our empire. We will travel to the mountains to perform a ritual."

"What mountains?" Alaina asked a right on top of Lewis' "Where are we going?"

"I'm surprised you don't recognize the scenery," the empress answered vaguely.

"We've been here before?" Alaina asked.

"You took this route to get to Argosi," Sainade told them.

"We're going to Alta? We're going home?" Lewis asked with excitement.

"We're going to the Mist Mountains on the Mainland. After you help me with the ritual you can go home to Alta Island," the empress promised as she waved her hand in dismissal.

Sainade locked Alaina and Lewis into small rooms below deck. Alaina tried to stay calm. The idea of going home sent flutters into her heart. Still, she could not simply take the empress at her word. The empire would never give them their freedom for nothing.

What choice was there? The band would make her do whatever Sainade wanted!

Alaina took a deep breath and tried to sleep through the voyage home.

Matt walked without trying to hurry. The women always took their time and it seemed silly to run only to wait. He walked at his own pace and looked at the woods around him as he walked. Matt was looking around and not looking at the trail in front of him. He jumped out of his skin when he saw a large form standing almost on top of him.

"Where is the nanok daughter?" the shadowy form in a gruff voice.

Matt could not tell if this man could be trusted or not. He needed a little test.

"I'd ask the nanoks. They always know where she is."

"The daughter's scent is all over you. Not the nanoks. Tell me where she is."

"You can smell Mira? Then why do you need me to tell you? Just follow your nose."

"You will tell me where she is. Are you holding her prisoner?"

"What's going on?" Mira asked as she walked up to the pair.

"Nanok daughter! The vines came to life. I cannot stay in the forest but I need to help you save the world and fight the Argosi."

"The Argosi are bad but there is a worse enemy," Matt warned him.

"Come with me," Mira motioned the other two. "We need to tell him the whole thing," Mira told Matt. "Tell him your vision. It's a good place to start."

Chapter Thirteen

Matt walked out of the clearing with Mira close behind. The strange werebeast agreed to help them. He knew nothing, and he had no desire to learn more. Matt tried to explain the different sides and who the true enemies were but the beast did not want to listen. Matt did what he could to explain the situation. He could not find words and he worried that the werebeast did not know what he was really up against.

Still, someone trusted in them both. Mira seemed to think the werebeast knew what he was doing. She had met him before. Mira spoke a series of quick words to the werebeast when Matt was too far away to hear. Matt was sure that Mira was telling the were-thing to watch out for the Argosi or to look after the women or some other noble idea.

The other women probably thought that Mira was asking for help. Matt knew better. People like Mira and Matt did not need looking after. Things happened to them — dangerous things — and they would happen no matter who was watching them.

Matt was lost in his thoughts and not watching where he was going. As his luck would have it, Matt promptly slipped and twisted his ankle badly. Matt began to fall; the pain making him lose his balance. A vision took shape before his body even hit the ground.

He was high in the mountains, mountains he recognized: the Mist Mountains! He saw Lewis and Alaina standing in chains. They both looked disheveled and scared. The woman with the crown of golden branches, the empress, stood in front of the pair holding a wicked knife. She plunged the knife down and Matt had to look away. Blood had never bothered him but he couldn't bear to see his friend die!

Even looking away he could not miss the red blood slashing over the snow high in those mountains. He could not stop tears from flooding his eyes and flowing down his cheeks even as he came back to himself.

"Tell the women and the nanoks that we need to get to the mountain fast," Matt ordered Mira. "Lewis will die if we don't warn him about their ritual. They'll try to kill him!"

Mira quickly spoke to one of the nanoks before turning back to Matt. "The nanoks say that they want to ask the Creator's advice."

"Advice on what? The Creator would not want anyone like Lewis to die!"

"Calm down, Matt. This is how to nanoks handle things. It is just their way."

"Do they think there is another way? Is saving him even a possibility?"

"We must see what the Creator tells the nanoks."

They confined Alaina to her quarters on the ship for most of the trip to Alta Island. She was beyond bored. She had heard people on the docks complain about cabin fever but the buzzing ache she felt seemed more like she was slowly dying. Sick and bored did not describe how to terrible she felt.

Light from an open door brought a flicker of hope into her heart. She prayed that they would let her out of the hold. The guard who opened the door motioned for her to follow and she felt her heart rise with hope.

He gripped her arm before she walked over the door's threshold. "You're allowed out to use the restroom. Don't try any funny business."

Alaina could only nod at his words. Running had never occurred to her. Where could she go on a boat? There was nowhere to run until they docked. What was the point of all the intimidation?

He pointed the way to the bathroom, or was it a head? Ship terms always made Alaina a little confused. She tried to find her way even with all her confusion. Still, Alaina could not stop herself from pausing when she heard raised voices.

"You know that this ritual is not all that is required. A sacrifice must be made. I will tell you right now that I will not stand for an Argosi losing their lives. You will be on your own. You'll be left at the world's mercy and you have shown little mercy yourself."

It surprised Alaina to hear that the empress was the speaker. Alaina strained her neck to see who the empress was arguing with. Did someone want to kill Argosi?

"Your only objection is that your people could die?" Asked a voice that sounded deep and pure; nothing like the empress' voice. "What if I told you that no Argosi would die? What if all I was asking for was the blood of a few magic users?"

Alaina tried to mute a gasp. She didn't want the others to hear that she was there. She didn't want to think about what the words she had over-heard meant. Alaina tried to control her breathing.

"You done yet, girl?" the guard called. Alaina quickly used the restroom and ran back to her room. She had a lot to think over and she found that being stuck below deck might just be bearable. If she could just wrap her mind around it...

~*~

Mira absolutely hated being in the middle of an argument.

By: Jennie Arnold

It was one of the reasons she did not make friends with the girls from the Mainland. Matt and Lewis were calm but the stress was getting to them all.

Matt was upset because the nanoks were second guessing his vision and the nanoks were upset because Matt wasn't even trying to understand their ways, and poor Mira was stuck with the job of trying to keep both sides from attacking each other!

It sounded so simple on paper. Matt and the nanoks had gotten on fine before. It seemed to take a fly-swat to get the two groups to argue.

Things seemed so much simpler when she was just a baker on the Island of Alta. Mira could feel her problems mounting and she always seemed to yearn for simpler times. The truth was that Mira did want things to be simpler but she did not want things to go back to the way they were.

Mira could see changes in the women, some good and some bad but they were all different people now. Changing too much would make everyone stop being the people they really were. Mira wanted the Argosi gone but she did not want to stop talking with the nanoks. She did not want to stop being who she was.

She wanted the nanoks to stay the same too but she did wish that each group (nanoks, magic women and Matt) could all be more patient with each other. Even the werebeast seemed to bring trouble!

The Creator has a message for the Almost Nanok, Snow told Mira in a disappointed voice. *He says that he wants to save the werebeast but only if Fate lets him. The Almost Nanok is supposed to know what the message means.* Snow did not like the werebeast and she made her feelings known to her sleuth.

"Were you expecting a message for him? I thought you were asking about Lewis and Matt." Mira was unsure how all the communications with the Creator worked but she knew that the messages were accurate.

We were asking about the mountain and what was required there. I don't know why the Almost Nanok was mentioned at all.

"I need to talk to Matt. He doesn't like to think about the vision but I need to know if it is possible that the blood in the snow was not Lewis'."

You think the Argosi will kill the Almost Nanok? Snow seemed intrigued by the idea.

"I know the Argosi will kill someone and I don't want it to be someone who does not deserve it."

We all deserve death. We have all made mistakes but there is hope for us, Dancer said, startling Mira as the nanok walked closer to the man. *But the Creator gives us better than we deserve. Fate has found a way for us and paid a price in our place. Fate brings us where we need to be and works to get us there without harm.*

"Fate!" Grunted the werebeast. "Fate can be fought and beaten!"

Not without bringing danger to others. You might think you beat Fate but the truth is that there is a balance. You will still pay the price, only at a later date. Dancer growled out the last words.

"You need not explain Fate to me. I do not know what your diverse and strange party is doing here but I know that I am for whatever you are planning. You can consider me one of your sleuth."

Dare you declare yourself a member of the sleuth without the leader's permission? Snow growled.

"He has already proven himself," Mira reminded them. "He saved us as we ran from the Argosi."

You speak for him, daughter? Dancer asked. Mira nodded and Dancer gave a nanok grin in reply. *Welcome to the sleuth.*

By: Jennie Arnold

The nanoks were roaring their welcome when Matt ran up.

"Did they tell you anything about Lewis?"

The Seer was right about the ritual. The Argosi will force a sacrifice. Blood is sure to be spilt but loss of life is not a certainty. Your friend may not be the one to lose his life.

Matt gave a visible sigh of relief as Mira interpreted the nanok's words.

"How do we keep Lewis alive?"

"We have to get to that mountain before the Argosi! We have to be there for Lewis." Mira said the words that Matt and Kiarlin were thinking and they each gave one solemn nod to prove it.

Lewis grew up as the son of a farmer. He rose with the dawn to get chores completed. The list of things to do on a farm never seemed to end! Lewis was used to long days and early nights. His body seemed to wake up before dawn no matter how tired he was. On a farm, rising early meant more chores were completed by nightfall but on a ship it just meant long hours of boredom.

Lewis tried to sleep more, but he ended up listening to the surrounding sounds: the crashing waves, the pounding feet of crew-men running, muffled voices talking and laughing. He even heard Alaina's door open and close.

He put his ear to the door so he could hear the sounds from the hall more clearly but he still had no clue what they were doing with Alaina. Could Sainade be forcing her to use magic?

Lewis was so busy thinking and worrying that he never heard the footsteps that came to his own door.

"Don't waste time, boy. You're being allowed out to use the

facilities.... or do you want to stay here instead?"

Lewis quickly got up to follow the guard. They were making their way up a set of stairs when Lewis dared to ask a question.

"I heard you let Alaina out of her room. Where is she now?"

"She's already back in the room. We let her leave it to use the restroom before you. Ladies first, you know." The guard put his hand on Lewis' arm and steered him forward as he talked. It was clear that the guard did not plan on letting Lewis out of his sight.

Lewis could see the reason for the guards' paranoia on the horizon. They were coming into port. Lewis could see the mountains he had dreamed of in the distance and the beaches that he had played in as a child in the distance.

He knew that now was his chance! He had to make a run for it. Lewis reached for the magic inside of himself. He felt the guard's hand tighten on his shoulder as if he knew what was about the happen. Still, the guards, none of them, could stop what happened next.

Lewis used his magic to push the guards away from him. They grunted and struggled. Some even screamed in frustration but all of them moved to the side. A path formed before him but he did not use it to run.

He pulled Alaina to the top deck with his magic. The door's lock was busted open with wind and fire flicked before her to lead her on deck. The path in front of Lewis allowed Alaina to get to him.

Lewis called rocks and sand from Alta's beach to make a bridge. He and Alaina ran to freedom. The rocks moved and shift beneath them but Lewis had no trouble keeping balance. It was like the wind that was helping to move the rocks was also keeping him up. The elements themselves were helping him!

By: Jennie Arnold

Lewis felt a thrill that rang through every pour. He was home, back in Alta. He was free and moving away from the Argosi. Lewis could not help a smile from breaking out over his face. His smile faded instantly when he heard Alaina scream.

The sound bounced off the air itself and echoed in his head.

Every atom in him wanted to turn and look, to go to her, to make sure she was unharmed, but he knew that it was a trap. The Argosi had made her scream because they wanted him to look!

He could not give into their plans. He needed to continue moving. The Island of Alta was at stake!

By: Jennie Arnold

Chapter Fourteen

Alaina felt a blinding pain surge through her brow and down to the soles of her feet. She felt like her head would explode! She could feel Sainade seize her magic. The surrounding air sizzled as Sainade used the magic on Lewis.

Alaina saw Lewis tense and heard the soft moan that escaped his clenched jaw. Lewis did not show pain in the movement of arms or the arch of his back, like she did, but his eyes spoke of the extreme pain that he was in. She was surprised he could stay on his feet!

Neither one of them could move from the pain. Guards could walk onto the bridge and carry them back to the ship without one hand raised in protest.

Sainade's face was a mask of fiery. Alaina's magic was still being used to keep her own body from moving but it was being used in torturous ways on Lewis. The only thing that kept her from killing him outright was the looming guard.

Alaina lost track of the waves Sainade was sending into Lewis. He fell to his knees from the pain and could no longer keep from groaning so loudly that the people on the Island must be able to hear.

"You have made a grave mistake today, boy!" Sainade swore. "You both may have made the attempt but I can see who planned all of this. I know who really tried to flee!"

Sainade motioned to the guards. "Take the girl back to the hold. Keep a careful watch this time and don't let one toe even go past the threshold of her door."

The guards nodded and rushed to do as Sainade commanded. Alaina was afraid of what Sainade would do next.

The problem was that Alaina could *not guess* what the velvet woman would do. She had never seen Sainade so angry! Alaina was not sure that Sainade could stop herself from killing Lewis; no matter how the empress reacted when she found out!

"Please stop hurting Lewis, Lady Sainade!"

Alaina could only hope that calling the woman by her title would remind her of her duty but the velvet woman did not even look at Alaina.

"The empire needs him and the empress will not be happy if he cannot even walk," Alaina continued hoping to talk sense into the woman.

"The empress will not fault me for punishing him. The truth of the matter is we do not need him to walk, only to do magic."

Lewis screamed out in pain as his legs shrunk and shriveled. It was plain that Lewis could never walk on them. He was breathing hard with his head resting on the ground in a slumped position.

"I will remove the disability before we reach the mountain. Do not even think about running to your little Island. I will burn every home until your own countrymen give you to me."

Lewis glared up at Sainade, defiant to the end. Alaina could feel the fight leaving her. What her magic had just done was terrifying and Alaina could not even think about doing it to someone else.

Alaina did not realize she was crying until she saw tears land on the deck. "I will never do that again...." she sobbed." Please never make me do that again!" Alaina could not seem to make herself stop crying. The crying turned into racking sobs.

"Quiet!" Sainade snapped at her. The velvet woman slapped Alaina when her sobs did not quiet.

"Stop!" Lewis yelled as he shifted his weight, trying to move. "There's no need to hit her!"

"Allow me, High Lady Sainade." It surprised everyone to see the ship's captain. "I have young girls of my own. I know how to make her stop crying."

"Be my guest, captain," the velvet woman invited. "I will escort the boy back to his room while you see to the girl." With that, Sainade, Lewis and all but two of the guards left.

"Come with me to a quiet corner," the captain said as he led her to a pile of barrels in the ship's bow.

"When my girls are upset I always tell them a story. They laugh at the end and all the tears are gone. Their favorite stories are about the Shadow People... the Wild Fae. It has been some years since I needed to tell this story. Let's see if I remember how it began:

"Once upon a time, there was a beautiful land full of hope and promise. It seemed like every inch of the land was covered in green things; soil was ready to support life. The Argosi, my people, wanted this land for their own and they felt that it was only their right. The Wild Fae, of course, saw things differently.

"The Fae felt nothing for growing things. They wanted a world covered in mettle, a world that allowed them to take without ever giving back. The Fae believed that they could use the resources of the land without working for them. They did not know that you cannot harvest what you have not sown. My ancestors, knowing that the Fae crazy scheme could never work, allowed them to use the land. After one season, the Fae saw that the land here on Earth, no matter how lush, needs care to thrive."

The captain took a pressed four-leaf clover from his uniform breast pocket. He handed it to her. "After giving the Fae a few months to evacuate the land, my ancestors moved in. That clover is from that first land, the land my ancestors plowed; the land the Fae lived on. Look at it. Count the leaves. There are seven." He smiled as if remembering a happier time.

"My ancestors were in a strange land but they knew that they would flourish."

"Who were your ancestors?"

"My father called them Merfolk. They traveled the sea, like me. There's sea salt in my blood! The ocean calls to me. The call almost drove me insane until my wife traded her family farm for this boat. She knows me better than I know myself! I bought her a merchants villa by way of thanks but she still deserves better!"

Alaina smiled at the happy ending, only then realizing that she was no longer crying. "Thank you, for your help and your story," she told the captain.

He put an arm around her. "You will thrive and flourish too, child. I see something of my girls in you. They had a hard time accepting their roles here. The girls struggled for years, looking for happiness where they were but then they realized that there was a choice. They could make new roles. The ones originally assigned to them were not really theirs' anyway. You will find your role."

Alaina could not see a way to change her role but she could not help but feel better as the remaining guards brought her back to her room.

Mira and the nanoks had no trouble keeping the fast stride that Matt set. The glimpses Matt saw of the future turned him into a thing possessed. He set an almost inhuman pace.

The nanoks sent runners ahead to speak with the Creator while the rest of the party caught up. Three runners had gone ahead but none of them had received a message until Dancer herself traveled ahead.

By: Jennie Arnold

What did you see? What did the Creator say? Snow questioned before Mira could even open her mouth.

I believe I have more information about the true enemy your friend has been warning us about. There were different hunters roaming this land long ago. There were man-things who would not talk with us even if they heard. We call them the Not nanoks but I have heard you humans call them Wild Fae. They plan on conquering this world.

Mira knew that she needed to translate this conversation for Matt. He had been worried about these unknown enemies and about what they could do to Alta. She suspected that it was at least part of the reason her friend was so manic. So she translated as quickly as she could.

"I thought the Wild Fae were myths. You know that they couldn't conquer the world even when no one fought back. Surely you remember the story! The Fae don't understand farming. How do they plan on surviving here?"

"I don't think they plan on staying here, Matt. They plan on taking all the resources they can and leaving us on an empty shell."

Matt's face seemed to get even paler. "We'd better travel faster." Mira could not help but agree.

Exhaustion pushed Matt to sleep with a force most nights. No one could sleep deeply with such strange dreams filling the night. Little wonder nightmares persisted when the waking world was what it was. Even with all of that Matt's exhausted body needed rest. He had to put the dreams aside so he could fall into sleep.

Matt could not relax. That place of blackness and peace

eluded him. He was stuck in that place between sleeping and waking. He did not know that he had entered the gloaming fields but he had.

Matt found himself in a bright, sunlit field. Wind blew with the scent of wild flowers. Matt knew that he wasn't dreaming. This place felt more like a vision than a dream. Where ever... or whatever... this place became, it was pleasant now. Then, the sky filled with dark clouds.

Matt tried to run but pictures filled the sky and he could not look away. It was as if a shaman had come to the Island to hypnotize him! The pictures held him and he had to see! Blood fell in the snow. Daisy fell from a cliff. Lewis' legs disappeared. Alaina and Kiarlin each grew a third eye. Matt tried to shut out all the images. He began to scream with frustration.

There is no need to be so noisy, young nanok. The future will order itself if you concentrate.

"Are you talking to me?" Matt whispered in disbelief.

There is no one else here. Matt could swear that the nanok was grinning.

"Alright," Matt said to himself. "I just need to concentrate."

Matt took three calming breaths and looked up to see that the sky was blue and clear. The valley looked peaceful once more.

Think about your friends, nothing but them, and the future will reveal itself.

Matt did as he was told and the clouds returned. Matt saw a slew of pictures again. Alaina and Kiarlin hugging each other; Lewis running towards the mountains but running backwards. He was facing Matt, yelling warnings while moving in the other direction.

"What is all of this supposed to mean?"

I must speak with the sleuth and the Creator before I can

By: Jennie Arnold

give you an answer. I will find you again to tell you.

"I don't know if that will work. Find Mira. Tell her your messages and then she can translate." The nanok nodded, and the valley began to fall away.

Matt woke with a start, breathing hard. Tiredness rolled over him but a smile formed on his lips.

~*~

Lewis could see that Sainade was not simply angry with him. She was furious! He was sure that Sainade would have caused him even more pain if she thought the empress would let her. He could not help but be a little afraid of her. His legs would not work and he was entirely at her mercy.

"Bring me the potion," Sainade commanded. A guard moved quickly to her side holding a steaming cup.

Lewis clamped his lips closed, refusing to open an inch. Sainade's fingers gripped his jaw, squeezing and pinching, but Lewis still refused to open.

The guard that stood at Sainade's side had enough. He punched Lewis in the stomach, forcing all the air to leave his lunges. Lewis opened his mouth to gasp for breath but Sainade forced the potion into him. The liquid burned going down and a strange, light-headed-ness followed.

Lewis found that the few movements they allowed him were getting slower and slower.

"Give him another dose in an hour's time," Sainade ordered the guard as she walked away. The guard nodded and watched Lewis' hazy eyes with mistrust.

Lewis was having a hard time focusing his thoughts but he could tell that this guard did not like him. The guard next to Lewis' bed motioned to the guard by the door.

"Get the next dose ready." The guard by the door rushed to obey the first guard's command. It was clear that Sainade had left the guard by the bed in charge.

The guard returned with a steaming cup. "Should we give it to him soon? It loses potency if it's not fresh." The first guard nodded in answer.

"We should give it to him now. The High Lady would not be pleased if we waited too long."

The guard forced the potion down Lewis' throat. He could not even put up a fight this time but the guards clamped their hands around Lewis' arms like he could bolt at any moment. The liquid really did burn Lewis' throat going down, but he only felt the pain for a second before blackness jumped to meet him.

Dreams came then, vivid dreams with flashes of color and growling rumbles. All the images seemed to blur and the passing time was immeasurable. Lewis could not tell if everything happened in weeks or in the blink of an eye. He felt like he should worry... like he should be doing something but he could not tell what it was for the life of him. He did not know where he was but he could not make himself care about that either.

Finally, things started to slow, pictures came in focus and Lewis could grasp that he was dreaming. He saw a picture he recognized.

"Matt? Is it really you?" Lewis whispered in a hoarse voice.

"This will sound crazy but let me finish before you say anything," Matt took a deep breath. "This nanok has been training me to control my powers. He told me you were drifting and that I needed to call you. I did and now you're here... I guess you're not drifting anymore."

Lewis felt like he needed to say something in response but he had no idea what he could say. "The nanok was right," he started slowly. "You called me back. You can control your power now? Do you see a way we can get away from the Argosi?"

By: Jennie Arnold

"The Argosi are going to kill you. You and Kiarlin's sister have to get away as fast as you can. They are going to make a sacrifice on that mountain!"

Lewis could not hear the rest of Matt's warning before something pulled him from the dream. He struggled against the force, trying to get back to his friend; needing to hear the message but the force only pulled harder.

Lewis would have bolted upright if his legs were their normal shape but the movement changed Lewis' balance and he ended up falling off the bed. He groaned quietly from the floor.

"I told you to wait an hour. You could have killed him with a dose that high!" Lewis saw that Sainade was ordering the other guards to beat the one who had forced the potion into him.

"Please, m-my Lady! I just didn't w-want him doing any m-magic, my Lady!" The guard stammered out over the noise of the beating and his grunts of pain.

"Stop!" Sainade ordered the guards. "I am not without mercy. Give this man two doses of the potion; the same amount he gave the boy. If he survives, let him back into his unit as if nothing happened. If he dies feed him to the fish!"

The guard's face paled visibly, but he went with the others when they lead him away. Lewis forced his thoughts away from the guard. Lewis' head hurt like crazy and his thoughts were still muddled but he picked a few things from their conversation.

"You don't want me doing magic that badly? I must scare you. I thought Alaina's band gave you all the control you needed. I guess you did too."

Sainade balled her fists into Lewis' shirt front. She pulled him up until he was looking at her in the eyes. "Don't think you have won, boy," she hissed at him.

Her hand flew out towards the fallen cup that once held the

potion. "You will drink this every hour and you will never have the opportunity to escape again. You got lucky today but you still never made it to the beach."

Lewis would have responded that he would make it past the beach next time, legs or no legs but Sainade released her hold on him. Lewis went tumbling to the floor. He felt his head hit the floor with a smack and the world was black.

There were no dreams this time.

By: Jennie Arnold

Chapter Fifteen

Alaina stumbled as she walked behind the stretcher that carried Lewis. She worried constantly now a days. She worried about the ropes around Lewis and about how tight they were. They bound his neck, chest, and hips to the stretcher until welts appeared. The ropes looked smooth but she knew from experience that it would get painfully tight if he struggled. The bumpy road might force him to move and so could the guards.

He was being carried by four men, one on each side. She could only pray that the guards would not hurt him. The empress wanted him unharmed but Lewis was already the worse for wear.

Alaina saw Lewis wake with a start. He would have fallen to the ground if the ropes hadn't prevented him. The ropes cut into Lewis so sharply that blood began to pool around the ropes.

He opened his mouth to yell in surprise but they forced a warm potion down his throat before he could utter a sound. Alaina could see him try to turn his head to the side but a hand covered his mouth and nose, keeping him from breathing until he swallowed.

Alaina worried about Lewis and the potion and her home. She worried about the Island and her family. Alaina worried about herself.

Alaina let her eyes wander. She looked this way and that. There had to be something useful somewhere! Her eyes caught a movement by the trees. It was a nanok. Alaina knew that nanoks were wild hunters, but she also knew they avoided men. This was no normal nanok! Lewis' friends sent it. Alaina swore she could feel the magic from the other women.

She moved forward to tell Lewis, but the band stopped her

after two steps. Alaina knew that she was too late when she saw Lewis' throat work. He had swallowed. Alaina saw Lewis' eyes cloud with the drug.

Sainade looked down at Lewis. "I have been much gentler than you deserve. The empress wants you to stay unharmed and out of trouble. The potion and a few ropes will see to that. They are as difficult to break as the band. Ask the girl if you do not believe me."

"You think these ropes are enough to keep me out of trouble? You think potion will make me complete your ritual? I will make sure that I never see your mountains!" Lewis spoke in tones of challenges and not questions.

Sainade walked away from the stretcher. Alaina quickly asked permission to walk with Lewis. Sainade nodded knowing the young man needed to be soothed.

Alaina walked alongside the stretcher then. "You heard about the ritual. How?" Alaina whispered down. Her fingers tapped his where the guards could not see. She motioned to the trees where she had seen the nanok.

Lewis nodded slightly before whispering back. "Matt told me in a dream. I know it sounds crazy, but it is true. You weren't surprised by the news. How did you hear of it?"

"I over-heard the empress talking about it. I couldn't over-hear much and I'm sure there was more to the plan than I heard."

"Keep listening," Lewis advised her, "and keep watching."

Alaina smiled before answering, "I promise."

Matt spoke quickly about his dreams to Kiarlin and Mira. "We have to be in that pass," Matt told them for the hundredth time. "Their caravan will be there."

The nanok was showing Matt how to use his power and he had seen improvement. Matt cleared his head and concentrated on Lewis and he could see where his friend would be. The trouble was that Matt could not always see *when* they would be there. Matt was lucky this time because he could see the stars in the vision. He knew when Lewis would show up for certain but the time he needed for walking did not leave much for dilly dallying.

Time had become a precious thing for Matt. He knew that Lewis would be in that pass in less than twenty-four hours. Matt set a wickedly fast pace to make it to the pass in time. The women knew about the visions and they knew that Matt's visions were right. He only needed to tell them he had seen that Lewis' life depended on them being in the pass, at two hours to midnight, before the women jumped to match his pace.

He was glad that they understood without him having to go into detail. Matt could see that Mira wanted to know details, but she had the grace not to ask about them. The nanoks had no such reluctance. They wanted Matt to tell them what was coming.

Matt still needed Mira to intemperate for the nanoks in the waking world and Mira would tell the nanoks they needed to stop asking.

Matt was fairly certain that the nanok in the gloaming field could not hurt him, no matter how rude he was to the beast, but he was not sure that the nanoks in the waking world had the same reluctance. He would not test them to see what he could get away with.

Mira continued to have him attempt to talk with the nanoks in the waking world every evening but none of the attempts were ever successful. Kiarlin, on the other hand, never seemed to stop trying and never let Matt stop either when he worked with her. Kiarlin had been having visions in that stormy sky too. No nanok spoke with her but she saw the shapes in the sky. She could see the future in that sky just like Matt could.

She also assumed that she had a chance of talking to nanoks as Matt was supposed to. She would attempt to speak with the nanoks as Matt attempted the same thing. She would get images now and then but she rarely knew what they meant. She and Matt mostly talked about the gloaming fields.

"I saw Alaina and a nanok staring at each other across a field. I can't explain why but it felt like they were competing with each other; like they were having a staring contest."

"Have you noticed the way Mira looks at the nanoks when they talk? It looks like a staring contest to me! Maybe Alaina will learn to talk with the nanoks."

"I didn't hear any words but all this magic seems so strange. She still might be communicating with them," Kiarlin remarked.

"Kiarlin!" Mira called as she walked up the hill towards them. "You won't believe what Snow saw when she went scouting!"

"Did she see the Argosi? Did she see Lewis?" Matt asked in excitement.

"She saw the Argosi guards and a royal party traveling with them. She saw Lewis tied up and, more importantly, someone saw her."

"She's not hurt, is she? Did someone catch her?" Kiarlin asked worriedly.

"No, no!" Mira assured her. "Nothing like that. Alaina saw Snow. She communicated with Snow with pictures."

"She drew pictures for the nanok?" Matt asked incredulously.

"Snow says that Alaina pushed pictures into her head. She was very surprised by it. Alaina showed her that the empress wants to make a sacrifice. Alaina seems to think it will be Lewis but there is no proof that they won't sacrifice her."

"We need to get them both out of there!" Matt decided aloud as he quickened the pace even more.

Lewis shifted on the stretcher, trying to get Alaina's attention. He saw a handful of nanoks in the trees. The Argosi did not know much about nanoks. They would have seen the nanoks if they had known how to look for them. There must not be very many in Argosi. Lewis had to be thankful for their ignorance.

He knew that the Argosi were taking him to the misty mountains, but he was still unsure about what they wanted him to do there. The empress spoke about a ritual but Lewis could not trust her. Matt warned that a sacrifice had to be made, and Lewis trusted Matt, but how was he to avoid being sacrificed?

Was the sacrifice even supposed to be him? Matt seemed worried that the Argosi would kill anyone they got their hands on. Lewis tried again to catch Alaina's eye but the velvet woman held the girl's leash tightly now. There was no chance that the girl could get to Lewis' cot. Still, Lewis was glad to see that Alaina's eyes were not on the ground in front of her. She was looking into the trees.

He began to move his head again too, looking for nanoks. Sainade must have noticed his jerking movements. He cursed himself for forgetting. His movements were not slow or thoughts vague. The potion must be wearing off and Sainade could see the effects leaving Lewis.

It seemed like she moved up to stand beside him in an instant. A guard stood next to her with a steaming cup in his hand.

"I can see that this is a job I will have to do myself," Sainade decided. "Those impeccable guards either give you too much or too little." Sainade sighed once more after her complaint and turned to the guard next to her. "Make sure he drinks it all, every drop."

Lewis turned his head this way and that but the guard was strong. He used one hand to keep Lewis's head still while the other forced his jaw open. Sainade poured the drink into him.

Lewis hated the fuzzy kind of buzz that covered all of his thoughts. It was like he had to crawl through noise and mud just to think and then the thoughts floated away even after all of his effort.

"I'll drink the potion," Lewis' tired mind forced him to say. "I'll drink the potion without fighting if Alaina gives it to me."

"You think you're clever, boy, but you are not half as clever as you seem to think. If I find you are trying to trick me, then the pain you felt before will be a tickle compared to what comes."

"I trust Alaina. She wouldn't trick me or add anything to the potion."

"You really think I need to add something to that potion?" Sainade asked incredulously. "You're already doing everything I demand. You can't reach your magic!"

"I don't know what you're after, Sainade but I know you're capable of anything. You'll do anything to get your goal."

"You don't think the girl is capable of the same thing?"

"Alaina's not like that. She's not cruel!"

"I'll allow the girl to give you the potion, boy; it will make my life easier and put your mind at ease, but ask yourself how well you really know her..."

Lewis lay in silence on the stretcher, thinking. He remembered all the times she had gone out of her way to help

By: Jennie Arnold

him. He thought of all the times they had both got into trouble to help each other.

"Alaina's better than you! She's better than any Velvet women. She's proven where her loyalties lie," he whispered into the sky above. He could get messages to her every hour when she fed him his dose.

Mira could see that Snow was shaken by the things that Alaina had shown her. Mira knew that Snow was holding the details back from her; she was not mad at her because of it. She knew that Snow was trying to protect her.

Plus, it made it easier for Mira to tell Matt what was happening. Matt was becoming desperate to get to the others. Giving Matt details about their pain would only make him more desperate! She did not enjoy lying to her friend or holding back information but she was not lying if she told everything she knew!

Still, Mira could not let Snow suffer alone. She had saved her life multiple times now!

"Snow," Mira began, breaking the she-nanok out of her thoughts, "I need to ask you some questions about the Argosi force you saw." Mira felt silly making up excuses to talk to her but she also knew that she would be embarrassed if there were no excuses.

This battle is the duty of all nanoks, daughter. I will help you any way I can.

"Thank you, Snow. Let's go down by that lake where things are quieter."

The two walked down. Snow held her head low. She knew that this was not about a battle. Mira jumped right into the problem.

"I need you to tell me what Alaina showed you."

I did tell you.

"I need to know the full thing." Mira spoke the words outright and in her head as the nanoks speak. She could see the effect the words had on her.

It is not a happy story; the nanok declared. *I saw much death and I could see that the people who died were not only loved by the girl I was seeing but loved by you. I did not want to be the one to tell you bad news about people you love.* Snow stopped and tilted her head as if she were thinking. *Recent events have made me change my mind. Telling you may just be a mercy.*

I saw the Darkness Chaser and the Argosi enemies. I saw the girl who sent the images; she is a strong magic user but that will not save her. The Argosi plan a sacrifice. The girl thinks they mean to make Darkness Chaser kill her. She thinks she is the sacrifice but I know the truth, now. The Argosi don't know that they have allied themselves with pure evil. The sacrifice is meant to raise the Wild Fae. They will kill us all.

"I thought Wild Fae were just myths. Are you telling me they are real?" Mira asked in astonishment, already knowing the answer.

Your people think men who talk with nanoks and seers are myths too. You've seen both in the real world with your own eyes. You know that the world is scarier than the stories can say. The Wild Fae returning really scares me.

The real trouble is that the Wild Fae will be unstoppable if the portal is opened. The only way to stop them after that portal opens is for their own prince to give up his magic. What Wild Fae would ever do that?

"That might not ever have to happen. No one would open that portal if they knew the risk. We need to tell the others;

about the Wild Fae at least. It might be best to keep the sacrifice to a need to know basis. We'll warn them about what they can change without worrying them about what they can't."

You know I won't tell the Seer or the magic women. I don't even want to tell Dancer. I don't want to tell anyone!

"Thank you for telling me the story, Snow. I know that it was hard for you but the others really need to know what we're facing."

The Argosi do not know what they are facing. They might decide not to go through with the sacrifice if they knew. They think the Wild Fae will help them but they will only help themselves. That's who they are.

"We'll do all we can to get a warning out but I think our first goal still needs to be getting Lewis and Alaina away from the Argosi."

Make sure the others agree with that plan before you decide anything.

By: Jennie Arnold

Chapter Sixteen

Alaina walked beside the stretcher that held Lewis. He had not moved a hair in hours. Sainade allowed her to give Lewis the potion like it was a reward but she hated doing it. She hated watching his eyes glaze over and knowing that she had done that to him. She knew that he had agreed to their rules. It was the only way the two of them would ever communicate. She did not want Lewis to know her desperation. She was sure that he shared it! She wanted to tell him about some great rescue scheme but none existed. Until, maybe, one did...

Alaina saw them before the guards did. There were nanoks in the trees and women hiding behind them. Alaina could only see them if she knew what to look for. Desperation made her eyes keen. If she squinted she could even see her sister's scarf. They were here! And the Argosi were walking right towards them! She had to do something!

She reached for magic without thinking. Sainade was hardly paying attention. She was not prepared when Alaina reached for the magic. It rightly belonged to Alaina, and she felt no guilt over taking what already belonged to her. Magic suddenly woke within her. It was like a rubber band slapping into her face while ice water covered her skin.

Alaina made plants wraith with quick growth. She made lightning fall and fire roar! She would use anything to keep the others from looking at the trees. The nanoks were there to protect her but she would do what she could for them in turn. Alaina expected the guards to run at her but none of them did. They all stood yards away and just watched.

Lewis, even with his limited movement, could grab her arm, "Go!" He commanded.

"I won't just leave you," Alaina swore. She pulled more magic into herself and pushed it into him. She felt the disability spell fall away from his legs instantly.

"How did you do that?" Lewis whispered in amazement.

Alaina did not answer as she pulled him to his feet. "I know that the potion is making you tired but you need to run as fast as you can," she insisted.

"I don't even think I can run," Lewis tried to move his legs, but every muscle was cramped and sore.

Alaina knew the potion was working on him, making his mind and his body too tired to fight. She could see fear and shame in his eyes. She knew he was going to make her leave him.

"I won't leave. You have to run!" Alaina was not about to let him push her around!

"Then get help! We can't do this on our own." Lewis tried to persuade her to leave, and they both knew that it was true.

"I'll be back!" She promised reluctantly. She would not have given her word if she thought he could move one step more.

Alaina called the fire to her and sent it as close to the guards as she dared. They fought to put it out while she ran to the trees. She heard guards behind her but when she turned, they were far away.

Lewis had a long, thin tree branch, and he was using it to fight as many guards as he could. He knew the fight was hopeless, but she could nothing without time. Alaina knew that she could not leave him for long.

"Kiarlin?" Alaina whispered into the trees.

The figure of a nanok ran around her and back to a ravine. She followed the nanok and saw several women and the thin man who had helped to rescue her.

Kiarlin left the other women and ran to hug Alaina but

By: Jennie Arnold

Alaina could not let herself be comforted until she finished what she came to do.

"Lewis is still back there! We have to get him out of there before the Argosi hurt him."

"The nanoks could rescue him like they rescued us," Daisy declared looking at the nanoks around her.

"I don't think they can understand us without Mira here to translate. We need to find her." With those words, Matt turned around and ran towards the camp the others had made the night before. The women and nanoks quickly followed after.

Matt was shocked – not amazed or flabber-gasted – that Kiarlin's sister had found them. It was too wonderful and amazing to be true! What were the odds that they would all be at the right place at the right time?

Half the job was done and he had barely had to work at all. Now all they had to do was free Lewis!

Mira had told Matt that the nanoks knew a prophecy. They honestly believed that three Islanders could stop the world from ending! Matt did not worry about such things because he did not believe it himself. It was not that he did not want to help or that he did not trust the nanoks' words.

The truth was that Matt did not think it was needed. The nanoks saw their territory as the world. He only needed to save a mile or two.

The Argosi invasion must have been the ending the nanoks saw. The nanoks' small world must have ended as soon as those ships arrived. Matt had heard the nanok from that strange vision talk about hoping in what Fate had in store for you but how hopeful could he really be if they thought that the world was going to end?

"Mira!" Matt called out. "We have an important message that you need to give the nanoks."

"That's funny," Mira said with a smile. Matt wanted to wipe the annoying grin from her face. "Snow was just telling me that she had a message to give you."

"Now is not the time for jokes, Mira. Lewis is in trouble! He distracted the guards so Alaina could escape but we had to leave him with them to get her here!"

"You saw Lewis?" Shock made her voice rise an octave or two. She turned to Matt and just seemed to realize that Alaina was there. "I'm sorry. I'll tell the nanoks that they're needed."

Matt turned to Kiarlin. "You should take your sister down to the stream. I'm sure she wants to wash up." Matt saw a glint in Kiarlin's eyes and quickly changed tactics. "I mean, it is more private down there so you two can catch up."

Matt's logic of the words must have filtered through to the two of them. Kiarlin led her sister away with a loving arm over her shoulders. With Mira off talking to nanoks and the women talking to each other, Matt found himself alone. The women from Alta Island were practicing their magic miles away and the river might as well be so far.

"What's a man to do with rare free time?" Matt asked himself. The answer came to him and made him feel slightly guilty. "I should get back to the gloaming field and talk with that nanok myself."

He had not seen his nanok in almost a week. He had meant to visit more often but after a long day of marching sleep was all Matt could think of. He was tired enough now to sleep for true but he was not exhausted. He could lie down and find that place between without crossing over. To test that theory, he laid down and found that in between sleep and awake. Imagination controlled the world but thoughts that came were still your own.

By: Jennie Arnold

I knew you would come, young one, the nanok intoned startling Matt.

"That makes one of us. It was a bit of a surprise to me. We found Lewis and the Argosi. Mira and the nanoks are going to rescue him now. Alaina has already been found and I can already see a change in Kiarlin."

Your news makes me happy, friend. I am glad anytime someone finds freedom. Getting the magic girl away from the Argosi will help your other friend as well. The nanok looked at Matt to make sure he was being taken seriously. *I am afraid they were using the girl's magic to hurt him.*

"It's alright, then. She's with us so they can't hurt him now."

Your friend still needs help and we can give it to him. The Wild Fae are coming and they will bring harm to many. We need to stop them to save many, including your friend. The nanok gave Matt that look again. *We need to work together to make a net.*

"I'll get the string and needles," Matt volunteered, jumping to be useful.

We cannot catch any Fae with string. We must make a net of hope and dreams. That is the only way to trap Wild Fae and this is the only place the nets can be made. You and I must make them here in the gloaming fields.

Matt gave the nanok his cockiest smile. "Let's get started."

Lewis was forced awake when a warm liquid was poured down his throat. He choked and spluttered but most of the liquid wormed its way into his stomach. The rude awakening coupled with a knock to the head did nothing to help Lewis'

memory of the last few days. He wracked his brain and felt a sinking in his gut as it all came back to him.

"The potion!" He remembered aloud. Lewis tried to sit up but ropes held him fast. He twisted this way and that, looking for an enemy. He was shocked to find that he was in his sitting room; the sitting room of the home he had grown up in. The sinking feeling became a sharp panic even with the numbing drugs in his system.

"Where's my family? What have you done with them?"

"Now you're worried about your family?" Mocked the empress as she walked into Lewis's limited line of view. "You weren't thinking about them when you made that escape attempt. They will suffer for your mistakes."

Guards marched in pushing the stumbling figure of Hewin Thalda, Lewis's father, between them. Lewis strained against the ropes harder with each step his father took.

"You let him go," Lewis demanded. "Let him go now or I'll use every scrap of magic I have!" Lewis had used his magic before even after drinking the potion. He knew that he was angry enough to break through the haze.

The empress laughed in his face. "After all that potion your magic has to be unreliable and inaccurate. You cannot be sure the magic will not harm your father — if your magic comes at all."

Lewis tried to keep his face blank, tried not to see the truth in her words. He spoke as calmly as he could, "You want me to work with you. I'll never help you if you hurt him. Let him go."

"You and your friends have proven to be more stubborn than we anticipated. This motivation will help you keep things in perspective. You will remember your place."

The empress turned to a guard behind Lewis' head. "Silence him. I want the boy to watch, not talk." A rough piece

By: Jennie Arnold

of cloth was pushed into his mouth. Lewis turned his head and fought all he could but he knew it was pointless.

Tears streamed down Lewis' face and blurred the vision of his father. "Don't you worry, son," Lewis heard his father say. "We'll get out of this together."

"Bring the girl in," the empress ordered.

"Andrea!" Hewin called to his daughter with worry in his voice. Her face was bruised and her eyes were red from crying.

Lewis called to his magic over and over but nothing seemed to be happening. He was not worried about hurting his father with magic; he knew the Argosi would hurt him far worse. He could see the worry in his father's face and terrified tears streaming down his sister's. He knew he needed to help them but he did not know how!

He saw a streak of color on one side of him. He felt the sizzle of magic and a flash. Lewis knew magic had been used near him but he could also tell that although he did try to call his magic, the magic did not come from him now.

Lewis turned when he heard the guard next to him fall to the floor. The guard had been standing right next to his sister. Worry for her filled him. Lewis stretched his neck to look at his sister. He looked for his sister and father but he saw that they were no longer there. Lewis could not help himself. He laughed with joy.

The empress turned to him in shock and anger. "Did your magic do this?" The question demanded an answer.

Lewis could only shake his head. The gag had been removed, but he was laughing so hard that words were beyond him.

"Search the Island," the empress ordered the remaining guards. "They have to be here somewhere. People don't just disappear into thin air!"

The guards ran outside. Lewis could no longer see what

was happening but he could hear the growling nanoks and screaming guards.

"They're safe," Lewis cried in relief. "You tried to... but you couldn't. They are safe." He repeated to himself with joy over and over until the empress ordered another dose of potion forced into him. Still, the joyous feeling did not leave Lewis even as blackness settled in.

"Send out scouts," Mira ordered as the nanoks got into a hunting formation.

No need to fear, daughter. We have hunted predators that leave a trickier trail than this, Dancer reassured her.

I will make sure that the invaders pay for the lives that they have taken and for the foolish mistakes that they continue to make, Snow swore in a growl that would have made most others bulk but Dancer would always see Snow as the cub she had helped raise.

No, Snow, she commanded with an equally fierce growl. *Vengeance is the Creator's job. Our duty is to protect our people and our brothers and sisters. We must rescue our daughter's friends. We must each perform the destiny that was assigned to us.*

I will listen to Fate and complete my destiny. The Creator cannot do it all on his own. I will help the sleuth by bringing justice!

That is not the way, Snow. Dancer said the statement like a command and Mira could feel the power of it. Snow evidently could feel the strength as well. She hung her head down and wined apologies.

I will guard the sleuth daughter. I do not know what the

Creator has in store for us but I trust him and I trust you. I will complete whatever mission you give me.

Dancer rubbed her muzzle against Snow to show that she forgave her and all was forgotten. Mira felt bad about breaking into their moment but this was important.

"Can you track Lewis? Alaina is sure that the Argosi will hurt him."

Dancer nodded in a way that only a nanok can. *I will lead this group myself.* With that, six nanoks ran towards the Island of Alta.

It did not take Dancer long to realize that the man was on the Island itself. He had a difficult time discerning the man's distinct scent among so many but in the end, Dancer found a house that smelled more strongly of the daughter's friend than any other. It was clear that the man visited this place frequently.

Dancer and the others bounded back to the alcove where Snow and Mira waited. Mira could tell that Dancer was bringing good news back. The nanok's head was held high and his eyes were bright.

We have found your friend, daughter. He is in your Island but the Argosi enemies are with him. Mira knew that Dancer thought it was too dangerous for Mira to go on the rescue mission but the truth was that none of them knew Alta as well as her.

Our daughter is right, Snow began. *She knows this Island and its people. We are only strangers there. She can make sure that the enemies are the only humans we need to worry about. You know how jumpy these humans get around our kind.*

Dancer grudgingly agreed that the two of them had a point. *Our daughter will go to the Island with us,* she agreed, *but you and our daughter will be in the center of the hunting formation where it is safest. A dozen nanoks will accompany us.*

"A dozen nanoks cannot beat the Argosi' lightning sticks.

Charging in is not a good plan."

Charging is not our plan at all. Listen until I finish, cubs. Dancer leaned closer to take the sting from her reprimand. *Plumblossom is strong among us. She can go into the gloaming field and use magic there that can be brought here.*

"Plumblossom can use nature magic like Kiarlin?" Asked Mira in shock.

Our magic is different than the magic you humans use. We only borrow magic from the other worlds for a short time and we can only do small things with it. Dancer looked at Plumblossom. The lighter nanok nodded before she continued. *Plumblossom has been able to move living things from one space to another.*

I have been granted powers in the past. I see no reason why Fate will not lend them to me again. I will lose many nights of sleep because of this but it will be worth it. Two worlds ride on the shoulders of you and your friends.

"You are helping me save the humans too, Plumblossom. It does not seem right for you to be in pain."

Do not worry, daughter. The world is worth more than that to me. Let us finish this before the Argosi move him.

Mira sprinted in the center of the hunting formation. She ran past fields and shop fronts she had played in as a child. She saw Lewis' house come into view.

This is it, Dancer sent.

I am ready for my part, Plumblossom sent. *Make sure that you are ready for yours.*

The others nodded as one.

Everything happened at once then: Plumblossom vanished, lightning flashed, Dancer smashed into the house, Mira moved to the Southern window and Snow stood before the door with the remaining nanoks. Mira saw Hewin and Andrea, Lewis's father and sister disappear with the flash through the window.

By: Jennie Arnold

She went running to the ridge. Plumblossom said she would reappear there.

Mira had not seen Lewis but she had assumed that the nanok had been able to get him out with his family but Mira's assumption was proven incorrect when laughter sounded from the house. *That's Lewis's voice*, Mira knew and shivered.

She could not help but be disappointed that Lewis was still trapped. The sight of little Andrea and her father made her smile though. It would help Lewis in the long run too, Mira knew. Lewis could break through with his own magic but Mira remembered Lewis as a gentle friend. He would not hurt someone if he could help it and he would not have to worry about hurting innocents now. Plumblossom seemed worried that she might have to hurt Hewin though. He was looking at her nervously.

"Don't worry," Mira reassured them. "The nanoks are on our side."

"How is this possible, lass?"

"It's a long story. You need to hear the whole thing and I'll tell you, just not now. The story can wait until we are not surrounded by enemies."

By: Jennie Arnold

Chapter Seventeen

Matt found himself in that odd place again. He had laid down to sleep, exhausted after a day full of activity; planning to do nothing but rest but his mind would not stop spinning. Questions went around his head in circles and would not let him fall into oblivion.

The nanok that helped and trained Matt remained a mystery. Matt did not want to look a gift horse in the mouth. He was grateful for the help but he did not like secrets. Another part of Matt warned that very few people would do something for nothing. What was this nanok getting out of helping him? Why was the nanok helping him?

Matt felt certain that he could answer the first two questions and many others if he only found the answer to one important question: Who is this nanok?

Every other mystery would just fall into place if he just knew that.

Mira had told Matt that the nanoks in the sleuth had names. She introduced him to the nanoks traveling with them. Matt could honestly not tell one nanok from another but he trusted Mira. He was sure that she was telling him the truth. She must know each by name. Mira had told him the names of all the nanoks but Matt still did not know the name of the nanok in that other place.

Matt was not sure how he had ended up in the place now. Usually, he had to force himself to travel to the gloaming field — where he could see the future — instead of finding himself in a boring dream — where he had no conscience control. This time was different. He had not made the decision to be here. He was not even sure where here was… He could tell he was there though. The feel of the place, as well as the control he had, told him he was in the gloaming fields.

I did not expect to find you here, the nanok told him.

"I was not expecting to be here. How did you know where I would be?"

I did not know. I live here. You come to me and I teach what I can.

"You live here? I only come when I sleep."

I used to come when I slept. I died in my sleep but I live on here.

"Will I live on here? Is this where everyone goes?"

No! Of course not. Most souls go to be with the Creator or to judgment depending on Fate. Souls like me, souls with unfinished business, go here.

"You have unfinished business? I suppose you're here to finish that business."

I am here to finish what was started so many years ago. I began teaching you solely to finish the Wild Fae. They are the ones who killed me in my sleep. My sleuth was fighting them for the territory they stole from us! The nanok took a deep breath to calm him. I regret that I even considered using you. This fight came to you long before I did. Destiny wrote you here at this place and at this time. We may yet help each other but I swear never to use you, Mattatemus Augustus Kaletu.

Matt tried not to cringe at the use of his full name. He knew that the nanok just meant to be formal. He wanted Matt to know he was serious and Matt could see from the nanok's eyes that he was.

"That is a good oath, my friend. I would make a similar bond to you but I do not know your name."

I have not used my name in a long time but I do still remember it. They used to call me Juniper Wood.

"Then I swear to you, Juniper Wood, that I will help you finish the fight with the Wild Fae. I promise that as long as you

By: Jennie Arnold

help me I will help you."

A good promise, friend, Juniper said with a nanok grin.

Matt awoke with a start but the images were still playing through in his head. He could not get the nanok, or the name he had learned, out of his head. Still, it did not take long for something else to fill his mind.

"How did they get here?" Matt asked Mira when he saw Hewin and Andrea Thalda.

"Mira rescued us!" Andrea said proudly, practically dancing.

"I don't think that I did anything," Mira corrected. "Dancer and Plumblossom did all the work."

"The nanoks killed the Argosi?" Matt asked with surprise.

"One of the nanoks made us move," Hewin started, but he could not continue. His words spluttered into silence.

"Plumblossom went into the gloaming field to use magic. She transported them from the house into the ridge where we waited," Mira finished for the older man.

"Wait, wait, and back up." Matt felt hairs on the back of his neck prick up. "One of your nanoks went into the gloaming field? Can you help me talk to her?"

Matt's excitement became clear with the light of anticipation in his eyes so Mira could do nothing but say yes. She led Matt to Plum.

"You can go into the gloaming field? Do you go there regularly?"

Mira tried to hide a smile as she translated. "She says yes to both."

"Ask if she has ever met another nanok there." Matt could feel his excitement raising as he waited for the answer.

"She says she sees many nanoks there. Where are you going with this, Matt?"

"Ask if she's ever heard of a nanok named Juniper Wood."

Mira pauses before she can repeat the nanok's answer. "She says that Juniper Wood was her brother's name. They were littermates. He died --"

"Right after the Argosi came?" Matt finished for her in a breathless voice.

Plumblossom laid a gentle paw on Mira and made strange sounds.

"What is it?" Matt asked Mira.

"Plumblossom wants you to go into the gloaming fields with her and lead her to Juniper."

"I've never taken someone else into the gloaming field before. I'm willing to try but I don't know if I can take her."

"She says that she has taken other nanoks into the gloaming when they sleep nose to nose."

"Of course it won't be easy," Matt mumbled to himself. Getting nose to nose with the nanok was not easy but Matt managed it.

Matt went to that trance before waking and after sleeping. He found himself standing next to Plum on a hill in the gloaming field. The she-nanok looked impatient and excited.

You are sure you saw Juniper, Seer?

"That's what he said his name was. He has been teaching me for weeks but he just told me his name last night."

That sounds like my brother, Plum said with a smile.

"This way," Matt pointed to the field where Juniper had always met him.

I did not expect to see you again so soon, Juniper called to Matt. *Is there something wrong?*

"I brought a friend who really wants to see you," Matt told him. He stood back and let Plumblossom have some private time with her brother.

Little Plum! Juniper called. *How you have grown! You are a master in this place by your own right. I called to you but the*

By: Jennie Arnold

peace you made with Fate was something you had to do on your own. Matt and the sleuth are lucky to have you.

I am the lucky one. Our new-found daughter has allowed the sleuth to work with a Seer and Darkness Chaser.

Juniper gave Matt one of his most cocky grins. *You must not say things like that, Plum. You will only make my friend's head swell.*

Plum laughed and rubbed her muzzle against her brother. *It's like no time has passed at all!*

Time passes swiftly; sister and we must race to catch up. The end is coming and our sleuth and the lands of men must survive it! Matt and I have been weaving a net to do just that. It will catch and trap the Wild Fae.

They can't turn into smoke with this net around them?

They can't use magic at all in this net, sister, Juniper insisted.

Then you must let me help make it! Plum yipped with joy.

Lewis felt like he was floating. He felt buoyant and weightless, the way he did when he was swimming. He opened his eyes and saw the blue sky moving above him.

Could I be floating down the river? He asked to himself. He tried to sit up to get a look around him but he could not. Ropes cut into him and it all came flooding back.

The Argosi had tried to hurt his father and sister but something had stopped them. Magic had taken his family away. He could only pray that they were safe. Something told Lewis that he should be worried about his own safety.

He saw that he was tied to the stretcher yet again. The ropes were cutting into him so he moved to relieve the pressure but it seemed to be pointless. The ropes seemed to get even tighter when he moved. Things became even bleaker when he saw the velvet woman. Sainade stood next to the stretcher holding a chain that attached to a headband. He could not see the banded woman's face but it must be Alaina!

"No!" Lewis called out in shock. All eyes turned towards him at his outburst — including the banded silken. He could see her face now and he could not help but breathe a sigh of relief. The girl was not Alaina. Lewis breathed deeply, realizing that he had been holding his breath.

"The truth can be a shock but it is better to accept reality," Sainade told him from a dry voice.

"You didn't kidnap another girl, did you?" He asked pointing his chin at the banded girl in the corner. "That's not Alaina or any of the girls from Alta."

"Don't you recognize her, boy? She is the baron's silken. You and Alaina beat them in a competition earlier."

"I remember that the baron's velvet woman tried to hurt Alaina," Lewis reminded Sainade with venom in his voice.

"This silken will allow me to control you. Alaina was powerful but she never did learn her place. Sarilla knows exactly where she stands." Sainade stroked Sarilla's hair as she spoke, making the chained woman cringe at each touch.

"Someone approaches from the south, mistress," Sarilla told the velvet woman.

"Man or animal?" Sainade asked.

"Please don't be angry. I cannot tell if it is a man or a nanok."

"You better hope that it's not Mira and her nanoks!" Lewis said with fervor.

"Don't make me silence you now that you're awake, boy!"

Lewis did not even try to stifle a laugh. After the magic he had seen the nanoks perform there was little that could

By: Jennie Arnold

intimidate him. Sainade could hurt him but she could not do more than that. She needed him alive.

Sainade took his laugh as a challenge. She tightened her grip on Sarilla's chain and took a hold of her magic. Lewis felt pain ratchet up his body in waves. He ground his teeth to keep from calling out.

"You're no match for them. Mira and Matt can beat you." Lewis spoke as loudly and as clearly as he could with clenched teeth.

"Thieves like the velvet women are not worthy to fight the nanok daughters," said a voice from the surrounding landscape. The mountain ranges provided ample places for hiding. Lewis could not see the source of the voice. That is, until a figure came rushing towards them.

A man with the head of a nanok launched himself at their party. He screamed a battle cry that was unlike anything Lewis had ever heard before. He spun and shifted around any guards who came towards him. His body slammed into Sainade at an alarming speed. The velvet woman fell and did not get back up again. She was knocked out cold.

Lewis saw Sarilla's eyes widen in surprise. He knew she was feeling her own magic rushing into her. She must have pointed all her magic at the fighting duo. Lewis saw the nanok man's head shrink and change. A second later, Lewis saw that the man no longer had a nanok's head. He was a man again!

"Thank you, child." He nodded to Sarilla and kissed her hand.

"We're free," the girl breathed in disbelief.

"We won't be free for long if we don't get out of here!" Lewis reminded them. The former werebeast quickly moved to his litter and untied Lewis's bonds.

"I promised the nanok daughter that I would help you," the man told Lewis. "The nanoks will need the girl too. They want all the magic users they can find to help them survive the end times. My name is Oreland and I always keep my word."

"More guards are coming from the west. We need to run," Sarilla warned them in a worried voice.

"Let's go!" Lewis yelled as he sprinted to the south after the former nanokman.

~*~

Alaina clung to her sister, too numb to cry. She did not want to cry or even talk. She just wanted to feel her sister's touch, to know she was there with her. She could hear Kiarlin murmur to her; offering words of comfort. Alaina was not really listening to Kiarlin's words but she liked the comforting tone.

"I missed you, Kiarlin," Alaina said after what felt like an eternity. Matt had used his key to unlock the band from around her brow hours ago. She had not said a word even then. Alaina had plenty to say but she did not know where to begin. The idea of not only beginning but finishing seemed too daunting to even think about. So, she just remained silent.

Kiarlin hugged her and washed her in the river and dried her tears. The other women in camp left the sisters alone. They could sense that the women needed time. After hours that felt like days to Alaina, she and her sister came to the women's side of the camp. The women from Alta welcomed Alaina with hugs and tears before Alaina let herself tell what had happened through tears of her own.

She felt like a new person when it was all over. The events of the past could stay in the past and now she could live in the present.

"There is a fight coming. We have to be ready for it," Alaina told them with a smile.

"We have been training," Mistress Tilde told her with pride. "Kiarlin is a great elemental and Sonja is a skilled healer."

By: Jennie Arnold

"You are not trained to fight or to use weapons." Alaina took a breath and watched the faces of the women she was speaking with closely. "I hate what the Argosi did to me, to all of us, but I also know that I needed to fight with them to fight against them. They taught me to fight because they wanted to turn me into a weapon. I will make sure that the Argosi regret what they did forever! I want to teach you all to be weapons against the Argosi."

"Where do we start?" Asked Mistress Tilde with a sad smile.

Mira could not help but feel the tension in the air. The women were all anxious about Alaina. Matt seemed to sleep more hours than he was awake. He said that he was building some kind of trap for the Argosi in the gloaming field. He said it was such earnest that Mira could not help but believe him.

You seem worried, daughter, Dancer commented. *Your mind is troubled.*

"Do you feel the tension in the air?" Mira asked her.

Tension? Dancer seemed unfamiliar with the word.

"The air feels like it's vibrating."

Yes, I feel it too. There is danger in the air. You should stay here to warn and protect the other humans. There is a battle coming. We must prepare before it is too late.

"How do we prepare for battle? Make halberds and arrows? Maybe a siege work or two? There are so few of us, Dancer," Mira said the last in a defeated voice. The tension in the air was getting to her too. The nanok could sense this and put a paw on Mira's back to comfort her.

All is not lost, daughter. We have magic on our side and not just the women. We have the gloaming field. Humans do not enter there, save Seers and nanok daughters. The Almost Nanok does not even know the place exists. A strong soul is needed to enter such a place.

"If I entered the gloaming could I learn to do what Plumblossom did?" Mira asked her question cautiously, unsure if she was ready for the answer.

Plum is very talented. Not everyone can do as well as she does in the gloaming field but any nanok can enter it. It takes practice to have any skill.

"Would Plum be able to teach me?"

Dancer did not answer. She only looked at Mira with a nanokish grin on her face.

I thought you would never ask, daughter, Plum said behind her. *Teaching you would be an honor.*

Mira smiled her thanks.

By: Jennie Arnold

Chapter Eighteen

Matt had been making good progress with the net between sleeping and waking. Juniper had told him how important the net would be. The nanok knew how to motivate Matt. He understood the importance of the thing and could focus his thoughts to precise points. He would have liked to spend all his time in the gloaming but he needed to be moving to travel. The nanoks still insisted that the party get to the mountains.

Worry was written all over Mira's face and even Matt could see it. Matt felt her worry too. He worried about Lewis. He worried about the Argosi. Matt knew firsthand how cruel the Argosi could be but he also knew that there were bigger enemies to worry about. The Wild Fae were coming and that threat could not be ignored.

Matt wanted to help Lewis but Lewis could not be helped if the Wild Fae came. The Argosi were a problem, but they were not *the important* problem. Beating the Argosi would not fix the real problem it would only delay things for a short time.

Still, Mira and her nanoks had a point of their own. Lewis could not be saved if the Argosi sacrificed him before they made it to the mountain. Time was not on their side and they needed to hurry. Matt understood all of that but he could not shake the feeling that he needed to stop the Wild Fae. All of this needed to be done, but it was just practice for the bigger battle.

He rushed, as the nanoks wanted him to, and kept his thoughts to himself. He had voiced his concern to Mira, of course, but after that, he had not said a word of his worries. He just walked. Matt lost himself in the repetitive movement of walking. He was not paying attention to the world around him. He just thought and walked but he should have been watching.

The next second, Matt put his foot down and he felt a stab of pain. A loud pop echoed, and it took a moment or two for Matt to realize that the sound came from him! Pain shot up and down his leg. The vision's numbness filled his head while pain tingled in his leg. Before long the vision filled his being.

Matt saw Lewis standing in the Island green in Alta. Lewis looked happy, but the smile was wiped from his face when Argosi guards stepped out of ditches and trees. They surrounded him in seconds. A young woman stood next to him, crying. A man with a walking stick and a smooth face looked like he wanted to run. Lewis just looked angry.

Lewis screamed and charged the Argosi. They had their lightning sticks out in a flash and hit Lewis with them before he could blink. Lewis was soon on the floor writhing in pain. Matt saw the edges of the vision fade. He fought to keep the vision going. He needed more information. Matt looked here and there as quickly as he could but all the work was for nothing. The vision ended there.

He came back to himself and felt Kiarlin tenderly rubbing his ankle; healing it with a mere touch. Mira, Daisy and a few other women sat around him. They all wore anxious frowns but none of them seemed too forlorn. This had all happened before by now.

"Lewis is free," Matt told the others. He was not sure how he knew this information but he was sure that he did. "Lewis is free right now but he won't be for long. He is walking into a trap!" Matt let the news sink in before he went into any details. He found that he was breathing hard. He felt like he had run for miles but he took a deep breath and told them the whole thing.

"Lewis is going back home... back to Alta Island. The Argosi are spreading lies about retreating. Lewis thinks they're true, so he returns home to help... but it's a trap. The Argosi are there waiting for him. We have to warn him before he gets

By: Jennie Arnold

there." Matt continued to breathe hard, but it was getting easier now that it was all out in the open. He took a few deep breaths to calm himself.

"We just have to warn Lewis. That's not too hard if he walks fast," Mira said with her hand on Matt's shoulder, trying to comfort him. "We could help Alaina. We can help Lewis too."

Matt nodded. "You're right."

He was not sure that he really believes what Mira is saying but he knows that sitting and moping is not going to help anyone. Matt fought to push the worry away but there is only so much he can do.

Walking and keeping busy would have to keep the worry at bay for him.

"We'll find him, Matt," Mira promised.

Lewis followed the former werebeast and the silken into the forest. He had been arguing with Oreland for some time. "We need to go back to Alta. The Islanders there will help us."

"That is the first place the empress will look," Sarilla mentioned, taking up Oreland's argument. "You know that going back will only put yourself and your friends into danger. It is not a real option so stop suggesting it."

"I'm not abandoning my home!"

"You're not abandoning it. You're keeping your distance to protect it."

Lewis could see that both Sarilla and Oreland were tiring of the argument. He really did already know that he couldn't go to Alta but he also knew that going into the Wuthering Woods was not a good plan. Oreland insisted that they all needed to go to the woods. Lewis had refused but Oreland would not yield. Arguing got Lewis nowhere.

"You're sure we need to go to the woods?"

"Yes, I'm sure. The trees told me we all need to be here," Oreland insisted.

"You saw these trees in a dream?" Lewis tried to hide his incredulousness but Oreland obviously heard it in the tone.

"I was in the gloaming field. All the nanoks can go to it and so can I. Fate has brought the talent to me."

"You weren't a nanok when you had the vision," Sarilla commented.

"Mira can talk with nanoks and Matt sees the future. Why can't Oreland do a little of both," Lewis defended. "I still don't want to go into the woods. My father used to tell me it was haunted. He would tell me ghost stories that left my skin crawling."

"Ghost stories are just stories. Your father made them up to amuse you and keep you from getting lost in these woods as a child," Oreland insisted.

"Stories usually have a grain of truth in them. Twenty people could tell me about a boogieman in the woods and I still would not believe in the boogieman but I would never go into those woods. Something must be in there to make them tell such stories," Sarilla said thoughtfully.

"Some strange psychic vision told Oreland that we all need to go into the woods. So we have to go whether the stories are true or not. We just need to be sure to be extra careful."

Lewis did not want to go into these woods either way but he also knew that something needed to be done. Lewis could not think of anything else so the woods seemed like the only option.

Shadows fell as soon as they entered the woods. The canopy above was so thick that the sun seemed to be unable to

By: Jennie Arnold

break through. Lewis could not help but feel like the Wuthering Woods really were haunted. It was impossible to see the forest floor because of the lack of sunlight. Anything could be lurking at your feet and no one would know until they were on top of it.

It's no wonder ghost stories were made about this place, Lewis thought to himself. *It's creepy enough for a slew of stories to be made without ever going more than a yard or two in.*

Lewis kept tripping over roots and bric-a-brac on the forest floor. He could not see well so he kept tripping over his feet. Sarilla seemed to have an even harder time of it in her gown but Oreland looked like he was having no trouble at all. Lewis did not see him trip once!

"How can you see where you're going in this mess?" Lewis asked Oreland.

"I need not see. The voices of the trees are telling me where to go. I'm just following them."

Oreland's answer made Lewis look at him with concern. "I don't hear any voices, Oreland."

"They're talking to me, not you. Why would you hear anything?" Lewis felt even more concerned after hearing this question but he did not know how to begin voicing his concern so he remained silent. The three of them continued walking in silence until they came to the center of the forest.

"This is it," Oreland whispered. "This is where we need to be." Oreland's eyes were alight with hope. Lewis followed Oreland's gaze and saw why.

A tree stood in the center of the forest but this was not just any tree. This tree had white bark with leaves the color of fire. No earthly leaves have ever been that color. Lewis could not take his eyes off of the tree. He looked to the right and saw that Sarilla and Oreland were having the same problem.

"It's beautiful," Sarilla whispered in awe.

"He wants to help us," Oreland told them with a smile. "He wants to show me how to make a tool that will help you against the Wild Fae."

"What Wild Fae?" Lewis asked in shock. "Those are just children's stories. I need to fight the real enemies — the Argosi!"

"The Argosi have made foolish deals with the Wild Fae. I was there when they made the deal. The tree has seen dealings with the Wild Fae and knows that they always go back on their word. The Wild Fae will deceive the Argosi."

"Great! Then I don't have to worry about the Argosi," Lewis said with true relish.

"The Argosi want to invade your home. That is a terrible thing. I can see why you don't like them... but you should know that the Wild Fae don't plan on invading your home. They plan on destroying it!"

"They'll kill everyone!" Lewis could hardly believe the words even as he said them.

"The others need to know!" Sarilla cried out in shock. "The Fae won't just kill guards or velvet women. They'll kill my sisters, all the silken, all those people on the Islands... So many people would die!"

It was clear that the girl was panicking. "I need to warn the Argosi. They'll send the guards to fight the Wild Fae. The Argosi can save us!"

"The Argosi put a band on you, Sarilla!" Lewis shouted. He felt anger flood his face with heat. "You can't keep defending them! They kidnap women and destroy towns. They kill anyone who gets in their way. Those Argosi deserve whatever the Wild Fae give them!"

"How many people in Argosi are forced to be there? How many are just like the women from your Island. How many people there have never hurt a fly? Are you going to let the

Wild Fae destroy them too? Or do you think they'll stop with the guards?"

"Now is not the time for this," Oreland said in a voice that commanded them to be quiet. He held up a white rod covered in intricate knots and swirls. The symbols were so fine that they looked like words.

"We have what we need to stop them both. This wand will stop the Wild Fae. We will bargain with the Argosi by telling them the truth. We can tell them they are being tricked. We'll tell them we have the weapon and that we will use it to help them if they leave."

"They don't need to know that we need to kill the Wild Fae just as much as they do," Lewis agreed.

"We might not need to do that," Sarilla told them. "The signs on those trees are Argosi short talk. It says that they are leaving. Guards are returning to ships."

"We need to find out why they are leaving," Oreland said quickly, leaving no room for arguing.

Mira found that she got on well with Plumblossom. She was patient and calm no matter the circumstances. She did her best to learn fast.

"Get comfortable on your pallet. Clear your mind and focus on each limb. Breath in and out slowly as if you are preparing to sleep," Plum directed her. Each lesson began the same way. This was how she prepared herself to enter the gloaming field.

Mira did as she was told. Plum had been traveling the gloaming for longer than Mira had been alive! A wise person would listen to the advice of someone so experienced.

Plum's directions got Mira to the gloaming field, but that

was not enough. It took a blink or two before Mira could move in the gloaming field. The shock of the place made her lose focus. It was like dreaming of flying only to plummet into wakefulness. She had to focus on the calm to keep it in place.

She was surrounded by rolling hills but she stood in a low valley. The sky above her was lit with the vibrant colors of a sunset. Birds flitted in the air to fly loops around her. One of the birds was dark as midnight with round eyes and glittering talons. A raven! The nanoks had said that ravens were bad luck. Mira moved to shoo it away.

"Get out of here!" She waved an arm at it.

"You're the one who is out of place," the bird told her with a note of condescension in his voice. "This is my home. You're the guest and you're being quite rude!"

Vile bird! Plum nipped at the thing. *You do not belong here! No one invited you so be gone! This human is my guest and is under my protection!*

"Look to the sky if you don't believe me!" The bird danced in the air until it was level with the swirling fog.

A hole had formed in the sky to morph into a void that the fog leaked from like a broken water main. Pictures begin to show through the fog until images filled the sky.

She saw Lewis falling into a net and nanoks roaring into the moon only to be silenced with a slicing motion. Mira shuddered at the violence of both visions in the mists. Matt's visions always seemed to be more specific but Mira's always left her shaking. She could not imagine seeing more.

She tried to force the fear from her mind but the feeling only seemed to grow. Fear began to overwhelm her. She could not stop shaking. She began to quiver all over. Mira began to notice that she was not the only one shaking. The whole world was shaking! The gloaming field seemed to morph and change.

The land around her was no longer a valley surrounded by

By: Jennie Arnold

hills. It was now a pass in the mountains. Cliffs and peaks seemed to go straight up into nothingness. The place itself felt bleak and sad. The feel of the place was changing into something Mira knew she did not like. The gloaming field was morphing into chaos!

All of Mira's greatest fears seemed to be taking shape. The ghosts she was afraid of as a child, the dark alley behind her father's shop, the sound of thunder; all the things that haunted her childhood nightmares chased her. She ran until she came to a dead end. She thought she had nowhere to go but the wall of solid rock in front of her exploded. Men in Argosi uniforms came running through the gaping hole. Mira knew what surrounded her; nightmares on her left and Argosi on her right. Rocks fell onto her from above with the Argosi spears. She had no hope of escaping. Panic set in deeply. She couldn't breathe!

This is the wrong path, daughter! Plum sent to her, yelling in her mind. *You must leave here. Come to me now!*

Mira steeled her determination and ran to Plum, flinging her arms around the nanok. The nanok shifted them both out of the gloaming field and into their beds. Mira flew upright, gasping and sputtering.

"What happened? Are you all right?" Matt asked with shock and fear in his eyes.

"I'm all right," Mira told him in surprise. "I'm all right. It wasn't real... only a nightmare."

"I want to learn how to heal one day. I can see the value of it but right now we need to focus. We are at war with the Argosi!" Alaina had had this conversation with Mistress Tilde so many times she lost count. Still, the Mistress seemed to bring it up every day.

"Learning to heal is not just for medicine. It could become a weapon. With healing, we can thicken the blood so that it does not flow or force the lungs to react to poison that is not there. Healing is a weapon too," Tilde argued again.

"That's just cruel. Killing is ugly enough without adding anything so dirty. Healing should only be used to help people. There is enough magic that can only be used to kill. Don't dirty up good magic too!"

Alaina could only think of the times Sainade had forced her to use magic to hurt. She could not stop it or do much of anything besides pray and pleaded for her magic to do good. Alaina did not want to be responsible for good magic turning bad.

"Just let me show you," Tilde promised before running to a goat that the nanoks had caught earlier. Two cubs had been playing with it, learning to hunt when Mistress Tilde took it to use.

"I usually heal by sending energy into blood and heart. I send vitamins into the areas that are troubling the patient. I just reverse the process — " Tilde stopped as she saw the results of her magic.

The goat was now little more than ash.

"Did you expect the magic would do that? You have shown more wisdom than I gave you credit for by telling me not to use that flow of power."

"I was not expecting anything so drastic." Alaina swallowed down her disgust before continuing. "That type of healing should never be used. Winning this war is not worth losing our humanity."

The other women nodded. The conversation was over.

By: Jennie Arnold

Chapter Nineteen

"We have to return to Alta Island," Sarilla told the two men for the umpteenth time. She could not see why the two of them wouldn't listen to her! She spoke since, but they acted like she simply said that rain is wet!

"We are going to Alta," Oreland insisted. "We're just not jumping in without knowing what we're getting into. We'll get there. We just need to prepare first."

"Getting into the Island should be easy. I know this Island much better than the Argosi." Lewis knew that his words sounded like boasting but it was all true. "The only thing I'm unsure of is what to do once I get there. What are we looking for? You never explained the whole plan."

"We need to know if the signs are true. We have read them but we've been mistaken before. I want to see the Argosi leave with my own eyes," Oreland suggested in a sagely voice.

"Just look for women. The people the Argosi took should be back," Sarilla said in an excited voice.

"I should be able to look without trouble," Lewis promised.

Oreland and Sarilla both seemed to be full of worries but Lewis kept thinking that things were finally going right. He was finally free of the Argosi! He was no longer in their clutches, prophecy or no, and it looked like they were leaving his home as well. He could not think of anything more welcoming!

"We have no guarantee that the signs are telling the truth," Oreland reminded him when Lewis brought it up.

"They aren't posting it for all to see. Why would they lie in a coded message that only their country-men can read? It's not like this was meant for us." Lewis argued with Oreland but he felt his eyes fall to the ground with his gut. Could the Argosi have known that he would read their message or maybe just hear of it?

Lewis pushed the thought from his head. The thoughts were not his own. Running for so long only left room for gloomy thoughts. He tried to be upbeat. His father had taught him to look for the best in people while preparing for the worst but it was hard. He could have controlled his own thoughts but Sarilla and Oreland reminded him of every terrible thing that could happen! The Argosi couldn't have known that he would escape. They did not have time to prepare for all of this!

"You two are worrying for no reason. The Argosi could not have had enough time to plan all that. I'm sure that the empress is looking for someone else to intimidate." Lewis said the words with more fervor than he felt but he tried to push down worry and be confident.

They needed a leader. Sarilla was still just a child and Oreland was obviously still reeling from his change. Lewis knew that he was the only serious option. He was stuck being a leader whether he wanted to be or not.

Listening to the two of them gripe and worry only made it more clear that they needed someone to point them in the right direction and comfort them when they needed it. He knew that they needed comfort now.

"We won't rush into anything. I'll go into the Island in the most back-roads way I can think of. The Argosi won't even know that the trail is there. They won't even imagine looking for me. I'll come back with the information we need. Then, we can decide with all the information in front of us. We won't need to worry about any surprises."

The other two nodded and Lewis knew that he had made the right choice. They needed a leader, and he was the only option. Lewis could only pray that he was not making a

By: Jennie Arnold

mistake; that he was not walking into a trap.

Matt was back to walking with an un-halting pace. "We need to hurry," he would tell the others when they stumbled. "We need to warn them before they get to the Island."

Mira and the women seemed to be less enthusiastic. Matt wanted nothing more than to get to Lewis and warn him but Mira would warn about falling into a trap themselves. Kiarlin would warn that the other women could not keep the pace.

He could not believe that the two of them worried about things that were so small. They were trying to save lives! Tired feet and a few risky nights of mischief were a small price to pay.

"I know," Matt would start. "I know that I need to slow down but we still have to get to Lewis before he gets to them."

"We have resources that the Argosi do not," Mistress Tilde reminded Matt. "We can slow them down without hindering our own travel."

"You want to use magic to help us travel faster?" Matt already knew the answer to the question but he wanted to hear it from her own lips.

"We could make the roads near Alta muddy but leave the ones we are traveling on dry. Alaina knows some of their patrol routs, we can make sure those have fallen trees and logs to block it," Kiarlin suggested all of this as if it would be easy. Matt was unsure if the women really knew what they were getting themselves into. This would not be a game!

"Please, Matt," Alaina said with those big doll's eyes. "Lewis has helped me so much. Can we just do this little thing to help him?"

"I don't know why you all think you need my permission." Matt knew he should be grateful that they were telling him anything but he could not help but feel like they were trapping him as well.

"You need to talk to Mira's nanoks. They're the ones with the plan. Get Mira to translate for you to the Ahaya. I think Mira calls her Dancer," Matt instructed them.

He could not help but feel uneasy as they all walked off to do just that. The women were brave and confident but their enthusiasm could lead them into danger quickly. Still, he could not fault their courage. He just hoped that Mira could talk some sense into those women.

Mira seemed to have a way with the women. They were still as stubborn as ever but they did what she said more often than not. Matt did not have that way with any woman, much less a whole group of them! He tried to school his jealousy but he could not help but feel like an outsider. He knew that Mira would never keep something from him intentionally but her gift with the women was like the gift with the nanoks — you either had it or you didn't. It couldn't just be taught.

But Matt could speak with the nanoks in the gloaming... maybe he could speak with the women in the same way. They would be more likely to listen to a stranger than to Matt in any case. He would just take a look into their mind to see what this plan was.

Juniper had told Matt stories about ancient wise men that could send each other messages via dreams. Matt had been trying to copy their trick ever since. He had been trying to find Lewis's dreams for several nights now but that only led to frustration. Matt knew that it was time to do something different... something that actually worked and made a difference.

That's when he began practicing going into other people's

By: Jennie Arnold

dreams. He was not very good at finding the person he wanted but he always found a dream to explore. Practice had allowed him to get better and better at changing the dreams he entered. He could go into a person's dream and change towering trees into tall buildings. Matt could make a cloudless sky in rain-soaked terrain. He could change the world around him even though it was not his world.

Matt had not told Juniper about his treks into other people's dreams. He knew the nanok would not respond well. Juniper worried about Matt as if he were a child. He was still new to the dream world but he knew how to handle himself. Juniper had taught him more than the basics. Didn't the nanok trust him?

Matt could not blame Juniper very far — Matt was doing the same thing to him after all — Matt was keeping secrets. Juniper kept things back because he thought Matt was not ready to hear them and Matt kept things back because he knew exactly what the nanok would say. Still, Matt refused to stop going into the dreams.

He found a quiet spot in the place between and relaxed into the gloaming field just as he did in the waking one. Now Matt found himself in the middle of a black expanse. It looked like the night sky covered in stars. Each star represented someone's dream. Matt chose a star that looked about the right place and time Lewis's dream would be.

He stepped in, body tensing so he could easily step out again if he had chosen the wrong one. The dream was of an Island that Matt was sure he knew. Matt recognized Alta instantly. This had to be the right dream! He moved in closer to start changing the scenery. Lewis was sure to notice the changes and come to investigate. Matt could give him a warning then.

He tried to make spring green leaves fall red but nothing

happened. *I must be more tired than I thought*, Matt said to himself and tried to make a simpler change. He tried to let frost move over the ground to make a path straight from the Island to him but that didn't work either. Matt was wondering what to try next when relief swept through him. A figure was coming towards him.

"Lewis! Don't worry, it's only me. It's Matt!" He called with a smile and a friendly wave.

"It is a relief to find you," the figure said in a voice that was definitely not Lewis's. "I keep watch over Lewis's dreams. Enemies have been known to attack in the gloaming field."

"I'm sorry... Who are you?"

"Don't you recognize me, Matt? We met in the forests with the nanok daughter." Matt saw the man at a different angle and saw a nanok's head in place of a man's.

"You look a little different here than you do in the waking world," Matt told him dryly.

The former nanok-man laughed. "I did look quite different when we first met, Matt, but the magic woman has given me a man's head even though she still wears a headband. The Argosi took me and changed me. This is what I was before all of that."

"So you're back to being you. That must be a relief!"

"I am me again but I gave my word that I would help the Darkness Chaser for the nanok daughter. This is the best I can do."

"You must know this world well from being a nanok before."

"I never came here as a nanok but I am learning quickly."

"Good, because he is going to need all the help he can get." Matt leaned in close to the man. "Listen. I came here to give Lewis a warning. I'll have to tell you instead. The Argosi are trying to lure you to Alta and into a trap. Don't go to Alta!"

"We were suspicious of the messages but Lewis and Sarilla

By: Jennie Arnold

insisted on looking into them. We'll have to change course." The man put a hand on his strong chin as he thought. "I will have to wake and tell them as soon as possible. May we meet again, Matt? Goodbye."

"Wait!" Matt yelled as a wind pushed and pulled him at the same time. The wind was forcing him to leave and he knew that it was the nanokman's doing. "I have to talk to Lewis!"

"Tell the nanok daughter that the Darkness Chaser is safe. Tell her that Oreland has kept his word."

With that Matt plummeted into his body in the waking world. He gasped and sputtered.

"Are you alright?" Kiarlin asked in concern.

"I need to talk to Mira and those nanoks right now!"

Mira was rolling up the cloak she had been using as a blanket when Matt ran up to her. Mira could see that Matt was anxious by the look on his face. *There has been another vision,* Mira warned the nanoks near her.

Dancer nodded as if this was not new news to her. *Plum mentioned that your friend has been adventuring into other people's dreams. That can be very dangerous but Juniper has been watching out for him. Your friend will be safe despite his foolishness.*

Mira could only pray for Matt's safety and she could not help but worry for Lewis. If she and Matt could both speak with nanoks and venture into this dangerous gloaming field, it stood to reason that Lewis could too. Matt went in on his own, almost like an accident, but Mira needed to be trained to enter in. Mira hoped that Lewis had to learn to enter, so he did not get in over his head.

Mira had only just begun to go into the gloaming field and always with a guide but she still found her way to danger more often than not. She still shivered just thinking about the chaos she had fallen into. Plum was experienced enough to get her out but if Lewis fell into that there would be no one there to help him out of it.

"Were any of you able to talk with Lewis?" Mira asked Dancer aloud in their own speech.

His dreams are being guarded but not by one of us.

"We could have an unknown ally then? If they are guarding Lewis then they must be helping us," Mira reasoned.

I am not sure if they are helping him. Evil things cannot come into your friend's dreams, that is true enough, but we could have warned your friend had his dreams not been guarded. I would never attack this guard until I learned that he was an enemy but I will not count him a friend until I know his intentions.

Waiting may not be an option, Snow said as she ran up to the other pair. *Your friend, Matt has some news that you should hear.*

Mira walked to meet Matt. The anxious look on his face seemed to be even more so. Mira was not sure why her friend was so nervous but she knew that Matt did not get riled easily. Something must truly be wrong for him to be acting like this.

"What is it, Matt? What's wrong?"

"I can send myself into other people's dreams," Matt took a deep breath like he had just admitted a terrible sin. "Juniper told me not to, but I did anyway and I thought I could help Lewis so I went into his dream but the werebeast, he's not a werebeast any more by the way, and he stopped me and gave me a message for you. I told him I would deliver his message if he told Lewis he was in danger." Matt said the whole thing with one breath and spoke so quickly that Mira had a hard time

By: Jennie Arnold

following him.

"What was the message?" Mira asked slowly, hoping that Matt would take the hint and slow down his answer.

"He said to tell you that Oreland kept his word and the Darkness Chaser is safe. Does that make any sense?"

Mira started laughing. "Matt, that's wonderful news. Dancer was worried because Lewis' dreams were blocked but there is no need to worry. His dreams are being protected by a friend. He is safe!"

If the dreams are blocked how was Matt able to get in? Snow asked with her head tilted to one side. All of them looked to Matt as Mira translated the question but the young man simply shrugged as answer.

"How would I know why any of this happens? Maybe Juniper or Plum have an idea. They have been at this longer than me. I can go to sleep and ask Juniper while you go to Plum," Matt suggested.

Save the questions for later. We need to get moving to those mountains.

"Why the rush?" Mira asked Dancer. "Lewis is free from the Argosi and has been warned so he can stay that way. The Argosi cannot help the Wild Fae without him if they do go to the mountains. There is nothing for us to stop."

I have a bad feeling about this place. Snow's ears lay back as she spoke, showing how nervous she really was.

I feel it too, Dancer put in. *We should not be going forward but going back to the mountains is not a real option either.*

"We need to do something no one will expect," Matt said in a steady voice.

"We still need to find Lewis," Alaina put in quietly but firmly. "I know that he has beam warned not to go to Alta, but he is still where you say the danger is."

"Go back into his head and see if you can warn him," Mira

told Matt quickly.

"He is probably already awake but I should at least be able to get more information about the mysterious danger you all feel." Matt lay down on the hard ground and tried to find the gloaming field.

Rest easy, Dancer told him. *The sleuth is watching your back. We will guard you as if you were one of our own.* Dancer, Plum, and Snow ran off in different directions to form a hunting group, working to keep the danger away. Mira knew that the nanoks would keep them safe so she was not paying attention when several figures stepped into the clearing. She did not even notice the figures until they were almost on top of her and Matt.

"Am I ever glad to see you!" Lewis' voice rang out. "We followed your warning and tried to get away from Alta but we ran into some Argosi guards. They have been following us all morning but Oreland lost them about an hour ago."

The friends all met with greetings and hugs. Lewis introduced Oreland and Sarilla but the two of them were already getting warm greetings. Sarilla clung to Oreland's arm almost as eagerly as Alaina clung to Lewis's. Mira felt a pang of jealousy that she quickly pushed down. She cleared her throat awkwardly.

"The nanoks felt them approaching and wanted to leave. We did not feel right about leaving without warning you though. Matt went into the dream to warn you. I'll wake him to let him know the good news." Mira bent down to do just that but Oreland's hand clamped down on her arm before she could.

"Waking him now could be dangerous. It might be better if I go in after him."

Mira nodded, knowing that she was still too new in the gloaming field to find anyone. Oreland promised that he would be back quickly and gave Sarilla a reassuring smile. The

By: Jennie Arnold

former werebeast may have been quick but trouble began as soon as he closed his eyes. No one could pay much attention to see when the two woke.

"Drop your weapons," a commanding voice boomed out. No one moved. No one could think to move! The voice in the woods was obviously unhappy with their response. His voice got angrier as he continued ordering them. "Kneel on the ground with your hands on top of your head or the nanoks die."

Mira heard growling to her right and screaming in her head. "Stop it!" She begged. "Don't hurt them!"

She moved quickly to do as they asked. She saw Kiarlin and the women doing the same but Alaina kept her feet. Her face was red with fear and anger. Her hands were clenching and unclenching rhythmically.

"They will never make me wear a chain again!" She declared in a voice cold enough to make icicles freeze over. She raised her hands over her head and Mira could not stop watching the guards.

Plants moved around the guards like serpents and squeezed them in place. Fire rained from the sky like hail and fell on the Argosi. Alaina meant to use everything they had forced her to learn to destroy them. Still, Alaina was forgetting that the Argosi still held Alta and Brington along with the sleuth of captured nanoks.

"Wait!" Mira called hearing the nanoks panic. "You're killing Dancer and Plum, not just the Argosi!"

Alaina heard her and stopped the fiery hail from falling. The snakes of vines still held the guards in place but a few of the men had used knives to cut free. The Argosi who had yelled commands now held a weeping toddler in his arm with a knife to his throat.

"Stop now or this baby dies along with the nanoks," he commanded.

"That's the coppler's new boy," Mistress Tilde said recognizing the toddler.

Alaina put her arms down and the vines shriveled where they stood. The attack was over. Guards came to restrain their new prisoners. Mira and Alaina did not fight and Oreland and Matt were still asleep. The other women did their best to put some slack in the bindings but the Argosi made them cruelly tight.

Find an answer in that gloaming place, Matt, Mira begged her friend silently. *Find something that can save us.*

Oreland plunged into the place between. He had visited this place every night since Sarilla had given him his life back. Still, he knew that there were corners of this world that he had yet to explore. He had a feeling that Matt had found his way into one of these secret corners.

The familiar valley with its orange sky was empty. The mountains by the river where Oreland originally came, were also empty. Oreland searched every corner he knew and came up with nothing. So, he began to search the strange places.

He fought a squid beneath the water of the river and then fought a lion on the mountains. He walked beneath cloudy skies and apple trees and forests shaped like umbrellas, but still, he could not find Matt.

Like lightning, an idea came to him. "He's in someone else's dream. He went looking for Lewis but he must have found someone else's."

Oreland sat and relaxed his mind. He found the night sky full of dreams that Matt had come to so often. A nanok was waiting for him there.

By: Jennie Arnold

You are the Almost Nanok and you have come to help the Seer. The two of us are here for the same reason. I have been training the young Seer, but he takes on more than he should. He runs before he can walk! Matt needs all the help he can get, the nanok declared with annoyance in his voice.

"He will have our help," Oreland agreed.

They trap him in a nightmare. Juniper said this in a whisper as if he was afraid others might hear.

"You're right. The Seer seems to find trouble at every turn. Lead the way to this nightmare and we will bring him out." Oreland could not stop the smile from spreading on his face.

They came into a world full of lava and fire. The lava rolled like the sea while thunder roared in the sky. Most would have been daunted by a nightmare like this. Fear was so thick in the air that a knife could slice it. That type of fear seeped into a person's soul like water into a sponge but Oreland refused to let the emotions touch him.

"I'll bring him back, daughter!" Oreland yelled in the wind even though Mira was not there to hear. "I'll keep my promise and protect your friends."

By: Jennie Arnold

Chapter Twenty

Lewis knew that he only had one chance. It was now or never! The guard no longer held a knife to the child's throat, and the nanoks were being wrapped up in a thick net. He could use his power while the guards were busy watching the women. No one was watching him and he had to act before they remembered that he was a threat.

He pushed all his anger and rage and fear into his center, into his magic and the power shone forth. He sent fire and stone slamming into the guards. Lewis focused the strength of his power on the guards but he used all his concentration on freeing the nanoks. They would be the best way to free the others. The nanoks could fight on instinct and they wanted to help him and Mira.

He made flames dance along the net by the weights; using small sprints of power here and there to eat away at the rope without hurting the nanoks themselves. Lewis could not use his powers even after the Argosi forced him to practice. The velvet woman had always been in control. No one anywhere had power over them. He had learned to use more than raw force while traveling with Oreland and Sarilla.

Lewis had thought his Island was in trouble then. He thought the Argosi were pulling out of the continent. The sudden changes and regulations would cause no end of trouble for the small Island and Lewis was determined to be able to help by the time they reached the Island. He wanted to help his people rebuild and start over. He wants to send out messages to his friends and family. He had so many fine plans.

He thought none of those plans could possibly happen after Oreland told him Matt's message from the dream but now he saw the truth. Lewis's planning had prepared him for this. It had prepared him to fight his enemies and save his friends. He might not end up as the hero of Alta Island but titles and grandeur paled in comparison to his friend's opinion of him.

This was not some stranger on the street or even a neighbor who knew his name. His friends were the people who knew him best, who knew everything about him. Their opinions of him mattered more than the opinions of thousands of strangers. He could not let them down — that was just who he was — who he wanted to be.

He used his magic to stop the Argosi in any way he could think of. Rocks were flying and fire erupted out of even the clearest sky. He was careful not to use the magic near his friends. He did not want to hurt them by mistake....

The velvet women and their charges had no such qualms. Tilde and Daisy writhed on the floor. Alaina and Kiarlin clenched at their ankles. Lewis could not tell what the Argosi had done to them but it was clear that they were in pain.

"Please stop," Daisy begged. "I promise to listen this time."

The women all said something like this in their own ways. Tilde nodded even though she could not speak for the pain. Kiarlin could do little more than moan but she seemed to moan louder after Daisy had begged. Alaina had bitten her lip to keep quiet, but she had bitten too hard. Her teeth left grooves on her lower lip. It was clear that the women could not take much more of the pain.

Lewis pulled the magic back inside of him and fell to his knees. He put his hands on his head and drank the cup of foul potion in one gulp.

"That was my own special blend," said Hiro's familiar voice. "This won't just keep you from using magic. It will keep your mind fuzzy as well. You should be much more compliable now even without the girl's assistance."

By: Jennie Arnold

"None of you will be escaping this time," Sainade agreed with a devilish smile. Alaina could not hide a shudder.

Lewis wanted to tell the Argosi that they were wrong. That they escaped once and that they would again. He wanted to comfort the women and hold Alaina but he could do none of that. The ropes that bound him held him where he was. Lewis fought the fog in his mind but it was futile.

He was trapped again for true. He could not move or use his magic. Enemies who had everything they needed surrounded him and more to force him into doing whatever they wanted. He was sure that Fate was looking down at him and laughing at some cruel joke. It jolted Lewis out of his self-pity when he saw a shape on the ground.

It was a pile of ropes and weights; burnt ropes and weights that caught his attention. It was the net that held the nanoks — or the net that used to hold the nanoks. They were free. The nanoks could still help them. Lewis could not help but smile. Fate *really was* looking out for them after all. They could win as long as fate was on their side.

Alaina willed herself not to cry. She was terrified, but she swore that she would not show it!

"There is no need to be frightened," Sainade told her with a mocking smile. "All we need is for you to take a little blood from your friend there. He needs to take his own blood with his own magic."

"Don't lie to me!" Alaina said angrily. "I heard you talking. You said that you would probably have to kill him. You're not just going to take a little blood."

"I would watch your tone," Sainade warned. "I have had to

threaten your family before and now they sit right in front of me. I would not have to cross a sea or send a message to hurt them. I just have to reach out my hand." Sainade's hand moved towards Kiarlin as if she would do it here and now. "I could even make you harm her."

"No!" Alaina cried, but it was too late. "I'm so sorry. Please stop!" Alaina felt magic being pulled out of her center and mangled by the band. The mangled magic was then forced through Kiarlin in waves.

Kiarlin tried to hold in a moan.

Unfortunately, soft whimpers escaped her throat instead. Alaina knew that Kiarlin would tell her that none of this was her fault but Alaina knew that her sister was in pain because of her. Alaina felt herself curling into her center and away from the world. She knew that she could never find her way back if she continued. She screamed at herself to stop but nothing seemed to make a difference; until a voice broke through the fog of her mind.

"I will spill my blood without your magic but we must make a bargain," Lewis said the words through clenched teeth but his voice seemed to boom.

"We do not need to bargain with you," Sainade told him in a clipped voice. "We have everything you hold dear."

Hiro gave a sad smile. "Never love something, or someone, too much or we will use it against you."

"Listen to my terms before you decide that you need not negotiate."

Hiro nodded and said simply, "I'm listening but I cannot negotiate with you. Tell me your deal and if it has merit, I will send for the empress so that you can officially bargain."

"Fair enough," Lewis agreed. "I will spill my blood of my own free will as your ritual demands. I will use my magic to do so if you stop giving me that potion." Lewis took a deep breath,

By: Jennie Arnold

knowing that the negotiations were just now beginning.

"In return for these things you will let the others go. All the women you kidnapped will be sent back to Alta Island with Mira and Matt. You have me for your ritual and you don't need anyone else."

"The empress can have all of that easily and keep your friends. We have your Island and your family. We have the first silken. The velvet women can force you into doing anything. This deal is pointless. You have nothing we want." Hiro actually began to laugh in Lewis' face. He made a hand-motion to the guards who gripped Lewis's arms firmly. They pulled him away.

"You're making a mistake!" Lewis's yelled to him in a shaking voice.

"I doubt that. I rarely do." No more words needed to be spoken.

Alaina could only bite her lip and try not to cry.

Mira experimentally pulled at the bindings on her wrists. She should have known that they would not give an inch. The guards who had bound her seemed to think she possessed a nanok's strength as well as their speech. They placed enough ropes on her to stop a herd of horses!

She knew she would need another way out. Mira tried to use the gloaming field, but she could not enter. She lay down but guards kicked her until she sat back up. They would not take any risks with her! She glared up at the guard but the man seemed not to notice.

Another guard walked in and made Mira do a double-take. She recognized the man! It was the same guard who had held her prisoner before; the commander who demanded that Mira teach his soldiers to call nanoks in the battle.

"Your friends cannot save you. You will teach my men how to speak to your nanoks. Call to them now or you will watch as your Island burns to the ground." The commander's voice seemed even colder than before.

"I told you, I never learned how to speak with them. It can't be learned!"

"Then you'll have to talk to them for us," the man said with a sly grin.

Mira gave a growl deep in her throat. That type of request was not worth a real answer. Mira fought down her anger, hoping not to do anything foolish.

"There is no need to get defensive," the commander told her. "You must learn to accept the realities of your situation."

"I see reality better than you seem to think. This prison cannot hold me." Mira motioned to the guard who had kicked her. "You plan on making sure that I can't go into a trance? I won't be able to train men very well in that condition. I must rest sometime."

"You can sleep when you're too exhausted to do anything more than sleep."

Mira felt like a ton of icy water had been dumped on her. "Where did you hear about that?"

"Our werebeasts have told us a thing or two about your nanok sleuth. The nanoks like to think that the Creator favors them and helps them survive but reality says that they are no match for our guns. They aren't gods! Your nanoks will be brought to heel one way or another and I think you'll want to work with me."

"They'll never help you if you kill a member of the sleuth no matter what I tell them," Mira told him with conviction.

The commander nodded. "But they will do what we say if

it means saving you."

"They're smarter than you think. You won't be able to trick them like that."

"We'll see," the commander said with a smile before turning to walk out.

"Make sure she doesn't sleep. Wouldn't want her to warn her furry friends now would we?" The guard saluted in affirmation and the commander walked out.

Matt was alone in a nightmare full of lava. It was not the gloaming fields he had seen before. *This can't be Lewis's dream,* Matt thought to himself. *Lewis would be dreaming of home like before.*

Matt turned to leave this place but a force harder than any wall stopped him. He bit back a curse! What was this? The gloaming field may still be new to Matt but Juniper would not have failed to mention this. Matt could only come to one conclusion: This trap was meant for him. Someone had lured him here and someone was watching him right now.

Matt looked this way and that, not at all surprised that he could see no one watching. This person must know the dream well. Hiding would not be a problem for them but it might be a problem for Matt.

These people, whoever they were, knew about the gloaming field and about him. He could only assume that they knew about Mira and Lewis as well. They may have Lewis trapped in this place!

Matt stood as straight as he could, just in case they were watching and had a look around. There was lava all around and Matt could not see a way to travel around it or through it. Of course, Lewis could have come in through a different direction and may have been able to navigate around the lava. Then, he saw it; a way around.

There was a peninsula sticking out on two islands in the lava. Matt stood on one small peninsula and the other island was close enough that he could jump to it. He walked closer to it and saw that it was quite a long way.

You've jumped farther than that for track and field competitions. Surely you have! You're the jumping champion three years running at the festival and you have jumped that far. You can do it again now!

Matt backed up and ran as hard as he could to get a strong start, and, if he was being honest with himself so that he did not have so much time to lose his courage.

He leaped and felt his feet leave the ground. His heart dropped into his stomach with the fear. Matt doubted he had ever jumped this far without the aid of a pole but now was not the time for second thoughts. He had committed and he would do what he had to. A shock vibrated up his legs as his feet hit the ground. The vibrations were so surprising that he almost lost his balance and fell in... Almost, but he didn't.

"I really do have enough luck for ten men!" Matt shouted through his laughter. He had cheated death and he had a right to be happy but now was not the time for celebrating. Now, it was time to leave.

Matt followed the peninsula, looking for another jumping point. This peninsula was much bigger than the first. The island seemed to go on and on but Matt wanted to find an alternate route just in case. He was so distracted with finding a jumping point that he did not see the shadowy shape before him until he almost ran into it.

Matt looked up at the shape, startled to find another person. The shape looked like that of a man so Matt looked up at it and

By: Jennie Arnold

yelled, "Are you trapped here too? Do you know how to get around that wall?"

The figure laughed. "I am not trapped, Young Seer. I am the one who trapped you."

Matt ran to the figure in shock and saw that it was not a man he was talking to but a Wild Fae.

By: Jennie Arnold

Chapter Twenty-one

Mira was tired, more tired than she had ever been in her whole life. The guard was very thorough. He kicked at her if she lay down and also if she slumped in the seat. They refused her a chair, but that didn't matter. She was sure she could sleep on the floor. If only the guard would let her be still for so long! Unfortunately, the guard did not give her a chance. They never gave her enough time! A kick was delivered to her already sore side if she even looked comfortable.

A commander came into the prison every half hour or so. They pulled Mira to her feet and talked with her while they walked around the room. He asked questions about Mira's favorite foods and colors. The questions and answers never mattered. He just wanted Mira to answer to make sure she did not fall asleep on her feet. Mira lost track of all the times the commander spoke with her but she was sure that she had been awake for at least 48 hours straight.

She fell to her spot on the floor when the commander let her. She was too exhausted to do anything else. She had to fight her muscles to get into a sitting position. The commander turned to the door to leave but quickly turned back around. Mira feared another kick but the commander's response surprised her.

"Let her sleep. That's all she'll do now."

Mira could have cried with relief after hearing these words. She knew that she should not give in to her weariness. She needed to get to the gloaming field and warn the others. She fought to find the spot between awake and asleep. Her body would not let her. She gave into her body's demand and relaxed. She was asleep in seconds and she did not dream.

Lewis fought to stay focused. The potion was still coursing through his system but he needed to tell the women about the nanoks. The news had given Lewis hope, and it was obvious that the women needed hope. Many of them were in tears.

He had wanted to tell them that first day — the first second — that their friends had been caught. Daisy had not stopped crying. Many of the others had clouded eyes. They were giving up and Lewis knew that it was up to him to bring their determination back. Women could be stubborn but everyone had a breaking point. They had already been through so much! They just needed someone to point the way.

The Argosi had trussed them all up and thrown them in a covered wagon. Lewis did not want the Argosi to know all their secrets. The nanoks still had a chance of escape. Small things could be forgotten in the chaos. The nanoks looked like big bears and they could blend in with the trees just as the average bear did. He wanted to check to see who else had been taken, but he was afraid. Lewis wanted to believe that hope still existed.

Someone could make it out!

He craned his head as far as he could, trying to take it all in, trying to see all that he possibly could. The view told him nothing but he held to hope because he needed to and so did the women. They all needed some hope.

"Mira's nanoks made it out," Lewis told the women in as loud a voice as he dared.

By: Jennie Arnold

"That's nice for them. And your point is?" Alaina asked in a voice even softer.

"The nanoks will get help!" Kiarlin told the others excitedly. Her voice got louder as she spoke and the other women had to shush her.

"The nanoks will save Mira," Daisy said in a soft, sad voice. "They don't care about us."

"No, they care," Mistress Tilde told her firmly. "Those nanoks have a prophecy that mentions us. The Creator told them we have to work together if we're going to survive. They'll save all of us."

"Fate let those nanoks escape and Fate is watching out for us," Lewis assured them all.

"Fate hasn't done a thing if the nanoks escaped without knowing they left us behind. Do the nanoks know we're still here?" Kiarlin asked.

"If I got free, I wouldn't stay close to camp. I would run away as fast as I could," Alaina said with a sad look in her eyes. "I doubt those nanoks are anywhere near to see that we are still trapped."

"Nanoks have better senses than humans do. They could find us by smell with no need to be near us," Lewis reassured the women.

"I would still feel better if we could communicate with them. I would like to know where the nanoks are. I would feel better even if they are far away," Mistress Tilde whispered.

"Maybe we can." Kiarlin looked at Lewis thoughtfully as she spoke. "Matt and Mira can both talk to nanoks when they dream. They both say they go somewhere between sleep and awake and they talk to nanoks there."

"Mira and Matt aren't with us. They can't give any messages," Daisy pointed out sadly.

"If Mira and Matt could both do it, Lewis might as well."

Every eye in the wagon turned to Lewis as soon as the words left Kiarlin's mouth.

"I'll try but I can't promise anything."

Kiarlin told him as much as she could about what she had seen Matt do. All the women squished together to make sure that Lewis had enough room to lie down. He tried to relax and send his mind into that in between place the others had talked about. He worried that he could not find the place on his first try but he was happily surprised to find himself there.

He was in a valley surrounded by mountains. The sky was full of rolling clouds. This had to be the place the others had spoken of. The sky itself looked like it was moving and Lewis could feel the peculiarity of this place. He was not dreaming. This was real.

"Mira! Matt!"

There was no answer.

"Anybody!! Hey!" Lewis yelled as he circled the mountains' base. He settled in for a long wait but then he saw it. A figure in the valley but not a man's figure; a nanok's!

"Dancer? Or is it Snow? Can you understand me at all?" Lewis felt silly not being able to tell the nanoks apart but he could only hope that the nanok in front of him was not too offended.

I am sorry, young one. I have not seen Dancer's sleuth in some time. I am Juniper and I live here in the gloaming field. I have been helping the Seer, Matt. I know something of you. Are you Darkness Chaser or Nanok Daughter?

"Dancer's sleuth calls me Darkness Chaser but everyone else calls me Lewis. I am sorry if I offend you but I am in something of a hurry."

This is your first time here, Juniper interrupted, *Rushing can be dangerous. This might feel like a dream to you but the things you do here have consequences in the world you came from.*

Lewis went on despite Juniper's warning. "I need to get a message to Dancer's sleuth. They were able to escape the Argosi, but we weren't. None of the humans made it out."

Dancer will want to know where you are.

"They separated us," Lewis admitted. "The magic women and I are being taken to the mountains. They put Matt and Oreland onto a ship but I'm not sure where they are going. They took Mira away but I'm not sure where she is. Can the nanoks help me find them?"

I will tell Dancer your message, Juniper promised. *The sleuth will work faster if they have more information. Come back if you learn anything new. I will tell Dancer all the information you tell me.*

Lewis left the trance and fell back into his reclining body with a smile. He had done it!

Alaina worried for Lewis as he slept. The Argosi had not been kind to him and now he slept without even the faintest movement. Alaina could not even see his chest moving. She was not sure he was breathing. Kiarlin said that the same thing happened to Matt when he visited the gloaming field but she could not tell if her sister was saying the truth or simply putting her mind at ease.

Fear washed from her when she saw Lewis open his eyes and smile up at her.

"I did it. The nanoks know where we are. I met a nanok while I was in the trance. He said to call him Juniper and he said he knew Matt. He says that they will be able to find Mira and Matt too," Lewis told them in a voice that croaked like he hadn't had a drink in days.

"I am happy for you, lad. The nanoks will rescue you and the potion will leave your system. They will have no hold over you." Mistress Tilde gave the women around her a sad look as she continued. "We will only get you caught again if we leave with these bands on."

"I could get my headband off," Sarilla said in an uncertain voice. The other women looked at her dubiously.

"She did get it off herself. I saw it," Lewis chimed in backing her up.

"How was it done?" Mistress Tilde asked excitedly over Alaina's "Can you teach us how?" and Daisy's "Did you use a key like Matt?"

Sarilla looked at them all with worry and fear. She told them what happened and her voice picked up volume and speed as she went on. "Lewis was shooting lightings and fire and I was so scared and I do not understand how any of it really happened."

"Shhh!" They all warned her at once. Guards began looking over.

"Matt got the chains off once. He can do it again. We just need to get to him and his tools and he can make another key," Lewis reassured them.

"We'll get you caught before any of us can get to a town for supplies," Kiarlin said sadly. "You remember that these headbands won't just stop us; they'll make us stop you too. They will force us to use magic against you."

All the women nodded their agreement. "All right," Lewis conceded knowing that he was outnumbered. "Then we need to find a way to get those off of you now."

"I think I have an idea." Alaina began feeling around the edges of the bands with magic. She wanted to learn more about the physical part of the headbands and she wanted to see how much magic she could draw before it hurt her.

"I can use some magic even with the headband on. I have to be careful not to use magic that needs too much power. The band will hurt you and warn the Argosi I think if we suddenly use a large amount of power."

"My chains came off after a sudden surge but I think that was more luck than anything else," Sarilla admitted.

"I think that the location of the magic makes a difference. The magic surge did not make the headband come off, the pressure point that allowed us to use magic made the band release. The amount of power does not seem to make a difference," Kiarlin theorized.

"The point could be different for each band too," Mistress Tilde pointed out.

"You keep talking with the nanoks, Lewis and we'll keep experimenting with the bands," Alaina told him with confidence.

Alaina and Lewis shared a smile, both full of hope for the future for the first time since being captured.

"Fate might be watching out for us after all," Alaina told him.

"No! No! No"

Oreland went from one plain to the next, looking for Matt. His heart raced faster with each failure. He only stayed in each portal a moment, waiting to feel another soul, but no feeling came. His hands began to shake. Oreland felt lost and overwhelmed.

Each portal looked like a star and the light it gave off was unique. Experienced travelers could find a specific person by looking at the light and hue. Oreland was not experienced. He did not know Matt well enough to find him by light alone. Finally, he had searched each dream he could find, but no Matt...

Then, he saw a star that looked like a dream and wasn't a dream. *He's in there*, Oreland knew before he even stepped into the gloaming field. Matt was in there and he needed help. This could be a nightmare but he knew that it wasn't. It was unnatural! Oreland knew he had to go in.

The voice of the tree came into Oreland's head and reminded him of the promise the tree had given him before giving up the wand. This wand would free them from traps and keep enemies from their throats. This fight could not be won without the Seer, Matt. The price of losing this fight was the world itself. He needed to get Matt and help the nanok daughter as he had sworn to do.

Oreland stepped into the not-dream with the wand drawn. A force field pulled and pushed him away but he held the wand before him and put all his attention on moving forward. He needed to get to Matt, and this was the only way to do it. The wand pierced through the shield and Oreland stepped through as quickly as he could, unsure if the shield would suddenly close shut on him.

He ran unto the not-dream and found himself over a river of lava. He stopped inches from the edge, breathing heavily. Oreland pulled back to the far side of the overhang. He put his hand on the cleft to steady himself. He took deep breaths and a look around.

The only way out was up. He moved his hand along the wall, looking for handholds. Oreland pulled himself to the top to find a long, flat peninsula. He could see Matt standing with a Wild Fae.

"What do you want with me?" Matt asked the elf.

By: Jennie Arnold

"You are a Seer. You should be able to tell me."

"You know it doesn't work that way!" Matt screamed. "Just tell me what is going on!"

"We know about your little plan. You and the nanoks made a net. You made a weapon but we will make sure that it will never be used against us." The elf stopped talking and gestured to an unseen assistant.

Three Wild Fae seemed to step from thin air.

All three of them materialized in front of Oreland. He held the knife in front of him like a weapon. The Fae jumped on top of him and kicked the wand from his hand.

Oreland struggled, trying to get the wand back, but the Fae had no trouble pulling Oreland along. They shoved him down to the feet of their leader.

"Your friend here will give our demands to the others. The Seer for the net. Matt stays with us or the net stays with us. Your trap cannot be set either way."

"This will never work," Matt declared loudly.

"I'm not leaving without him." Oreland was literally daring the Fae to fight him. He could only hope that Matt could get to the wand and use it to escape during the chaos.

"There is another option that might work!" Matt stood between Oreland and the leader. "There is no need to hurt him."

Oreland smiled, "And I thought you didn't like me."

"You came here to save me first. Fair is fair," Matt said without turning away from the Wild Fae.

"Let's hear this plan, Seer. Tell me your "other option". I'll decide if it will work."

"Well," Matt began to back towards the wand as he talked, pulling Oreland with him. "It's obvious that we need to get the Argosi to work with the nanoks. Just let us help you write a treaty."

"You're trying to buy time. That won't work. Looks like we must use two hostages and send messages through the nanoks as we originally planned."

More Wild Fae came out of thin air and attacked the two men. Large bodies slammed into them and pinned them down. "Get your hands off me!" Oreland yelled on top of Matt's "You're making a mistake. It doesn't have to be this way!"

Matt fought against the Fae but they were tired of his struggles. The Fae holding him knocked him on the head. He blinked rapidly, trying to clear his vision.

Oreland felt a strange numb tingle in his hand. He put his hand out and stretched his arm into thin air. He was not sure how he knew what to do to get the wand but he followed his instincts just like he did after the experiments turned him into a monster. He only did what he knew he had to. Oreland used the wand to send the Fae away from him. He grabbed Matt's arm and told the wand to send them into the waking world.

The screams of the Fae faded away as the two of them woke. Oreland found that his hand held Matt's arm in a firm grip in this world as well. He looked down to see that they bound his hands. They tied Matt in the same fashion.

"My lady will be glad to hear that the two of you are awake," a voice declared from the darkened stairs to the left.

Oreland tried to get to his feet but the ground beneath him moved. We're on a boat, he realized with shock.

"Your empress is in the mountains," Matt declared confidently, "not here on a ship."

The velvet woman Arcadia stepped out of behind the guard. "He does not mean the empress, Matt. He is talking about High Lady Ramilla. You remember her, don't you?"

Chapter Twenty-two

Someone tall awakened Mira after several painful kicks to her sore side. It felt like she had only slept a few hours but the angle of the sun outside told her it had been longer than that. She stifled a groan and rolled her neck and shoulders. She was still bound and forced to remain seated but she did what she could to relieve the cramped muscles. She was not given much time to stretch.

An even larger crowd came into the small room Mira was held in. The room became even more cramped when a man in a fine silk robe entered with his entourage. Several guards came in with the group.

"Are you sure that she can do what she claims?" The man in silk asked.

"I have seen her do it myself, High Lord. I am positive," the commander answered with a clipped nod.

"I wish to see this magic at work myself."

The man in silk had a haughty, grating voice that rang on Mira's nerves. It did not help that Mira knew they were talking about her and around her. They acted as if she were not even there! She wanted to refuse to do anything on principle alone. She set her mouth and went stubborn. But she knew that she would be given no options.

"You heard him. Call your nanoks," the commander ordered her.

"You know that calling won't work this far from the woods. No sleuths hunt here."

"We were farther than this when your nanoks found us last time," the commander reminded her. "Legends say that your nanoks used to hunt all over the Island. They should hear you even from here."

Mira shook her head in denial. "I can't."

The commander took out a lightning stick and held it in a white-knuckled fist. "I suggest that you try."

Mira took a deep breath, closed her eyes and tried to call the numbness to her. Nothing happened. She could not even force the urge to roar. "I can't call them. I could bring them here if you let me into the gloaming field."

"I don't think that will work with us," the commander clipped out. The man in silk seemed to agree. He waved a hand towards the commander and the motion must have been a signal. The commander's fist collided with Mira's jaw with force. "No more games, now. Call them!"

Her eyes widened with shock when a nanok's voice she recognized answered her. She did not expect to reach anyone much less someone she knew!

We come, Nanok Daughter. Hold on. We're coming to help you. It was Dancer's voice.

"Dancer," Mira whispered in shock.

"I see we have something," the man in silk began. "I see it in your eyes. You're in contact with the nanoks at this very moment."

"They won't fall for your tricks. They won't just walk into a trap."

"How little you know them," the man in silk said as he shook his head. "They'll do anything to save you." Three guards came into the room and dived towards Mira. She bucked and fought but the guards overwhelmed her and hogtied her.

Run! She yelled to the nanoks in her mind. *Get away from*

By: Jennie Arnold

here. They are using me to send you into a trap. These men want to capture you again and you can't let them. Run!

Do not fear, daughter, Dancer sent back in her calm voice. *We come and we will not let them win.*

You have to listen, Dancer, Mira sent out desperately but she could tell that no one was listening. "Don't do this!" She screamed in anger. "Don't hurt them."

"We have no intention of harming the creatures. The empire still needs them after all. We would never harm a useful tool," the man in silk purred the words. He moved his hands with quick signs to the guards. Mira could hear the nanoks growling now but she already warned them it was all a trap. They could not hear.

The man in silk made more quick movements with his hands and the guards charged at the nanoks. Mira could hear them dying outside. She could feel them dying in her head. She wanted to cry out or roar! She could not just stay here and let this happen. She had to help them!

Mira felt the numbness folding in around her. It was happening again, just like it happened in the ship. The powers that mysteriously overcame her were doing so again. Anger and fear were overwhelming her along with the power and she was not sure what she would do with the magic that came. She was not sure what she could do, trapped as she was. Still, she knew that she had to do something.

The ropes seemed to fall away from her with no need to struggle. She felt strength surge into her. She moved in small ways but big things seemed to happen. She flicked her wrists and swords seemed to fly from men's hands. Mira just moved her arm to stop a block and the lightning sticks ignited in the guard's hands.

"Bring her down!" Yelled the commander, pointing to Mira as she moved towards the nanoks.

Mira saw things in slow motion. She saw the end of a whip coming towards her. Mira caught the whip with her fist before it could strike her and pulled it from the guard's hands. Mira used the whip and flicked it at the guards once. They all went flying through the air and landed on their backs. The only living things left standing were Mira and the nanoks.

Mira fell to her knees. "What have I done?"

Do not fear, Dancer sent to Mira. *The rage will leave you. Fate made you see this so that my sleuth could be saved. You are not at fault.*

"You cannot say that Fate made me do this because it didn't. I can control myself."

You did not do this to hurt those guards but to save our sleuth, Snow reminded her. *Fate and the Creator will not blame you for saving others. They will celebrate your triumph.*

"It was not a victory to me."

We can discuss blame and victory later, Plum said. *Right now we must leave. They are waking up!*

"They're not dead? Thank goodness!" Mira felt a surge of hope as she ran with her sleuth.

"Are you sure this is wise, Empress?" The guard asked the small woman.

"These things must be checked and more than one solution must be tried. We are an empire built on scientific principle. Death is a permanent thing. If we kill him, then no other solution can be explored! Start with a different idea." It was obvious that the woman was used to being in command and having others listen to her words. She turned and walked away without stopping to see if the orders were being carried out.

By: Jennie Arnold

Instead of listening to the guard's other ideas; ideas that had been tried before and already proven incorrect, the empress approached the cart where the prisoners were being kept. The guards watching the area bowed to her with their elbows touching their knees.

This kneeling position showed a form of respect, as was befitting her station. The prisoners looked at her in the eyes. This did not show respect! The man who could use magic showed the least respect of all by showing the hate he felt. His feelings were written all over his face!

"Sainade!" The empress called out. "Bring Lord Lewis and the First Silken to my tent." She coated the order with as much venom as she could muster. The boy obviously lacked understanding of what harm a title could do to him. Still, he would learn quickly enough. The two captives had no choice but to follow the empress to their fate.

"Is this another punishment for the escape?" Lewis asked with a sigh.

The empress herself delivered a full-handed slap to his left cheek. He staggered from the surprise and suddenness of it. "We will deal with your escape attempt within due course." She took a deep breath. "For now, be quiet and pay attention. Do you remember why we were traveling to the mountains?"

"For a ritual," Lewis answered slowly. "One that will involve my death. Is that still your plan?"

"The ritual involves your blood, not your death," the empress said. She spoke the words slowly as if she was trying to make him understand words that she was not saying.

Alaina gave a quick, relieved laugh and explained the words Lewis had missed. "You don't plan on killing him. You only need Lewis to bleed."

Lewis got that light in his eye like he was about to try something reckless and stupid. The empress quickly disabused him of the notion. "You are worth more to the empire alive than dead. We will only kill you as a last resort but remember..."

An electric jolt went through Lewis' body at a gesture from the empress. She saw him stiffen with the pain but bite his lip to keep from crying out. He was a hard one. A hard slave was usually a bad thing, but the empress was glad to hear that the boy was stubborn. His hardness could be channeled into helping the empire once he was safely secured. Only pain could see to that.

"You must remember that there are things worse than pain," the empress finished. She moved her hand again, telling Sainade to keep the flow of electricity going. The strength of the flow got higher and higher until Lewis did call out. The empress motioned for the velvet woman to stop after that. They had made the point.

"Give me your hand, Lewis," the empress commanded.

After going through that type of pain, Lewis did what she asked without thinking or hesitating. The empress was sure that she had begun to tame the young man, but he quickly proved her wrong.

"Don't!" He ordered the others. "The prophecy says I have to give my blood with my own power. I will but I won't have any of you making me do it."

"Go on then," Sainade allowed after the empress nodded. "You haven't been given potion for hours now. We needed you coherent for the ritual itself."

Lewis took a deep breath, held out his hand and made two precise slashes with air. Blood flowed from the cut onto the mountain. The group waited, holding its collective breath with anticipation. None of them flicked an eyelash when a ghostly figure appeared from nowhere.

"You've found him! You have found one of our own!" The

By: Jennie Arnold

ghostly figure almost looked like a man but the empress knew that the figure was really that of a Wild Fae.

"I have followed the ritual," the empress informed him. "Our bargain is complete. I was promised power."

"You fool!" The figure raged. "The ritual does not save your miniscule empire. The ritual allows the Wild Fae to reign once more!"

"No!" The empress shouted in shock. "I read and re-read that ritual. The Wild Fae can only come back if a Wild Fae's blood is spilt on the mountain where the legend began."

"The boy is one of us," the figure said with reverence. "He is our prince. He is of the blood."

"No!" Lewis shouted. "My father and sister are not evil like you. They do not want to destroy the world like you. My family is nothing like you and I am nothing like you!"

"Why do you think you have special powers? Why do you think that the people around you receive special talents when they are around you long enough?"

"That has nothing to do with you!" Lewis covered his ears and shook his head in denial.

"The man Hewin Thalda raised you. He is not your father. He found you on the side of the road after his wife lost their child. He thought he had found a son to replace the one he had lost."

"Stop your lies!" Lewis shouted as he fought to back away from the Wild Fae. A force field was keeping him in place. Lewis looked left and right for a way out but everyone and everything around him was frozen. Only his head could move. "Stop that! Whatever your goal is; it won't be reached by telling me lies about my family. I know who my father is and who my enemies are."

"I could fill a library with all the things you do not know, young prince." The Wild Fae began to walk around Lewis's frozen form in a slow circle. "You are loyal to the man you think of as your father. That bodes well for your relationship with your real one."

"Hewin Thalda is the only father I will ever want or need!" Lewis screamed at the elf. "I will never be loyal to a Wild Fae."

"The loyalties would be one and the same if we were all on the same side."

"How could you be on our side? You want to destroy us!"

"That is not so. We do not want to destroy the entire world. We just need to retrieve some of its natural resources. There will be a war but we may be able to spare an Island or two. That is if the communities are loyal to our people. Think about it. Who would win in a war, humans or Fae?"

"I think I would lose either way."

The Fae ignored Lewis's answer and continued. "Our people have been using magic for longer than this race. We know the answers to questions they have not yet begun to ask. Who do you think will win this war? Which side could save your little Island?"

"No conqueror would be satisfied with most of the world! I would not trust your Fae to leave Alta Island alone."

"The Wild Fae will take care of Alta just as they have taken care of our lost prince," the Fae promised.

"How do you even know that I am a Prince?"

"Only the blood of our prince would have awakened us. War has come with our awakening. Will you be with us or destroyed by us?"

"High Lady," Matt greeted with a flourish. "So nice to see

you again. I remember the last time we met very fondly. Hard to forget what with nanoks rescuing me from under your very nose at the time. The look on your face when you saw me was priceless."

Oreland made a sound somewhere between a laugh and an incredulous gasp. Matt just smiled back at him and tried to reassure the man. Matt knew that Oreland must be scared out of his mind. The Argosi had done terrible experiments on him the last time he had fallen into their hands. Matt wanted to give the man whatever help he could.

He knew that he owed Oreland for coming to save him from the Wild Fae in the gloaming field. Matt needed to do whatever he could to pay the former nanokman for his loyalty. The two of them shared a bond now. They were more than friends and Matt would do whatever he could to protect him.

"What friend did you bring to me now?" Ramilla asked. "Can he see the future or do magic or call armies? Is his only use to be a stick? Should he be beaten to make you co-operate?"

"He can do something even better. Hurting him would be a mistake."

"I promise you now, boy, if I find out that this was one of your tricks..."

"It's not a trick or a lie. He can go into the gloaming field. I'm sure that your werebeasts have told you of such places. You know that they exist."

"Yes," Ramilla admitted slowly, as if testing for a trap. "Some of our guards have spoken of such a place. None of our were-men can get there but they all talk about it. They say that the nanoks rule the place with wills of iron. That it is a place full of impossible things."

"It is a place full of impossible, beautiful things but I will never take you there," Oreland declared loudly as he pulled away from a guard who was holding him. Oreland ran for Matt, no doubt planning to help him get away, but other guards ran to stop him. They quickly tackled him to the floor.

"You will do whatever we tell you! Matt thought that he could out-smart us but he is back where he can best help the empire. He can tell you that fighting is useless."

"Maybe a guard or two needs to show you what will happen if you resist. Maybe you need to see it first-hand." Arcadia walked towards the man with hate and rage in her eyes.

Matt moved to stand between the two of them. "There's no need for all of that. Just let me talk to him and he'll be ready to help you."

"What are you up to, Matt? You weren't this helpful before." Arcadia and Ramilla were both glaring at Matt as if they could see into his past and glimpse at every bad thing he had ever done.

"He helped me and I want to make sure he does not get hurt. Just let me help him. You get what you want and I get what I want. Everyone wins!"

Lady Ramilla gave a nod. Matt gripped Oreland by the shoulder and led him to one side so that they could speak with no one overhearing.

"Listen!" Matt whispered fiercely. "I know you're scared but you have to listen! Lewis, Mira, and Sarilla are far away and the only way to get to them is with this woman. We need her to take us to them. We need to trick the High Lady so we can save the others!"

"They won't make me a slave again? You can promise me this?"

"I will do everything I can to make sure you aren't a slave again. Your freedom will be yours again."

"Then I promise that I will give my life to make sure that Darkness Chaser does not lose his. I will keep my promise to nanok daughter!" Oreland spoke so reverently that Matt was surprised the other man remembered to whisper.

"You have to make the High Lady think you're going to do everything they ask."

"I know how to lie. I can lie to her."

"You have had more than enough time for a private conversation," Arcadia announced as she walked up to the two of them.

"Are you prepared to go to the gloaming field for us?" Ramilla made her statement sound like a question but it was really a demand.

"I will agree to help you learn about the gloaming field. I will even help your guards go into the gloaming field but I cannot help you hurt people through it."

"Teaching our men should be enough for now," the High Lady decided with a nod.

"You'll have to teach them quickly. I want those men to be able to get to the gloaming field by the time our journey is over. We'll be in the mountains in less than two days."

"We're going to the mountains?" Matt asked, not bothering to hide his surprise.

"We're going to your friends, Matt," Arcadia told him.

Alaina saw enemies all around her. The Argosi had been forcing both her and Lewis to do all the things they did not want to do. Now a new enemy was attacking.

The Wild Fae had Lewis.

They forced the world around them to stand still while they spoke with him. Alaina was connected to him through the magic so she and Sainade could hear everything that was happening even though no one else could.

Alaina worked to force her legs to move but she could not even wiggle a toe.

Alaina called her magic to her in desperation. Power surged into her but she could not release it as she usually did. Alaina could normally unleash her power if she focused on the problem or enemies at hand but focusing did not force her power to do anything. It would not flow out of her. The Wild Fae's spell was affecting her power as well as her movements!

She needed to stop him somehow so that Lewis and the others could be free along with her. Freeing herself would be a start. Being a prisoner herself would not help the others but the only sure way to be rid of the Argosi would be to free everyone.

It was clear now that Kiarlin, Matt and Mira were not exaggerating when they said that there was a worse enemy. Wild Fae planned on destroying the world! The Argosi might be conquerors and abductors but they did not want to destroy everything. The Argosi used people and tried to turn them into animals but Wild Fae fight Fate and kill people to destroy everything around them. Alaina knew that, at all costs, she must not let that happen!

It was up to her to help Lewis beat this Wild Fae here and now. Alaina drew in her power once again but this time, instead of focusing it on the Wild Fae, she moved to focus it on the only other thing she could...

Fight evil. Go up against the most sinister thing in the room, she told the magic. *Fight it with everything you have until it cannot fight anymore.*

The magic heard her and it fought for her.

~*~

The empress could not move, hear or even see what was going on but the lack of movement really told her all she needed to know: the Wild Fae were double-crossing her. The

Fae could only do this type of block and they would not use a block against a partner.

Advisers had warned the queen that the Wild Fae would try to double cross her but she refused to believe it. She was so blinded by the good things that they had promised that she could not see that all those things were too good to be true. The Wild Fae had planned on abandoning her from the start!

Their plan to turn two good nations into one great one was not even a real plan! Their agreements were little more than smoke and mirrors. They were all a distraction from their real game — the trouble was that the empress could not be sure what their end game was.

The man who could do magic obviously meant more to the Wild Fae than she had anticipated. They were going to quite a bit of trouble for him. She had been ordered to bring him to the mountains where the blood that flowed with this new, strange magic would allow the Fae to give their powers to the Argosi nation. The Fae were dying out and the Argosi were thriving. The Fae could survive if they partnered with a strong nation. The Fae agreed to give Argosi weapons of power if Argosi agreed to form a partnership. The empress was quick to agree. What a fool she had been!

The empress remembered when she was small and her mother called her by another name before they thrust the name empress upon her. She had wanted more badly than anything else to please her mother. Her mother, the empress at the time, told the young princess that the only way to make her happy would be to make sure that the empire not only survived but thrived. The young girl had taken her mother's words to heart and creating a thriving kingdom had become her life's goal... at any cost!

Those choices, so many years ago had led her to here and now. They had brought her to this: to being unable to move, speak, hear or see while her allies plotted against her.

By: Jennie Arnold

Chapter Twenty-three

Lewis fought to hold on to the truth... the truth about whom and what he was. He held onto the truth until his knuckles turned white because he could not defeat these Fae alone. He needed a little help from Fate. *Please*, he silently begged. *Please help me know what to do!*

Then, just like that, he could move. The Fae turned like he was going to run but then stopped mid-step and moved his hands as if to fend off an attack. "You cannot hope to defeat me with elemental magic! The magic of Fae is much stronger than that."

Lewis felt his magic connect and bond with Alaina's. He used to fight this weaving when Sainade forced him to use it but now, he just let it happen. He let the magic flow from him and become lightning to strike at the Fae.

The Fae put up a shield to stop the lightning, but the shield exploded. Both the lightning and the blast from the explosion slammed into the Wild Fae. The force of it surprised both the Fae and Lewis but Lewis was even more surprised when the force field around him disappeared. He could move again! He saw others around him moving as well and he knew that the magic he had thrown had freed them all.

The Fae did not stay down long. He jumped to his feet, but he did not have the strength to form another force field to trap so many. Lewis could tell from how the Fae moved that he could not do any more magic. At least not for a while yet. Lewis was stronger than him in magic.

"You have power but you lack finesse," the Fae said with a forced smile that looked more like a grimace. "I have reinforcements on the way. You cannot defeat even one Wild

Fae warrior. They have studied magic longer than you have been alive!"

Lewis looked at the Fae's eyes as he spoke, looking for truth. He could see doubt in the light of the Fae's eyes. The Fae's eyes usually sparkled when he gloated but his eyes were dead now. The Fae was trying not to show any emotion on his face which meant one thing: the Fae was lying!

"Your reinforcements won't be here for days, maybe weeks."

The Fae's eyes blazed up. It was clear that Lewis had guessed correctly. The Fae was on his own and he would stay that way. No help would come for some time. Getting to Earth, in general, must have taken a large amount of magic. Getting other Fae here would take even more power and magic. The magic users would never have enough energy to move so many at once.

Lewis knew that he had the Fae where he wanted him but he would have to keep talking to keep the enemy in front of him on his toes. "I could use my lightning again to injure you and then let the Argosi deal with you. I hear that they can be quite ruthless. I won't bore you with the things I've seen or the stories I've heard but I'm sure your imagination could fill in the gaps."

"You can play your games now but you will lose before the race even begins! More of my people will be here if you wait too long to make your move. We both know that you cannot kill me yourself and I could never kill a prince. The only option left is a duel." The Wild Fae said all of this like the answer was clear but Lewis found himself confused.

"You just said that we could not kill each other. What will dueling accomplish? Won't one of us die in a duel?"

"You and I will not be dueling each other. Our leaders will approve a duel. We will each pick a champion who will fight for us. If you win my people will leave Earth but if I win, then you will return with me and my people will overtake Earth."

"I cannot agree to that," Lewis told him. "If you lose than you leave Earth alone. If I lose, then I'll go back with you but either way, you have to leave the Earth alone."

"My people cannot spare all of Earth," the Wild Fae told him. "We can agree to allow some of Earth to live in peace though. The Argosi and your people in Alta should receive a reward for taking care of our prince. We will allow Argosi and Alta to live in peace whether my people win or not... Unfortunately, I can only agree to this if you agree to come back with me either way."

"There is no point in the duel, then. I would agree to come back with you if you agreed to leave my home alone." The Wild Fae seemed to want to make things more complex than they needed to be.

"The fate of this world is at stake. Alta and Argosi will be safe but the fate of the rest of Earth is unknown. If my people win the duel, the entire world will be under our rule. If your champion wins the duel then the world will remain as it has always been."

"You and your people do not care about the earth at all. You just want me. Call off the duel and let the earth live as it always has been. I'll leave with you. There is no need for any of this," Lewis pleaded with the Fae.

"It is a tradition, a tradition that is important to my people and it will soon be important to you." The Fae moved to put an arm around Lewis in a gesture of comradery. Lewis quickly moved out of the Fae's reach.

"I am not authorized to speak on Earth's behalf. I have to talk to the people in power before I can give you an answer." Lewis was in over his head and his only hope was to buy more time.

Mira ran with the nanoks and she was able to keep pace. Adrenaline kept her from tiring. She knew that her friends were in danger and she did not want to think about what the Argosi were doing in Alta. She was doing all she could to avoid thinking about the Wild Fae. The Argosi in her home were worrying enough!

She put each thought into moving her feet forward. The sooner she got to them the better. She could see that the sleuth was traveling with her through the mountains but she could also sense that they were not preparing for a fight. She was not sure where they were traveling but she knew that Dancer had a plan and she trusted the Kodiak so she followed without question or complaint.

The other sleuths are getting nearer, Snow told Dancer with a rakish smile. *Your guess was right. They are all looking for answers.*

We should be able to send a strong signal from the Creator's cave. The other sleuths will hear because they are all moving closer to it, Dancer explained to Mira. *We can ask the other sleuths to join us in our fight. The Creator will speak to them through us and tell them what it right.*

"You think they will fight with us? That they will help Alta to keep the world safe?"

The sleuths will do what the Creator tells them just like we do.

Dancer seemed confident that the other sleuths would join in the fight with them and Mira could do nothing but follow her lead. It was certain that Dancer knew more about the other sleuths than Mira did. She had no choice but to follow

Dancer's lead.

Stay here with Snow and Plum, daughter, Dancer commanded. *I must go into the cave alone.*

"What will happen in there?" Mira asked Snow after Dancer had left.

Dancer will go into the cave and call to the other sleuths. They are all nearby, looking for answers so they will hear us, Snow explained. *Dancer will tell them that the end is coming and the only way to save our kind is to work with humans to keep the Wild Fae at bay.*

"The other sleuths will believe Dancer?" Mira asked trying not to be impolite but she did need to know.

They will ask the Creator themselves and he will reveal the truth to them. Do not fear, daughter. They will fight with us.

Mira tried to feel as sure as Snow did. She had doubts in Dancer's plan but her doubts faded as roars sounded.

"That was fast," Mira remarked.

A good nanok sees reason much more quickly than your people do, Dancer remarked as she exited the cave.

"Then they will fight with us?"

Four other sleuths have already agreed to join our fight. I am certain that more will join as time goes on. It will echo in the cave so others will hear if they come searching.

What will we do with so many sleuths? Snow asked.

We will divide and conquer, Dancer answered.

A sleuth is always stronger fighting together, Plum reminded her.

The sleuths will not be divided but the fight will be. Our sleuth and Storm's will join and go free the Seer and the Almost Nanok. The other two sleuths will go directly to the mountains and surround the enemies who took Darkness Chaser.

We can send you and the Seer into the gloaming field to warn the women and your friend that we are here to help. We can all work together then to stop the Wild Fae, Snow said excitedly.

Exactly, Dancer sent with a smile. *You will be a fine Ahaya one day.* Dancer's eyes shown with pride.

I hope I will not have to be leader for a long time yet, Snow admitted, nuzzling Dancer quickly.

All things happen in their own time. The pride in Dancer's eyes did not diminish a jolt. *I think you are ready to lead the hunt to bring back the Seer.*

Snow smiled, gave out an excited yip and commanded the sleuth to run towards the river where Matt was being held.

~*~

Oreland gripped Matt's arm and whispered, "The nanoks are coming. They lost the fight last time but there are many more members now. More nanoks have joined the sleuth."

"You can tell how many nanoks there are?" Matt whispered back in surprise.

"I can't tell anything exact but I can get a sense of numbers. There must be double the number than when we left them."

Matt could tell Oreland was about to explain further but Arcadia walked up behind them.

"I am glad to see that the two of you still have information to share; information to make you valuable because the dreamers continue to say that they cannot enter the gloaming field."

"I explained to you at the beginning: only certain people can enter the dream. You must be born with the talent and then you can be taught to change the world to match your needs. You can't just expect everyone in the group to be able to do it. It's like any other talent. A great artist has to have some talent before they can be trained."

"The high lady and I both expected one person in the group to be able to go into the other world. You will no longer be useful to us if you cannot teach anyone!" Arcadia hissed out her words with venom. The young men could see that she meant every word she said.

"I'm sure we can find someone who can travel to the gloaming field. Just bring more people!"

"There is a small group that the empress will allow to learn. This power cannot be given to anyone who may not be loyal to the empress and the empire."

"The empress does not trust her own subjects?" Oreland seemed shocked at the very idea.

"Do not question the empress!" Arcadia ordered. "You are in enough trouble already." Arcadia did not stop for a breath. "Guard!" Arcadia motioned with her hands.

Guards moved quickly to get a hold of both Matt and Oreland. The ship gave them all little room to move in but Matt and Oreland both twisted and turned as much as possible. The fight gave both Oreland and Matt a small taste of freedom but it was short-lived. The guards had their arms twisted behind their backs. The smallest movement sent stabs of pain up Matt's arm but both he and Oreland continued to resist.

They twisted and tried to move their arms out of their current painful position but everyone, guard and noble alike, stopped dead when a roaring filled the air.

"It's your nanoks," Matt told Oreland.

"They are here for you," Oreland told him. "They still need you to survive the coming attack."

The nanoks worked as a team to bring down men with weapons. These men were trained warriors but they were not used to working against such an organized team. The Argosi conquered small communities who had never even seen an army before. The guards had never fought against an organized group who was prepared for them. The nanoks brought the guards down in the blink of an eye.

Matt did not recognize most of the nanoks that had saved him. They were not from the sleuth who talked with Mira. Matt looked around frantically for a friendly face.

"Plum!" He called, finally recognizing a face. "Plum, where's Dancer and Mira? Where did all these other nanoks come from?"

Matt sent the questions in a jumble. He was still learning how to send thoughts to the nanoks in the waking world. He could only manage a sending with nanoks that he knew and even then the thoughts came in a scramble. Luckily, Plum knew Matt well enough by now to understand what he meant.

"Follow me," Plum sent and went running, hopefully, to get Mira. Matt and Oreland followed after her at a run themselves. After running out of the ship and swimming a short way to the shore, Matt saw Mira standing next to Dancer and Snow.

"Matt!" Mira called. "We need to get to Lewis as soon as possible. Dancer says he is in trouble."

"I know. I saw it in a dream," Oreland said in explanation. "Lewis is meeting with Wild Fae. They want to make a duel so that they can force Lewis to return to the other realm with them."

"Dancer says that destroying the Earth is the Wild Fae goal but prophesies — the Wild Fae's own prophesy — says that they need their lost prince returned to them." Mira stopped translating there as if she had just heard what she said.

"Lewis is a lost prince?" Matt asked in shock.

"Shouldn't you know this as a seer?" Oreland asked in curiosity.

"I don't know everything. It doesn't work like that." Matt fell back as soon as he finished talking as if he had fainted. Everyone, human and nanok alike, clustered around his still form. His eyes popped open in seconds. "I need you and Dancer to tell me as much as you can. I'm supposed to be some kind of champion. I'm the only one who can see what the Wild Fae will do before they do it."

"The Wild Fae can become shadows, Matt. I've seen it happen. You can't just fight them!" Oreland insisted.

"I have to! So stop arguing and start walking. We have a lot of traveling to do if we are going to get to Lewis in time."

Dancer moved her head under Matt's hand.

"She says that she knows a way that can take you right in their path. The Argosi need to get to a certain pass but there is only one way to the pass that will allow them to take their carts. She suggests that we lie in wait to ambush them."

"As long as we get there fast," Matt said already beginning to walk after Dancer.

"We'll get there before the Argosi do, Matt," Mira promised.

"I just hope we aren't too late."

Alaina was shocked at the speed at which the Argosi traveled. She and Lewis slowed them as much as possible. She had begged Sainade to tell the empress what they had seen and heard while the Wild Fae was bargaining with Lewis but the velvet woman held her tongue. Alaina had told the empress what she had seen herself but no one seemed to believe her.

"The Wild Fae are setting you up," Lewis told them for the hundredth time. "This is all a trick!" The empress had listened to Lewis's please for days now but she had done nothing about it.

"Do not take me for a fool. The Wild Fae will not double-cross me. Although I must say that you were not meant to know about this part of the plan. You country-folk are so superstitious," the empress walked away from Lewis. His bounds prevented him from following after her but his voice carried.

"I've seen what they can do! You're playing into their hands. Don't go to that mountain!"

"The Fae want a champion and they have agreed to fight anyone I choose. My velvet women will destroy them before the fight even begins!" The empress declared.

"You can't play these games with the whole world's future at stake!" Lewis knew he had gone too far when the empress turned to him with fire in her eyes.

"I am the empress of Argosi and the whole world will be mine! I have every right to gamble with what is mine!" The empress motioned for Sainade to silence Lewis. The empress and her followers were so busy with Lewis that they did not see movement across the pass as Alaina and the other women did.

Nanoks formed a ring around them that none of the guards dared to attempt to break. There was a standing order that the nanoks not be harmed.

"These nanoks will be our allies. Killing them will not help our cause. Get nets and trap them!" She ordered harshly. "They will be weapons if they refused to become allies."

Guards scrambled about this way and that, getting nets and lightning sticks. Their agility and swiftness was not enough to out-maneuver the nanoks. A net might fall on a nanok but Mira and Matt were quick to slice through them with belt knives. None of the nanoks could be trapped for long. The guards tried to tackle the two young men but the nanoks were quick to defend them.

"We are not here to stop you!" Mira called. "We know who the real enemy is and we know that you need help to defeat the Fae."

"I am here to be Lewis's champion," Matt told them

without one grin or sparkle. "I am the only person who can see what the Fae do before they do it. If anyone can win with the whole world at stake, it's me."

Matt's pronouncement was met with silence.

By: Jennie Arnold

Chapter Twenty-four

Lewis was no longer bound. Matt and Mira stood with him in the pass surrounded by a guard of nanoks. They made an intimidating sight but so did the Argosi. The Argosi empress stood near them with an enclave of velvet women. It was time to meet the Wild Fae.

"Those primitive beasts will see that they cannot go back on their word when they make a promise to the empire!" The tiny empress swore. "You may agree to fight their champion but it is my velvet women who make the killing blow."

"Why does it even matter who kills who? The ending result is the same." Her earlier words only baffled Matt. The champion would be dead and the Wild Fae would leave... hopefully. "The Wild Fae might refuse to leave Earth in peace if you interfere like that. They won't consider it a fair win."

"Argosi guards and velvet women will defeat them all! You have seen the power of my army and soon, they will too."

"We don't want the Fae to "see the power of your army"," Lewis said through clenched teeth. "We want them to leave!"

"The Argosi Empire will be victorious either way!"

The three friends from Alta shared a look. It was pointless to argue with the woman! It was risky just trying to talk with her when she had an army at her back! They needed to finish this before the empress had her men do anything else!

Lewis made a single, quick slice across his palm. All three magic users felt a now familiar numbness flow over them as blood trickled to the rocks below. The real enemy, the Wild Fae, had arrived and he came wearing full armor with his sword hissing as it left the scabbard!

Matt twisted left and fainted right as the others backed away from the field. Soon, the nanoks, men, and nobles formed a ring around them. Matt ignored everything around him so that he could focus his power on seeing what his opponent would do in the next couple seconds. Five seconds was enough to change the whole tide of the battle!

He parried and thrusted and even began to move the sword like a staff. He was not used to fighting with a sword but the Fae seemed to be out of his element as well.

Matt assumed that he would be a swordsman but Fae were probably more used to working with magic than with swords. They were on equal, if uneven, ground.

Matt could only hope that it, along with his advantage of seeing the future was enough.

Matt focused on the future to change the outcome of what he saw but one thing stopped him cold. He could see the farm he grew up on in flames and the inn he had sat with Mira and Lewis no longer standing. He called to Lewis, "Get to Alta! They won't destroy it if their prince is there."

"They won't destroy Alta, Matt. We made a deal that Alta was safe either way, no matter who wins." Lewis tried to explain further but Matt interrupted him.

"I know what I saw! They are going to destroy it!"

Lewis ran to the horses, but the Earth shook with a BOOM that forced Lewis to stop in his tracks. Lewis sank to his knees. "No, no, no!" He screamed over and over. Mira stood a few feet away with her hands on her head and her mouth open. She looked like a feather would knock her over. Matt, on the other hand, saw nothing but red and felt fire burn through his veins.

"You killed them!" He screamed as his sword sliced through the Fae's neck. "They were innocent people there but

By: Jennie Arnold

you killed them all!"

All three of them felt the numbness spread and the power inside them worked on its own. Fire and lightning flew from Lewis while nanoks mauled anything that came near Mira.

It was clear that the nanoks felt the anger inside of Mira. Matt felt waves leave the gloaming field and force the two Fae into another dimension. They were gone....

"It's over," Matt told the other two in a voice that surprised him with its hoarseness. "They left." He heard Lewis groan and Mira sob before twin thuds told him that the other two had lost consciousness but he could not hear any more than that.

The blackness of unconsciousness also took him.

Alaina had to remind herself to blink. She could not look away from her friends in the center of the ring. She could feel the power radiating from them; feel the anger and the passion driving it. The force and strength in all that emotion scared her.

She could tell that the Islanders were too far gone into their grief and pain to see who they were hurting and that scared her even more. Still, she could not leave Lewis or the others.

They had helped her when she needed it most and now she would help them if she could. Alaina quickly made shields. She called up all of the magic she could while wearing the band, the long hours of practice finally coming to use.

Protection was placed around the nanoks and around the Argosi too. The Fae were the ones who needed to feel the force of this blast and all the power needed to go to them, not to any other source. She narrowed and focused all of the magic she could manipulate.

Alaina looked directly into the eyes of the champion Fae

and moved all the magic energy into him. He flew to the ground as if he was hit by a stampede of horses. The Fae twitched this way and that, until after what seemed like hours, he did not move any more. The Wild Fae who had first spoken with Lewis walked to his comrade.

Alaina felt the air around her harden as if the Fae were trying to hold her there again. She used the adrenaline she had left to push the force field away from all of them and snap it back into the Fae. He rocked back on his heels, trying to regain his balance.

"I wouldn't try tricks like that again," Alaina advised him.

"I can see when I am beaten," the Fae said with a smirk. "I will just take my prince and be on my way." The Fae began to step towards the unconscious men.

"I cannot allow that," Alaina said as she pushed him back a few steps with a few flows of air.

"He must have forgotten to tell you that we had an agreement," the Fae began but Alaina knew all about the agreement, having heard the conversation the first time, so she cut him off.

"The agreement was that he would trade himself for the safety of his people but you broke that agreement when you blew up his homeland."

"Neither me nor my people attacked that Island. It is a tragedy that those people lost their lives but it has nothing to do with the agreement," the Fae argued.

"Those weapons were of Fae craft!" The empress declared accusingly. "I have seen demonstrations of their work!"

"The agreement is the same no matter where the weapons came from! I will take the prince and go and I will kill anyone who tries to stop me!" The Fae's eyes were alight with a desperate glint.

"Three sleuths of nanoks, an army, and elemental magic

users will all try to stop you," Alaina promised him. "I suggest you leave before we need to hurt you." Alaina was surprised to see that the Fae did just that. He left with a pop of displaced air.

"That was very nicely done," the empress complemented. "I believe that all of you will do well in the Argosi Empire."

"We're not going to Argosi," Alaina told her defiantly. "We saved your empire already. Just let us go!"

"War is coming," the empress declared as velvet women and their charges moved in to take the nanoks, the men and Alaina. "My empire will have the best weapons available for the coming war."

The velvet women were forming a shield around Alaina. She called her magic to her but it could not get near her. She tried to protect Lewis but the magic she could reach was not enough to do even that.

She strained against the stronger combined force of the velvet women. She pushed all that she could until the strain became too much. Alaina had no choice but to give in to the blackness just as the others had.

Mira woke up to hear nanoks all around her crying.

She saw nanoks with burn marks from lightning sticks in cages. She saw that she too was in a cage!

Mira jumped up and banged her fist against the bars, looking for a weak spot. Each bar vibrated spectacularly after she hit it but none of them gave an inch.

She felt like crying with the nanoks but she held herself back. Now was the time to remain calm and focused. She just had to think of a different way out... Mira tried to send out a question to the nanoks but they were all so upset that none of them would listen to her.

"There's a way out," she assured the nanoks aloud. "We just have to find it."

"There is always a way out, young man," High Lady Ramilla told him. "All you have to do is ask."

Mira watched her as the High Lady walked to her cage. She pulled out a key and unlocked it. Mira could not shake the feeling that these women meant nothing but trouble. She stood in the open doorway of the cage.

"The empress will see you now," she told Mira in a sickeningly sweet voice.

"And if I don't want to see her?" Mira asked her from the back of the cage.

"If you do not want to come willingly then I will call guards. You will not have much choice in the matter with weapons pointed at these nanoks, will you?"

Mira pulled back her lips and growled, barring teeth. She should be keeping her head down but she could not let the empress threaten her friends.

Many of the nanoks roared in their grief and many more cried and wined all the more. All of them seemed to get more agitated hearing her growl. The High Lady rolled her eyes at Mira in a very un-lady-like manner.

"Do I need to call the guards or not?" She tapped her nails impatiently.

"There's no need to threaten them. I'm coming." She slowly crawled out of the cage. Every muscle in her body was stiff but she managed to get out of the cage quickly and stand straight.

"This way," the High Lady said with a jester and quickly turned into a hallway.

"I'm so sorry, Sarilla," Oreland told the girl sobbing in his arms. "I promised that I would protect you but now we're just prisoners again. We're little better than slaves."

"Don't let them take me away," Sarilla said through her tears. "Please don't leave me!"

Oreland wanted to tell her that they would never take her away and that he would stay by her side forever but he could not make another promise that he could not keep, especially to her. He loved her, he realized.

"I won't let them hurt you." He said it more to himself than to her but he knew it was true all the same. "They'll never put chains on you again." He rubbed her bare neck gently.

"The missing band scares me more. If the headband was on I would know what to expect but now I can't even begin to guess what they will do."

"Without the band you can do magic. No matter what the Argosi decide to do, you can defend yourself. You don't need to worry," Oreland tried to reassure her.

Sarilla fought to quiet her sobs as Oreland rubbed her back, trying to comfort her. Sarilla was still sobbing when the door to the cell opened. Oreland stepped protectively in front of Sarilla, trying to keep the guards who came in from noticing her.

"The empress has "requested" your presence. You will come with me now."

Three guards came into the cell and held their arms. Two men held Oreland's arms in grips of iron before one man pulled Sarilla from a shadowy corner. Oreland strained against the men holding him. The guards must have guessed how Oreland would react and placed men around him to make sure he did not do anything rash.

"Leave her alone!" He yelled.

"The empress just wants to talk. There is no need to worry. You and your friend will tell the empress what she wants to know and nothing bad will happen to you." Oreland fought all the harder. It was clear that these men were lying.

By: Jennie Arnold

Chapter Twenty-five

The empress stood in her quarters. She had moved the prisoners to her ship once the guards had found them knocked out after the fight with the Wild Fae. She was not sure what part each of them had to play in the upcoming battle but the prophecies have said that they were all important to the empire's survival.

They needed to be led.

The Wild Fae had surprised her. She had never trusted them but she did not expect them to abandon their word either. She refused to be surprised like that again! She had a plan to make sure that she would never be taken in so easily. Half the empire had worked to train her. She was smarter than the Fae and needed to act like it! Her whole empire depended on her strength.

It would force these new guests of hers to see the truth: that the only way to protect the things they cared about was to join with her. It was a shame that the little Island was gone. The peasants there would be very useful right now but what was done was done. Those people would never come back but the Wild Fae would have probably won if grief had not driven the Seer. It was time to bring them all together.

"Our guests should be awake by now. Bring the guests out of the prison quarters. I need them brought to me quickly. But be gentle. They will soon be our allies," the empress commanded the guard.

Only one of the empress's guards remained in the room with her. The rest left to bring the guests in. The empress refused to call them prisoners but that was exactly what they were. None of them wanted to be here and none of them understood their duty. They would learn though. The Islands were a part of the empire now and it was their duty to help that empire.

They pushed Mira into the room. Oreland and Sarilla's quickly followed her entrance. Alaina and Kiarlin came in seconds later. Several guards brought the prisoners in but only two stayed. The rest went off to bring Lewis in.

"I did my end of the bargain!" Lewis told the guards. "I saved your empire and now it's your empress's turn to uphold her end of the deal. I'm not making any more agreements with her until she upholds her first bargain."

The guards ignored Lewis. They tried to force him to the empress's quarters, but he used magic to keep them at bay. More and more guards came pouring in until they overwhelmed him.

Sainade met the group on the main deck. "Drink this," she ordered holding a hot cup that smelled nothing like the potion they had forced into him before. Lewis knew that this cup held something different, but he still did not trust it. He turned his face away.

"It's not poisoned," Sainade told him in a tone that said that he could not see the nose on his face. "This is made to calm you down. It won't harm you. It will only relax you."

"I don't need a potion! I need to know the others are safe. I need to go home. There are people who weren't on the Island, people in outlying farms, people visiting relatives, people who made it! I need to go back and help them!"

"You will be able to help more than a small Island now.

By: Jennie Arnold

You will save an entire empire," Sainade said all of this as if the empire were some holy thing.

"I saved the empress from an assassin and then stopped the Wild Fae from invading. I did all I could to help your empire. Now it's my turn to help my own people."

"Don't you understand that your little Island is part of the empire? When the Fae attacked your Island they declared war on the empire and they will be back. All we can do now is get ready."

"You think I can make you more prepared?"

"Just go listen to the empress. Try to be calm and respectful." Sainade made it sound like she was a mother and Lewis was her unruly child.

"You make it sound so simple. I just want to get this over with. Lead the way."

Sainade led him to a grand set of double doors. Guards still surrounded him but they were no longer holding or dragging him. The guard opened the door and pushed him in.

Lewis looked around and saw the empress's extravagant room. He was not surprised to see gold gilding on every piece of wood but it surprised him to see so many people in the room. He was more than a little disheartened to find that no one had escaped. Fate must be trying to throw a curveball at all of them!

"Sainade mentioned that you needed to prepare the empire for war but was it really necessary to force so many of us to help you?"

"I am not the one who decided that each of you was needed. If it were up to me, you would all be back in the ruins of your little Island. Every one of you are more trouble than you are worth!" The empress said all of this with a siren face but real anger.

"Then why did you bring us here?" Kiarlin asked.

"A prophecy told me that I needed to," the empress

answered.

"Who could make a prophecy like that?" Alaina asked. "Were they a seer like Matt? How do you know that they were telling the truth?"

"I know it is true because more than one person told me the same prophecy."

"These people told you we would save your empire?" Kiarlin asked, looking for specifics.

The empress took a deep breath fighting to remain calm before she continued. "The prophecy said that a man who could do magic would be found in one of the places we conquered. This man could not just be the first magic user we see, although male magic users are rare enough. We could know him by his companions."

The empress looked at Mira and Matt as she said the next part. "He would be the same age as a seer and an emissary to old gods. We wanted to find you both. All three of you are secret weapons. All three of you grew up together and the prophecies told us you would all need each other. That magic man would save the empire but he could not survive to do it without the other two. Therefore, for the empire to survive we would need all three."

"That explains why Mira and I are still here with Lewis but not why everyone else is here," Matt said in an angry voice.

"It doesn't explain anything!" Lewis broke in angrily. "I used to believe in love charms but that did not make them real."

Matt nodded, remembering sneaking to the beach to bury lumps of string and hair under sharp stones. One of the old peddlers on the Island had sworn that braiding a strand of your hair with a lock of your love's curls would entwine your lives. The love would fall for you if you burying it under the golden stones of the Teeth.

Every Islander knew where to find the golden stones. Every other rock on the beach was gray but the tall, sharp stones of the Teeth were a golden yellow and they stuck out of the sand like a rude gesture. No one who knew the Island would miss it!

No one ever admitted that they had been to the Teeth, so it was impossible to tell if the tradition worked. Lewis obviously did not believe and Matt was not sure if he did either. Alaina could see it all with one look.

"Let the others go and we can come to an arrangement," Lewis demanded.

"Don't be so coy! Isn't it obvious? The rest of these people are your motivation for helping. You would not help out of patriotic duty but you will help to save a friend."

Matt was so angry that he found himself shaking. How dare these women threaten the others just to get her own way? The empress could have asked nicely. She could have explained the situation to them before all this started. Now they were all trapped in her web and she just had to pull a few strings to get her way. Matt was already planning a way out of this web!

"You brought all these people into this, threatened all these people? For what? What does this get you? More power, more land, more money?" Matt's voice shook he was so angry.

"This plan gives me one thing: My Empire's survival. Don't go thinking that I'm a selfish queen who never left her ivory tower. I know what it is like in the slums. It breaks my heart to see my people living like that. My heart breaks every time a soldier dies fighting for my empire. Keeping you here, using you as weapons changes all of that!"

"I am not a weapon!" Lewis said angrily. "And if you want my help, you won't make me or my friends a prisoner!"

"You weren't given potion and your friends are not wearing chains," Sainade pointed out. "We would like to give you proper rooms and make you comfortable but we have no guarantees that you will not run away."

"How can we run when you are holding our friends hostage? Stop acting like they brought here us on polite invitation!" Mira had spoken for the first time since being brought into the room. She was normally very level-headed and cautious but it seemed like all the close calls were catching up to her. "The truth is that we have to do what you say, just like before, because it is the only hope we have of seeing our friends or our home ever again."

"I don't want it to be like before," the empress swore. "That was a mistake. I want this to be something new. I want us to be partners. You do what I say. You save the empire and then I will transport everyone surviving from your Island to the capital city. You will each be given a manor house there where you can live with your friends and family. You can come and go as you please. You will not be prisoners."

"How will our families, or anyone in Alta, be found?" Mira asked with hope in her eyes. It looked like Mira was fighting the hope there. She was afraid of being wrong again or getting hurt again.

"I will have guards searching for survivors for as long as you agree to help," the empress was making several promises but the men could see the desperation in her eyes and knew that it was mirrored in their own.

"I agree to help but only as long as no one becomes a

prisoner," Matt agreed.

"If no one gets chained I will help," Mira said. "Those bands are evil things. I won't be a part of that!"

"I agree to help the empire but not to kill for it," Lewis amended. The other two echoed him.

"We will do all we can but your prophecy may be off a little. We need more help. We could not have gotten this far without Oreland and Kiarlin's help. We need them to continue to help us," Matt said reverently.

"They need the same deal as us. They get a manor in the capital when this is over and the freedom to come and go with no threat of being chained or captured," Lewis bargained.

The empress smiled one of her small, secretive smiles. "I believe that can be arranged." The small woman stuck out her hand. "Do we have a deal?"

Each of them gripped the small woman's hand firmly in a handshake. Lewis, Mira, Matt, Alaina, Kiarlin, and Oreland all shook her hand in turn. They had struck the deal. One enemy had been beaten but the battle and the adventure was just beginning!

The three young Islanders should be restless and full of excited energy but none of them moved. The ship and the other people on it still felt like an enemy. Leaving the little group seemed equal to leaving all safety behind. Fate took a hand in the matter and ignored their decision.

The shadow flashed in any corner it could. Only this shadow was not a simple obstruction to the light. The shadow could become Fae.

The Wild Fae could become shadows to avoid arrows and

swords. They could travel through shadow more quickly than the best stallion. The power of the shadow gave the Fae something beyond magic. Magic took strength but the shadow was unlimited.

Lewis, Mira, Matt, and even the empress did not know it but the Wild Fae had not all left.

The Fae who had spoken with Lewis was still on Earth. He had come to Earth in the first place to bring the prince back. He had already decided that he was not returning without the objective he had been assigned.

He became a shadow and traveled to where he knew Lewis would be.

He stepped out of shadow and wrapped a solid arm around the prince. Lewis called out and struggled but the Fae knew that the young royal was still acting, and thinking, like a human. The Fae felt sure that the young prince was not prepared to use his magic. None of the Fae knew that Lewis already had training.

They had forced Lewis to use his magic in the Argosi competitions. He knew how to use it to hurt and even kill. Lewis hated the killing they had made him do. He did not want to kill again but he knew that this Fae had to be stopped. Death would be a last resort but something had to be done!

Lewis called lightning to stun the Fae.

The Fae tried to move back into the shadow where he could force the prince to travel with him. Vines erupted from the ground and wrapped around his legs, forcing the Fae to stay still.

"None of that now, little prince. The Wild Fae are your family. We have magic that you have never dreamed of. You've learned a trick here and there but a trick will not save you. Come quietly with me now and you will be shown true power." The Fae turned to Lewis with a smile that could turn his blood

By: Jennie Arnold

to ice. "You will be crowned and given everything your heart desires."

Lewis dragged his heels and slowed the Fae as much as possible. He could break free if he just had enough time!

"I don't want to rule your precious Fae! My father raised me on Alta Island and I will remain loyal to the people there. They helped me when I had no one. I will not abandon them for anything!" Lewis kicked his leg up to free an arm. His free arm shot towards the Fae with lightning sparking off the fingers.

The Fae broke away and turned into a true shadow.

He could no longer hold the prince but lightning could no longer hurt him and vines could no longer hold him. Their tricks would not work. He turned before he took to the shadows to say one final thing before fleeing.

"You may have bested me for now but I'll be back. I will not leave this plain without bringing you home."

Lewis scrambled away from the shadows never wanting to be so close to the Wild Fae again. Mira and Matt pulled his arms and shoulders to help him move into the light. Lewis used his legs to slide into the middle of the room while his hands fumbled for his friends' arms.

"It's all right." Mira did her best to comfort on top of Matt's, "I've got you." Lewis tried to smile his thanks while he squeezed their arms.

"Is everyone okay?" Lewis asked, looking around the room. He saw the women standing together on the other side of the room, away from all the shadows. He was relieved to see that they were all alright.

"We're fine," Kiarlin began. She opened her mouth to continue, but the empress spoken before Kiarlin got her chance.

"The Wild Fae cannot get to you — or any of us for that matter. I know that the three of you have been working on something..."

She was obviously waiting for one of them to elaborate on the plan. Lewis was not clear about the plan himself so he waited for one of the others to tell her the whole thing.

"Some nanoks worked with me to build a trap. We made it in the gloaming field," Matt told her.

"If you let some nanoks in here to guide us we can go in and get it for you." Mira looked at Matt as she spoke, silently begging Matt not to give the lie away.

Mira needn't have worried. Matt could see what she was doing. Mira wanted to get the nanoks into the same room. Matt could only guess that Mira wanted to talk with them and that she needed to see them to do it. Mira had roared for them to come when they were miles away but roaring was not the same as a conversation.

"Our werebeasts have never mentioned guides in this gloaming field." The empress sounded suspicious and Mira and Matt both knew that they had to allay her fears.

"The werebeasts cannot get to the gloaming field," Oreland said speaking for the first time since being brought. "They only dream of it and hear the nanoks speak of it. A half-thing cannot get to the gloaming field." Oreland said the whole thing in a fast whisper and it took the room a second or two to catch up.

"You lie! They could not have gotten the details they did without going!" Sainade swore.

"It's true," Oreland said calmly. "A whole soul is needed to enter the gloaming field. None of the weres have a whole soul. Sarilla healed me and gave me my soul back. You need the Seer and the nanok daughter to get your net." Oreland knew he had said the wrong thing when her eyes darkened.

"I don't need to do anything," the empress intoned. "That net is not the only weapon that can stop them. Your white wand can be used against them too."

By: Jennie Arnold

Three men all looked to the small empress in surprise. "Do not look so shocked," Sainade scolded them. "The Silken can have wondrous skills like the three of you. They can make plants grow or see what an object will do with a touch or heal wounds. One of them has touched the wand we found on you."

Sainade pointed to Oreland as she talked. They all remembered the tree that had given Oreland that wand and they knew that both the wand and the net had to be used to stop the Wild Fae.

"We're not trying to trick you," Mira told her.

"You need both the wand and the net to defeat them," Matt backed up his friend.

"We have been making a plan, as you know but the plan is not as solid as you seem to believe," Lewis admitted.

"Then tell me what sort of plan you have. I'll see if I can fix it," the empress told them with a smile. "We are allies now after all."

Lewis took a deep breath to buy time. He used to second given to him to beg Fate to stay at his side. Lewis and the others needed friends more than ever. He was not sure the empress was a friend or not but there was only one way to find out.

They were both desperate. He just hoped she was desperate enough to listen... to use them instead of betraying them.

By: Jennie Arnold

Epilogue

"I cannot tell you the whole plan until you answer a question for me," Lewis spoke to the empress, but he was looking at his friends as he spoke.

The empress understood what he was asking even if he would not look at her. "I take it I must not only answer but answer correctly before you will tell me anything. You think this answer will prove my loyalty?"

"I believe that you put great stock in your word. If you tell me the truth then I will believe you."

"We will all believe your word," Alaina agreed with Lewis.

The empress nodded, accepting that they would all take her at her word. These were simple people and on the Islands and Mainland alike a man's word was his bond.

"And your question?" The empress asked.

"Why did you come to our Island?" All eyes turned to Lewis as the question left his lips. None of them expected his question to be this one!

"You know your history?" She did not wait for an answer before continuing. "Then you know that your land was once part of Thomlin Murthal's kingdom. He was the only man who united kingdoms across both seas. Thomlin had three sons and when he died, they divided his kingdom to avoid civil war.

"The three sons agreed to bring their father's kingdom together again. One son ruled in your Island along with the neighboring peninsulas. Another son rules Dara — his descendants still rule there today — and the third son went to Argosi. The three brothers were far apart but their bond connected them. They had agreed to form an alliance once their sons came of age. The ruler in Argosi reached out to his brothers but neither of them replied to him.

He feared his brothers were dead so he planned on sending a scouting mission to check on them. A civil war stopped this mission before it had begun. Generations later, the king's covenant can finally be fulfilled! Your rulers broke the covenant but my ancestors were faithful to their word. My reign will unite the kingdom because of my ancestor's faithfulness." The empress finished her story and looked to the three of them. "Does that answer satisfy you?"

"You think war will unite the nation?" Lewis asked in surprise.

Mira put her hand up to calm Lewis and quiet the empress. They stared at each other like strange cats! It was clear that the two of them were rearing for a fight.

"The empress has told us her history," Mira said in a calm voice. "Maybe we should tell her history as our people see it." They all nodded and looked to Mira so she continued.

"Alta Island was never empty. The land teamed with life from the beginning. The Creator made it as a sanctuary for lost wonderers and for anyone without a place of their own.

"Our people were lost wonders before they came to stay on the Island. Boats took them from one place to another but no community would welcome them. Finally, tired of travel and no longer able to fight those that meant harm, the Creator guided them to the Island He had made for just a purpose.

"The people brought seeds, customs and gods to the Island with them. The seeds flourished, and the customs grew more complex as the population grew, but the gods were fading away. They needed magic and old gods on the sea when my people did not have a home or even a place to return to. People without a home need to cling to something solid. But Alta Island was a home now. Old gods, customs and magic were all forgotten. Technology grew."

Mira took a breath and looked the empress in the eyes as

By: Jennie Arnold

she explained the rest. "The nanoks have seen the end coming. They know that the only way for both nanoks and man to survive is for us to defeat the Wild Fae. You and I both know that the only way to beat them is to work together as a team. Long ago, the Creator made everything you see around you and He had a plan for everything. The Creator made Fate to guide each of us. Humans stopped listening to Fate but the nanoks have remembered and Fate had warned them."

"Yes!" the empress interrupted. "One empire under my reign would be forced to work together."

"We are already fighting a war with the Wild Fae," Matt reminded her. "You cannot afford to attack Fae and men. You don't have the resources."

"Opportunity waits for no one," the empress said as if she were quoting someone else. "I will be able to do what must be done."

"There are risks and there are risks," Matt tried to put a lid on his temper but it was clear that no such thing would be possible. "Defending yourself when you're attacked on multiple fronts is a risk no one can run from. Attacking multiple places at once is a risk that can be avoided."

"You admitted that the land must be united to fight the enemy. I do not see another option for how to unite them."

"Revealing that the enemy is real is the best option. Most of the people on this side of the sea think that Wild Fae are nothing but myths. Armies will fight once they know the truth!" Matt insisted.

"And your little group of friends has a way to reveal the Wild Fae as what they are?" The empress used a mocking voice to ask this question, but it was a good question none the less.

"We might have an idea or two," Lewis said backing up his friend.

The empress leaned forward, ready to listen to every word the young man said.

"The net that Matt is making will trap the Wild Fae but it will not reveal their plan or even necessarily show them to any people here. No one knows how to prove that Fae exist aside from showing a large amount of respected people of the Fae themselves."

Mira nodded her encouragement before Matt began to speak, "The craftsman's guild in Alta keeps in touch with the Dwarf masons. The Dwarf are said to know more about Fae and dragons than any other race, including the Fae themselves! The stories may be an exaggeration but some of it has to be true. Surely they are knowledgeable about the Fae."

"Not a bad idea," the empress relented. "Asking the Dwarf masons to look into their library. Supposedly, the Dwarf have the largest library in the world. They have a large library even if it is not the largest."

"The hard part comes with how to get in touch with them to ask. Will they require payment?" Lewis had to explain his reservations. The empress deserved to know how he felt especially if they were to be partners.

"Your ideas are useless if we cannot complete them. One moment you say you have an idea and the next you say that the first step of the plan cannot be completed!" The empress was furious now. Her face was red and her eyes blazed with anger.

"They aren't useless," Matt insisted. "We told you they were not fully developed. All we need is more time to finish the plan." Matt was getting angry too now. He held his rage by a thread and was barely holding on.

"I can do nothing until the ship gets to port anyhow," Lewis reminded them. "Let us think about our plan until the ship gets there," Lewis pleaded with the empress.

"You'll have until we reach port to complete your plan,"

By: Jennie Arnold

the empress told them. "Do not think that this means you will have free rein. We will not allow you near the wand or each other until I have more trust than you have shown."

The empress motioned to her guards. Men swarmed into the room and stood beside each of the empress's guests. "Our friends here are prisoners until they can show that they deserve our trust. Treat them as you would any prisoner but make sure they come to no permanent harm."

They pulled hoods over their heads and wrestled each of them from the room. Lewis could see nothing but he could hear the clatter of bars on cell doors. He twisted, stumbled and turned this way and that, trying to find out how many men held him and how he could get to his friends.

He found that two men held him but more men than that stood nearby. A strong blow swiftly struck the back of his head. He fought against the dizziness that threatened to overwhelm him. Lewis felt his body weaken and go limp. He knew that the battle was lost. Consciousness left him.

Lewis found himself in what he knew was the gloaming field. Matt and Mira both knew more about the world and how to manipulate it. Lewis was not sure that he could accomplish even the simplest thing here.

"Lewis," Oreland's voice yelled across the vast fields. "How in the world did you get here?"

"I'm not sure," Lewis admitted. "The last thing I remember is that a guard knocked me out."

"It might be a good thing that you are here. Matt has an idea about finding the Dwarf city."

"He couldn't have said anything when we were with the empress?" Lewis almost laughed with incredulity.

"I'm not really sure about it," Matt admitted with a laugh. "I didn't want to say anything until I was sure."

"You're not sure about what?" Lewis asked.

"I just need to talk with Juniper to clarify a few things. Mira's talking with her nanoks too. They always seem to have an answer so that should help too."

"How will talking to nanoks teach us anything about other races? How would nanoks know anything about finding a Dwarf?"

"The Dwarves have a moving fortress," Oreland told them. "No one knows where it will land. It even moves in the gloaming field!"

"The nanoks know more about this world than we ever will," Matt admitted. "Juniper has hinted that he knows when the Dwarf will be in his valley. He will be reluctant to tell us anything. If you tell that nanok something in trust he will not even tell to save his own mother's life!"

"The fate of the entire world is in this. I think Juniper will find a way to bend the rules. All the other nanoks have." The others nodded their agreement of Lewis's words.

"I'll talk to Juniper. Mira can find out what the other nanoks know and Oreland can repeat the information to you." Matt moved to get started but Lewis grabbed his arm.

"Wait, Matt! It's a bad idea to separate out. Dividing will not help us. We should work together as much as possible."

"Sorry, Lewis but you don't know how to travel between worlds yet and I don't have time to teach you."

"How did I get here then?" Lewis was getting angry now.

"I willed you in," Oreland said, "but I only have power while you're in a trance not in the valleys of the gloaming field."

Lewis saw since and nodded reluctantly. "Do it then."

Matt ran to do just that and was gone in a flash.

~*~

Matt zigzagged across the fields, looking for Juniper. He moved around the valley where Juniper was usually waiting for him. Matt knew that he was not visiting on the normal schedule but the nanok could not be awake in the real world — he was trapped in this one!

"Juniper! Juniper!" Matt's voice rang strangely in the gloaming field, like an echo of someone else's voice. "Come out, Juniper! We need your help."

"There are things I cannot help you with, Matt," Juniper said as he appeared before Matt with a grin. "I will do all I can to help you but you should not rely on this place. It can be dangerous and unpredictable."

"We're getting desperate here," Matt admitted in a whisper. "The empress has given us an ultimatum and we need the Dwarfs' help to meet it."

"The Dwarf are not easy to find."

"You've hinted that you can find them when I talked to you earlier," Matt reminded him.

"The Dwarf people are very polite. They tell me before they get to my valley. I've told them they need not warn me but they insist."

"Do you know when they will be here next?"

"In a few days' time. They always arrive at night as you do," Juniper told him.

"What do they do when they get here? They wouldn't travel all this way just to camp on your valley!"

"Dwarves need to be near nature. Their fortresses float in the air but the Dwarf people need to leave the air and commune with nature. They will die if they don't! That is why they come to my valley. It is worth the long trip to them," Juniper explained.

"How do the Dwarf leave the floating fortress? They would have to leave to get near nature..."

"A tree grows from the fortress to the ground."

"This will be easier than I thought then," Matt said

excitedly. "All I have to do is arrive here in a few nights and stand at the bottom of a tree that suddenly grows. It should be hard to miss." Matt gave a sigh of relief and returned to Lewis's mind to give him and Oreland the good news. Then, went to see Mira.

~*~

Get comfortable, Plum sent to Mira. *Find space before waking and after sleeping.*

She was leading Mira into the gloaming field and would travel there with her to tell Juniper the plan they were developing. Mira found herself in the gloaming field quickly. It seemed like the process took fewer seconds each time he tried to travel. Mira tensed to run to the valley where Juniper met them but Plum gave warning yip.

There is a strange smell here, daughter! It is something I have never smelled before but it does not smell dangerous.

Mira relaxed putting the hunting knife back into her boot. "You gave me a fright going on like that. Now you say that the smell is not dangerous!" Mira was annoyed with herself for not looking before running and the annoyance showed in her tone.

The smell is not dangerous but a nanok knows that caution is always best. Never get too comfortable in your surroundings! Plum crouched into a stalking position and practically slithered into the valley. Mira flowed behind, doing the same.

Mira's sense of smell was not as keen as the nanoks' but it was better than the average person's. Still, Mira could smell nothing. She relied on her sight and studied the landscape before her. Nothing looked different on the ground but an odd cloud flew across the sky. The sky always seemed to look strange to her in the gloaming field. The clouds would be odd colors and swirl in air but this cloud was still different.

The cloud was more of a brown than gray and it appeared to be moving more quickly than the surrounding clouds. Mira had seen hurricanes whip through Islands and the odd movement reminded her of those terrifying tunnel clouds. Mira was about to ask Plum if there were tornadoes in the gloaming field when a thundering sound made both her and the nanok stop.

The sound was coming from the cloud but lightning did not follow… A green plant shot out of the bottom of the odd cloud and grew into the ground; making a latter.

"Are those things coming down to attack?" Mira asked in fear.

Those are Dwarf, Plum explained. *They are not violent but they are to be respected. They will defend themselves and they know more than anyone else.*

Mira nodded in understanding. "Matt was looking to meet these Dwarf. He said that they knew more about the Wild Fae than the Wild Fae themselves."

"How would they know anything?"

"They have the largest library in the world!"

Matt wanted to meet with these Dwarf but they are early, Juniper said as he suddenly appeared. *Maybe they will give the information to you now that you are here.*

Mira could see that Dwarf were indeed coming down the plant. She saw their silhouettes against the purple sky of the gloaming field. Now that she knew what to look for she could see that the brown cloud was actually a fortress in the sky! She marveled at the floating architecture while the procession of Dwarf made their way to her.

"You are the nanok daughter?" The Dwarf woman at the front of the procession asked.

"Do I know you?" Mira asked in surprise.

"The Creator sent us a message. Fate came in a dream and told us that we had to be in Juniper's valley on this night. He said that we have to meet three humans who can travel the land

Between. One would be a nanok daughter and one would be a seer. One would be a Wild Fae who gave the other two their powers."

"What!" Mira interrupted. "Lewis gave us powers? How?"

"The people we care about and care about us in return can change us. They define who we are," the Dwarf woman explained. "Lewis was always different. He was born a Wild Fae, not a human. He grew to care about his father and sister. He grew to care about his family and friends and you have all cared about him in return. That is why Lewis still looks and thinks like a human. He will never be fully Wild Fae."

The Dwarf woman sighed in relief. "The only issue is that all of you took something of his Wild Fae powers when you gave him part of your humanity. That is why all of you have powers even though it is rare for any human to manage magic."

"What about everyone else on Alta? We're not the only ones he cares about!"

"They will all have extraordinary luck or insight, amazing intuition... Their powers will not be as hard to control or as dangerous as yours."

"Velvet women on Argosi have found many women who can do magic. It doesn't seem so rare to me."

"The magic comes from nature, not the women," the Dwarf woman tried to explain. "The women only have the ability to borrow the power in nature. The band the Argosi forces on them looks for a bridge that unites the woman to nature's power."

"How can you know all of this?" Mira had to ask them. It was not that she did not believe or trust them but it did seem strange that no one had known anything about their strange powers until the Dwarf came.

"Unfortunately, my people helped the Argosi make their bands. We would not have loaned one book to that shipman if

By: Jennie Arnold

we knew what he would do with the information!"

"Books?"

"The Dwarf have been gathering the library before you humans discovered fire," a young Dwarf in the back whispered. "Information makes our city float. The information came in handy when the Wild Fae came all those centuries ago. I was there, you know? Don't look so shocked! We Dwarves have long lives. The Wild Fae tried to take the Between World as their own. They fought hard, but we fought harder. My people kicked them out of the Between World but we could not save more than that. The barriers are too thick."

"You fought the Wild Fae and gave them the bands?"

"None of us went looking for a fight. We fight because we have to. We put information in the hands of a man we trusted but we are bad judges of character. The man was not trustworthy."

Mira wanted to ask a dozen more questions, but another Dwarf left the Floating City and distracted her. She could see that this Dwarf was young. Maybe close to her own age. Dwarves lived a long time but they would have been close in age as they were measured.

"Evrick!" The Dwarf woman who had begun the talking exclaimed. "You were not given permission to come."

"Fate has come to me." The young Dwarf's voice was soft but clear and confident.

"Do you have proof of this?" The Dwarf woman demanded.

"Yes, mother. Fate has shown me a book; a book that I must give to the humans. It will tell them what they need to know about the Wild Fae and the net."

Mira took the book with reverence. "You've saved us," Mira told the young Dwarf as she took the book.

"I just did what I was told. Fate saved you."

Fate has saved us all, Plum sent in a voice filled with hope.

"That is not the only gift I have for you." Evrick pulled three stones from his pocket. They all glittered with all the colors of the rainbow. The sun made the colors dance all the more in the gloaming. "Your web will protect you from the Wild Fae but the Argosi will come back too. With these stones in hand, you'll be ready for them."

"What do they do?"

"They're beautiful," Mira commented.

"These stones can send short messages to the Dwarven Towers in the Floating City. Anyone who holds them can talk to the stone and the librarians will hear."

Matt blinked. "You want us to go back to the Argosi and spy on them for you!"

Plum did not seem surprised or impressed. "Your bodies are still with the Argosi. You can't stay here forever."

"Well that's a fine how do you do!"

Matt paced but Mira seemed calm.

"The Argosi have us and we need to confront them either way. These Dwarves have given us a chance. They've given us answers."

She turned her gaze to the two Dwarves. "Thank you. Thank you for the books and the stones and for fighting the Wild Fae that first time. Thank you for making this place a kind of sanctuary."

The Dwarf woman paled and explained, "Do not mistake me. This place is far from safe but it is safe from the Wild Fae. There are more enemies at work and we Dwarves will help you fight them. Your magic might be the greatest weapon we have."

"I'm just an Islander! I'm not supposed to have enemies and I already have too many," Matt complained. "I did not mean to make more. Mira is right… I should be thanking you."

"It is we who should thank you," Evrick said. "You fought the battle that we could not and won. The Dwarven Army

By: Jennie Arnold

should have been there! My people will be shamed for all time. We will try to make it right in a small part with the books and stones. I pray that you will accept these as a token of friendship."

"I've already learned the value of friendship," Matt said.

"The Creator has sent you to us," Plum said, "and us to you."

"Fate be with you."

"And with you."

Magic came easily out of wood and stone but now Matt knew that it would need to come out of his bones. The thought scared him even though he had been using magic for some time. He had stolen when he had to and took when there was nothing left but only because he had a mystery to take in. His mind was turning into a beehive to remember it all.

"Don't worry, Matt," Mira said, reading the look on his face. "We have friends in high places now."

Matt couldn't help but laugh.

A ripple of notes danced in the air and called them back.

"What happened?" Worried faces asked without words.

Matt held up the stones in this hand and answered with motions instead of words.

Their faces lit with hope. Fate was still with them after all.

The End

By: Jennie Arnold

Note from the Author:

This book would not be possible without the hard work and dedication from a village of people. Readers, editors, friends, family, and bloggers all worked tirelessly to make this book what it is today.

I need to thank my editors, Cassandra and Rita, who answered all the questions I asked. Even when I called at 3 A.M. I owe my both beta readers, Ravi and Jeremy, a cup of boiling coffee because they pulled an all-nighter or two to give me useful feedback before all deadlines. This book would be so much less without them.

The bloggers Nancy and Langley both gave me the courage to keep writing when they read through the manuscript and told me all their favorite scenes. None of those scenes would be possible if my friends Missy and Ashley did not share their endless knowledge of all things medieval.

My parents, grandmother, and sister all put up with me while I was writing, editing and basically lost in another world.

Thank you to everyone and anyone who gave patients and kindness to help finish this book!

www.ingramcontent.com/pod-product-compliance
Lightning Source LLC
Chambersburg PA
CBHW021124190726

48288CB00008B/2481